Chains Around the Grass

Also by Naomi Ragen

Jephte's Daughter, 1989
Sotah, 1992
The Sacrifice of Tamar, 1994
The Ghost of Hannah Mendes, 1998
Chains Around the Grass, 2002

Naomi Ragen

CHAINS AROUND THE GRASS

To Michelle —

Naomi Ragen

The Toby Press

First Edition 2002

The Toby Press *LLC*
www.tobypress.com

Copyright © Naomi Ragen, 2002

The right of Naomi Ragen to be identified as the author of this work
has been asserted by her in accordance with the Copyright, Designs &
Patents Act 1988

ISBN 1 902881 53 2, *hardcover*
ISBN 1 902881 54 0, *paperback*

A CIP catalogue record for this title is available from the British Library

Lyrics excerpt of *Always* by Irving Berlin
Copyright © 1925 by Irving Berlin
Copyright renewed
International copyright secured. All rights reserved. Reprinted by permission.
Give My Regards To Broadway © George M. Cohan, 1904

Designed by Breton Jones, London

Original cover photography by Adolfo Crespo for the Toby Press

Typeset in Garamond by
Rowland Phototypesetting Ltd., Bury St Edmunds, Suffolk, England

Printed and bound in the United States by
Thomson-Shore Inc., Michigan

For My Brothers

Prologue

There Sara sits on the new blue carpeting in the house of the uncle she hardly knows, playing with the two little girls they've told her are her cousins. She's taken in their frilly party dresses, their smug delight. They hold grown-up dolls with diamond earrings and high-heeled shoes close to their chests until an "aunt" with hatefully pitying eyes hisses at them, "Share!"

Grudgingly, they do.

These are their dolls, their house, their new blue carpeting. That is very clear to her. Acutely aware of the cost to her dignity, she nevertheless surrenders, accepting the doll with the humility of a beggar. She dresses and undresses it. For so many years— perhaps her whole life—she will play and replay that scene with shame, harder on herself than need be, overlaying it with a knowledge she never had at the time: She will never be able to forgive that image of ignorant bliss, that joyful dressing and undressing of the doll with breasts all the while her father was being buried.

"Passed away," is all they told her, her uncle and her mother sitting in the front seat of the uncle's new car that was to take them from the housing project in Queens to suburban Long Island. She sat in the back between her brothers thinking: ridiculous, impossible. She didn't cry. Instead, her fingers dug vengefully into the new upholstery, trying—but failing—to make a hole.

For years to come, her peace sacrificed to well-meaning fools who couldn't bear to watch a child see its father buried, she will look out of windows, searching for him, like Shirley Temple in *The Little Princess* watching for soldiers back from the battle of Mafeking. But unlike Shirley, she will not stamp her little foot and shake her pretty curls, adorably insisting: "He isn't dead, I tell you!" She will not move at all, sitting by the window on the seventh floor of the ugly red brick housing project in Queens.

Only forty-five years later, her mother newly buried, a grandmother herself, will she stand by her father's grave, believing it. She will bury her head in the soft, heavy middle of the brother she has been angry at for forty years, weeping loudly. "We needed help," she'll cry. "And there was no one to help us!" Embarrassed (she is always, it seems, embarrassing him and he, her), her brother will nevertheless embrace her, sending his stunned grown sons hurriedly back to wait in the car. Only then, will she have that insight that has eluded her so long, allowing her to see beyond the six-foot bully with the mean mouth and hard hand. She will be able to glimpse in him, once more, the angry, grieving twelve year old; see him as someone's little boy, orphaned, at the age of her youngest child, her baby. Only then will she realize, that out of all those alive on the planet, only he can at that moment understand her perfectly.

There it is, the opening door, the bitter cold rush of February air chilling the overheated room of the suburban house that has so impressed the child and her mother. And there is the mother, long awaited, a little unstable in the black high heels, uncomfortable in the borrowed hat. She does not, and has never, owned a hat of her own. She pulls up the black veil that covers her tear-stained face.

"Where were you? Why did you leave me?" Sara sobs into her mother's black-skirted thighs, her arms like a tourniquet about Ruth's knees. The mother's answer has been lost to time and memory. Only the smell of earth, and the chilled fibers of her woolen coat remain behind, intact, as solid as any tombstone.

Chapter one

W

hen the excitement and dread in David Markowitz's stomach went one level higher, finally waking him, he
perceived it as joy. He looked over at his wife, cupping her
breast affectionately, but hearing her deep, satisfied breathing,
thought better of it. She must be so tired after all that packing,
he thought. Another move. Besides, he couldn't waste the time.
There was too much to do. The movers were due at five, and he
had come home the night before too tired to check whether Ruth
had got everything ready for them. He would do it now. After
just one cup of coffee. He needed that one cup. After that he was
a dynamo. One cup was all that it took to transform him from
a weary laborer into a tireless capitalist.

Today there was only the one cab, barely two weeks old,
still smelling brand new, but in two years, three at the most, there
would be a second and then a third, so that by the time Jesse
finished high school there would be a whole fleet of them prowling

the streets of New York City, gathering up passengers and dollars without end.

Then they would move again, this time into a picture book house of their own on a quiet tree-lined street in one of the smarter suburbs. Ruth would be happy, finally. A home of her own, a backyard in which the children could play on their own, expensive jungle gym, perhaps a fancy temple nearby where she could join the Sisterhood and listen to the handsome young rabbi's pious and tiresome sermons. But for now, there was the temporary hardship that they would just have to endure—let his wife and son understand this already! All the money from the sale of the candy store in Newark had gone into the cab, and until they could save up for a down payment on their dream house, they would have to live in a (his mind searched, restless, for a way to finesse it, to turn the low-income housing project in the Rockaways into something nicer, the way they did in commercials: "a beach front development" perhaps? But the word "project" stuck in his mind, like a grease stain, practically impossible to transform.) Well, he shrugged, comforting himself, at least it was new, brand new. And besides, it was only temporary.

They didn't like the idea one bit, not Ruth and not Jesse, the only one of the kids old enough to give him trouble (or support, but that was too much to ask, wasn't it?) Sara would be fine as long as they packed all her dolls. She was an open and curious child, and would soon make new little friends, he felt sure. And the baby, well it would hardly to matter to him where his crib was. But there was no way even David Markowitz could milk any optimism from the reaction of his first-born. He wasn't kidding himself. Jesse wasn't just a sulking kid; he was downright bitter. It had something to do with leaving all those pimply-faced friends of his—the same kids he had called *"wops and micks"* when they first got to Jersey. Now, having to give them up was suddenly the end of the world. Go figure kids! But he was too fair to swap his guilt over uprooting the boy for anger over his son's irritating unhappiness. Well, of course he couldn't be expected to understand what a man has to do in this world. That required a certain maturity, and he was still young. One day he would respect his father's decision and understand the wisdom of it, but that day wouldn't come for many years. In the meantime, Dave told himself firmly, ignoring the spasm of painful guilt, the kid would just have to accept his fate.

But Ruth was a different story. She had no reason not to be glad. How many times had she bent his ear with the wonderful information that they were practically the only Jewish family in the neighborhood? Just like her to see everything, big and small, through the same set of glasses. The world could be coming to an end and all she would want to know is what time she had to light candles on Friday night. Just like her to let him make all the decisions, all the arrangements for moving and then to suddenly protest: "Where is the shul?" So he had *shlepped* back and searched the neighborhood and lucky for him he had found one. A million years old, built when the summer houses that surrounded it had been filled with prosperous Jewish businessmen and their plump wives from Prospect Park and the Grand Concourse, instead of Black welfare families. They hardly had the ten odd geezers you needed for the *minyan,* but still, it was a shul, with an old rabbi with a gray beard and an accent you could cut with a knife. That, he'd thought, ought to make her happy.

It didn't.

What about a school for Jesse? she'd asked next. There was a school, of course, a perfectly fine junior and senior high school named after some unmemorable, portly U.S. president. But that wasn't what she meant, he knew. Will he have nice friends—nice Jewish boys like himself? That was what she really wanted to know. Truthfully, he had no idea. But a few miles away, where the projects were only a dim memory of the landscape that flashed by on the way to the city, there were single-family homes on quarter acre lots with lots of nice Jewish families who sent their children to an expensive Hebrew Day School. He had nothing against that, in principle. In fact, he looked forward to the day he could join them. But all that would just have to wait. Anyhow, Jesse had been perfectly happy in his public school in Jersey, and he couldn't see why it wasn't good enough for him here, too, at the new place. What did Ruth want? That he spend his time learning to pray? Better he should spend it learning to add.

Dave sat up suddenly in the dark room, awash in a sudden swell of happiness that surged up, despite misgivings, from deep inside him. He couldn't understand his son's bitterness, his wife's hesitations. He himself loved movement, pulling up stakes. If someone had asked him point blank what he really wanted to be, and he had possessed the self-awareness to answer with absolute candor, he would have said the leader of a wagon train crossing the prairies to California: adventurous wild winds in his hair, shoulder to shoulder with other brave men, smiling with fortitude, urging the women and children forward kindly, getting them to dance and sing around the campfire.

This was the third—no—he caught himself, determined to face his crimes honestly, knowing that it would allow him to then enjoy himself in peace—no, the fourth move in ten years. The wife and children weren't dancing around the campfire anymore. He laid back in bed, lifting his pajama top and kneading the suddenly quickening ulcers above his stomach, ulcers he had had since his childhood. No one had minded the first move. He closed his eyes and there it was again. Amboy Street in Brooklyn. The stench of overflowing garbage bins. The melting, tar-covered rooftops. The billowing dust beaten out of rose-patterned pillows on fire escapes. Most of all, the unforgiving eyes of the fat women who looked out of their windows straight into yours. He could still hear them, like ludicrously bad actors on a terrible comedy show:

"Mikey!! Charlie!! You come up here. Mikeeeeeeeeeee-eeey!!!" The endless, intrusive chant of poverty.

8

What he had moved the family to next wasn't much better, true. But at least the tiny Bronx walk-up had had a few trees, slightly less noise. And the low rent had allowed him to build up the little nest egg which had allowed him to ignore—for the first time in his life—his brother and sister and all his wife's relations. Their combined warnings and handwringings, their demands for caution, for stability and moderation—for safety—had not budged his resolve. Instead, he had taken every red cent he owned or could borrow, and bought a candy store in Newark and moved them all to a house in Jersey with green lawns and little clapboard houses. Of course, that had not been his first choice. He thought of his brother Reuben for a moment. The sick regret was almost gone, now, five years later, leaving just a hopeless ache. Reuben had gotten lucky in the import business and then opened a plastics factory. He had taken in a stranger for a partner.

He tried not to think about that. He wanted today to be a happy one, the day in which he began to carve out for himself and his loved ones that big solid chunk of the American dream. His piece of the pie. He had to restrain himself from jumping up and looking at it yet again. If a car could smile, that yellow taxi was smiling. At him. He could almost hear the silent meter click up from nickels to dimes, from dimes to quarters, almost smell the new leather seats and the friendly scent of endless strangers climbing into the back. He opened his eyes and they rested on the cardboard boxes into which their settled lives had once again been poured at his urging. And then with guilt and hope and simple fear, he thought of the future.

Ruth rolled over and he caught her around the waist, snuggling deep into her softness and warmth. Her hand caressed the back of his head, smoothing down the hair that touched his neck. He took it and kissed the palm. After fifteen years of marriage, it still surprised him how small, even childish, her fingers were. He wanted so much to protect her and the children, to keep them far from all harm. To make life good for them.

"You still love me, right?" he whispered.

She opened one sleepy eye, startled by the question, the tone.

"What . . . ?"

"Oysh, I didn't mean to wake you. You're so tired, Ruthie honey. Get a little more sleep."

She sat up now, completely awake, looking at him with alarm. "Something wrong, Dave?"

"No, no, no." I've done it now. "I'm just so happy, that's all." He saw a sleepy smile spread across her small, vulnerable lips and watched her lie down again. He lingered hopefully, looking at her sweet pretty face for a while, wanting her to be less easily satisfied, to open her eyes again and really look at him.

"Ruthie," he whispered.

"Umh."

"You don't (hate me, do you honey? It'll only be for a little while, the new place. Until we get the business going, pay off some of the debts on the cab, put down a mortgage on a home of our own. Then we'll stop moving. You'll see. Trust me.)"

"Don't what?" she murmured.

"Don't have to get up just yet. Rest a while." He felt her reach out for him and he kissed the tips of her little fingers, one by one.

Outside, iron-colored clouds parted and the sun streamed through the bright autumn trees, touching the windows of the little clapboard houses. There was nothing special about this place. The houses, like the people who lived in them, were a little foolish in their pride, in their carefully painted fences, their neat plastic statuary of birds and holy men placed on lawns the size of beach blankets. There were reminders of the booming twenties in larger homes faced with brick and generous embracing porches. But even those showed traces of the Depression that had forced them into shameful compromises: tin sheds and outcroppings of cheap screened-in add-ons. But mostly, the town was made up of new houses built to welcome home the veterans, to encourage them to put death and corruption behind them, to shed the glory of their uniforms and to forget the great debt owed them. They were houses that whispered in a cynical and mean-spirited way: Get used to it. This is the best you can do. This is all that is owed you and be thankful for that. At least we are not all the same. At least there is some grass, the shade of trees. There are worse houses, they whispered. Worse fates.

Yet, though the houses were mostly small, conveying a clear sense of "make-do," there was also the feeling of stability: bikes left overnight on dark green lawns, unlocked front doors, clean curtains blowing out of open windows, laundry left billowing on common lines. It was, it proclaimed itself, for all its small attainments, a wonderfully safe place that enveloped housewives and small children in its plain, serviceable arms. It was a place to gossip over coffee, to climb up jungle gyms and zoom down slides, to dig flowerbeds in the dark, rich earth.

Jesse, aged eleven, felt some of this as he sat on the dewy, cold lawn waiting for the moving truck. He felt too, with a child's keen if inarticulate perception, the small, dark undercurrents that belied the bright surface of things. The women who avoided his mother after learning she lit candles Friday night; who wouldn't afterwards let their five year-olds come over to play with Sara. It had confused and angered him the first time someone had asked him if he was "Joo-wish"—making it sound like something you could catch. Still, while he couldn't begin to fathom the sinister complexities of these dull, plain women in their button-down housedresses, their sons were his friends. They traded baseball cards, sweated through gym, and rode miles and miles on their bikes through thick, fragrant woodlands. It saddened him to think of leaving them; the injustice made him furious.

Jesse Marks (name legally changed to "make him more comfortable in Jersey schools") believed in justice, the way only a well-loved child who has never experienced anything else can.

He believed that things should work out; that there was no excuse for them not to. Parents should be omniscient. They should never lie, never be fooled. And thus, he had been up and out at dawn, freezing his butt off on the damp grass, waiting, because his father had casually remarked that the mover was a good friend who'd give them the royal treatment and would move them in by noon.

And now, well after nine a.m. as (finally!) a battered old truck clanked and scraped its way down the street, waking up the whole damned neighborhood, he felt himself fill with fresh fury and nameless betrayal. His feelings came less from childish disappointment than from a budding sense of adult injustice: it should've been there at dawn. It should've been purring like a big powerful cat. It should've been gleaming like the noon sun on the Hudson. For what else did it mean to be treated royally? His handsome, dark face pinched, his young knuckles stretched white with fury, he tore out savage handfuls of grass and flung them at his parents' bedroom window, at the truck, at heaven.

Dave came out, tucking his wrinkled shirt into his pants, lifting up and snapping his suspenders as he walked. He looked at his son with surprise as a clump of grass caught him on the knee.

"Some friend. Some big deal of a favor," the boy accused. "Looks like it's falling apart. A piece of junk!"

Dave laughed, bending down and wiping off his pants where the grass had stuck in muddy green clumps. "*Meshuganah* kid!" As he spoke, he unconsciously lifted himself up a little, rocking forward on his toes. "What are you worried about? I never saw a kid like you! Why it's a great truck! They don't make them like this anymore. Look at what this can hold! As much as two trucks. I'm telling you. It's like getting two for the price of one. Trust me." He's grown even taller over the summer, Dave thought with a pang of secret joy.

Dave Markowitz hated few things more than being a short

man. He nurtured the secret vision of his son towering over him, reaching a height he himself had never dreamed of.

"But Dad, did you hear that noise? It can hardly move. What kinda motor is that anyway? Sounds like it's croaking . . ." he said doubtfully, looking at his father with reluctant hope.

Dave just smiled and grabbed him, trying to knead the final resistance out of his delicate young shoulders. But the boy's body didn't relax completely, hanging on to its distrust. Dave looked up at the movers (whom he had arranged for through a friend of a friend who had promised to move him as a favor, practically for nothing, with the best service).

"How ya doin, guys?" he said, slapping the rusting metal without rancor. "Think this jalopy can make it all the way from Jersey to Queens?

Ruth struggled down the steps, propelled forward by Sara's frantic tug and the baby's incessant struggle to push off from her shoulder and squirm loose. The effort loosened the bobby pins in her curly, reddish-brown hair, which fell to her shoulders and flew into her eyes. She was always, it seemed to her, trying desperately to keep up—with her husband, her kids. Always pushing herself, making that draining, extra effort, an effort that never seemed to pay off anyway in terms of measurable success.

Dave was always a little ahead of her. He overwhelmed her with his confidence in life, in the future in which she had been brought up not to believe. Life, her own family had warned her, was a dangerous road to be traveled one foot in front of the other, head bowed, eyes on the pavement. To look up, to dream, was to let down one's guard, to fall into the pit reserved for fools who believed that there was nectar to be wrung from this flinty planet. Dave was just the opposite, rushing headlong, his eyes always on the distance, his feet hardly touching the ground, flying, and she willy-nilly, connected to him, flying with him, her eyes always a little terrified.

13

She wasn't like her family. But she could never quite be like Dave either. For her, life meant (she hadn't thought of this on her own, but had read it somewhere) a constant shoring up. And it felt to her as if the things around her were always about to collapse simultaneously—faucets and toilets breaking down and leaking just as storms loosed electrical wiring and sent cables writhing like snakes just above their heads. She never really knew how to stop up the holes in the dikes. Or, more accurately, she never felt she had enough fingers.

"Dave!" she cried out as the baby struggled free and squirmed to the ground, crawling towards the overflowing boxes— picture albums, books, extension wires, stockings and linens—the flotsam of their lives.

He shook his head. She was the most disorganized, helpless . . . But then he looked at her and her presence lit into him, physically, with that familiar buzz of recognition. His wife. He scooped up his tiny son, washing his beaming face with kisses, then freed one arm to pat the head of his little girl as she pressed softly into the warmth of his thigh, her arms clinging around him as if he was a breakwater in the middle of a raging sea.

Slowly, the family gathered. They looked at the new taxi, watching the strong morning light bounce off the shining yellow paint, turning it to pure gold. They stared at its flashing promise, breathed in its new leather seats, their eyes lingering on the silent meter.

"Musta costa pretty penny," one of the fat movers grunted mockingly, breaking the long silence. The sight of him—so stupid, envious and mean-spirited—depressed everyone but Dave and the baby, who simply didn't notice.

"Bet your sweet life," Dave answered, as if an innocent question had been asked, his hands all the while caressing the flashing chrome handles. Then, as if ashamed of being serious, he flicked an imaginary cigar, crouching like Groucho.

"But what you gotta understand here, Ladies and Gents, is

that this ain't just a be-you-ti-ful classy conveyance. This is the first member of that taxi fleet that took New York by storm! Markowitz and Sons, Incorporated," he practically shouted, putting one arm around his reluctant son and the other around his harried wife and pulling them towards him with the implacable force of his love and conviction. A hug.

The engine seemed to clear its throat then burst into a powerful hum, a song of youthful power and effortless movement. Dave draped his arm around his wife's shoulder then turned to look at his children in the back seat. "I'll make it up to you kids, I swear." Then he gripped the steering wheel, pressed firmly on the gas, and moved his family down the familiar driveway onto the open road.

Chapter two

Through a darkness punctuated by the wheezing rhythm of the life support machine that will keep her heart going for a few more days at age eighty-five, Ruth will see this moment again. So many things will be lost to her, chips flying away under time's relentless chisel, but this she will recall with almost perfect clarity: sitting, apprehensive yet hopeful—next to her smiling husband on their way to their new home. She will see again the strong, satisfied corners of his mouth, turned upward in happiness, the dreamy languor in his smiling eyes. She will think of him as more relaxed than he had actually been, his hands looser and more confident around the wheel ... But it will comfort her in her strange, drug-induced sleep, discrediting the notion that they'd been nothing but dust mites in a limitless universe, suspended for a second in space until blown away by the random, exhaled breath of time. In that rich, shining moment when her husband's struggle, his choice and his own good had come together in brief triumph, she will find proof of real joy and meaning in life. And that it existed simply in the ability to choose your own path freely, whether it end in failure or in triumph.

We are never fully awake while we live; never conscious at the time of what are destined to be our lives' pivotal moments. Ruth didn't know, didn't realize as she sat there, worrying whether the milk in Louis's bottle would go sour, whether she'd remembered to put iodine on Sara's scraped knee, or if they'd locked the front door and turned off the gas, that this would be one of them.

"GIVE MY REGARDS TO BROADWAY!" Dave sang.

Ruth looked up, startled, shielding her eyes from the dazzling light of New York City skyscrapers reflecting the afternoon sun across the Hudson River. But Dave looked straight ahead, smiling, absorbing the bright vision of silver ladders climbing into the sky, Manhattan's gleaming pile of promises:

"REMEMBER ME TO HERALD SQUARE." He pinched her cheek.

"TELL ALL THE BOYS ON FORTY-SECOND STREET THAT I WILL SOON BE THERE, DUM, DUM, TEDUM!" she joined him, pinching him back, putting an affectionate arm around his shoulder.

"WHISPER OF HOW I'M YEARNING TO MINGLE WITH THE OLD TIME CROWD!"

"GIVE MY REGARDS TO OLD BROADWAY," they harmonized, only slightly out of key, *"AND SAY THAT I WILL SOON BE THERE!!!"*

"Jeez!" Jesse shook his head, stretching his adolescent legs out in the back seat, cramped with bags and boxes. But he, too, couldn't help tapping his fingers in time on the glass, while Sara and the baby giggled and bounced, making the car shake.

Then, just as abruptly, the vision vanished as they burrowed through the dark underside of the river, leaving the sun behind in a burning hole that shrank until it was finally extinguished. They emerged into treeless streets and the shadows of old gray buildings. Ruth clasped her hands together tensely. Jesse leaned back, defeated, his face darkening. Brooklyn. Again.

"New York, New York, whatever you wanna say, there's no place like it," Dave exulted. He pressed joyfully into the traffic, ignoring a chorus of condemning honks, giving them all the feeling of getting someplace, fast.

"You know what, when business is going good and I pay off some of the loans on the taxi and the medallion, I'm gonna take you all to the country, to Ellenville, to one of those farm hotels . . ."

"Oh, Dave, they went out of business years ago!" Ruth protested, shaking her head. "In the Thirties."

"What are you talkin' about?!"

"Sure they did! But I remember them. My father, God bless him, took me there one summer. They weighed you before you checked in and before you checked out, and if you didn't gain ten pounds, you got your money back."

"I was there once too. I remember those breakfasts, Gotteinu!—herring, whitefish, eggs, pancakes, heaps of sour cream on blintzes and latkes, pot cheese and sweet rolls! There was this little skinny kid, Hymie. He would sit and look at it and roll his eyes and take a few bites and then want to go out and play. But his mother would always grab him. 'Eat, you rotten kid! Eat or die already! Your father works so hard all week in the city you should be here and enjoy yourself!' And every morning, he would, poor kid, eat and eat and then go outside and throw up. Every morning!

"Then there was this guy who'd order two raw eggs for breakfast. Yeah! Raw! Every single morning for two weeks. He'd stick a pin in one and suck it out, and secretly pocket the other when he thought no one was looking. When it came time to leave—he was already on the buggy going to the train station—his kid came running after him with a suitcase and he—*nebbech*—tripped. They looked like somebody died, I swear."

"No—not in the suitcase!" Ruth gasped.

"The yolks started drippin' out from all sides. Must've had five dozen!" Dave's shoulders shook in laughter, then Ruth started in with her crazy laugh that was almost like a sob. And every time one of them said: "Stop! You'll make yourself sick!" the other took a peek and said something like "Sunnyside up!" and they'd start all over again, holding their hands over their shaking stomachs.

"You can tell a story, Dave," Ruth sighed, wiping her eyes. "You're better than Sid Caesar or Uncle Miltie. You could make a lot of money."

"Naw," he shrugged, very pleased. "Comedians don't make money. Brains make money. What's that new show? *The Sixty-Four Thousand Dollar Question?*"

"And what if you give the wrong answer?"

Leave it to Ruth to worry about the failure just around the corner, he thought, irritated, wondering why she always had to be so negative. But he didn't want to fight. He was too happy. So he smiled and answered: "So then you're a Sixty-Four Thousand Dollar Schlemiel."

The road began to narrow, the scenery changing from gray city streets to neighborhoods of cheap, attached houses with patches of unkempt lawns pinched painfully between. Then the houses gave way to low-lying marshes full of pussy willows and the strong smell of fish and finally there was the bay itself. Old men in straw hats cast fishing lines into the muddy waters from peeling rowboats. It looked like an old picture, everything so faded and still.

"How'd you like me to take you fishin' one day Jess, huh!?"

"We don't have any rods," the boy answered sullenly.

"So we'll buy. What, there's something you can't buy?" Dave said with forced cheer and a desire to please that seemed downright pathetic to Ruth, who squeezed his shoulder with understanding and pity. The boy had been torturing him for days.

"Just the two of us?" Jesse murmured with faint, conditional interest.

"Sure!" Dave nodded, delighted.

"Can I come too, Daddy?" Sara suddenly interjected joyfully.

Dave squirmed. "Well, fishing's really a boy's game more," he hedged, without much hope of success, not surprised by Sara's immediate howl of protest. With kids, you can never win, he was thinking, when he suddenly realized he'd been saved.

"Now would you kids just look at that!"

"A Ferris wheel!" Jesse shouted, rolling down the window, "Playland!"

"And there's a Merry-Go-Round and boat rides. When I was a kid I used to take the train here from Brooklyn. Took me two hours. But you kids, you're gonna go all the time. There, and to the beach! It's just a few blocks from our new place. What did I tell you? What did I say!?"

But even as he spoke, the gay, colored wheel was already behind them. On either side of the road old shanties with iron fire escapes leaned desperately against boarded-up storefronts. Bars and junk stores flew past, leaving gaps like rotting teeth. Through narrow side streets, they glimpsed Black children chasing each other in torn sneakers. Even the fresh sea breezes smelled rancid, as if filtered through rotting wood and junkyards.

Dave shifted uncomfortably. "This is the old section. Wait 'til you see our place! Brand new! Everything! Beautiful! When the City builds, it really knows how to build, I'm tellin' you. Just you wait."

You'll wonder, watching them get out of the car and step onto the pavement, following their eyes as they gaze up at the uniform brick buildings, how it is they didn't know, couldn't see. And your wonder might turn to pity and then perhaps, contempt. They should have known, you might say in your heart of hearts, as much as you feel sympathy. It was, after all, a low-income housing project. And having thought this, you'll begin to feel sure that your own knowledge would have kept you safe, away from the edge and the abyss. You wouldn't have let it happen to you, you'll feel confident. You would have climbed back into the car and rode off, saving yourself, your family.

Of course, you'd be fooling yourself. It is a false security, that feeling of superiority we have listening to someone else recount the steps to personal disaster because all of us are so very similar—we humans. We feel safe only because the teller is untalented, the truth unconveyed. And so, you must consider the soft building dust underfoot, the newness of the place. There was a glitter in the brand new windows, and a pleasant soft morning light that bathed the place in a sort of innocence. You might even realize that it was not, physically, the place itself which presented the problem. Weren't there untouched playgrounds with a kiddie pool? Basketball and squash courts? And what of the brand new community center with its inviting red doors? And the new saplings planted all over, just beginning to bud? And the large, neatly roped-off stretches of newly planted grass?

True, it was very different from the place they'd left: the small homes, the rivers of beautiful fall leaves drifting down from towering, old trees. And so they, too, were a bit apprehensive, Ruth and Dave and the children. Only Dave took confident, long strides, displaying a certainty he didn't feel, until, without realizing it, he wasn't so much leading them, as wandering off by himself. Ruth and Jesse lagged behind, like people let off at the wrong subway station, forced to wind their way through interesting, but unfamiliar and potentially dangerous streets. They searched for familiar signposts, their footsteps reluctant: I don't have to buy this, their feet said. I can walk out of the store.

But eventually they, too, were charmed by the newness. And why not? It had that rational symmetry of a wholly man-made environment, the realization of someone's idea of functional beauty. It's a beauty that seldom lasts. Like the clean lines of modern furniture, of Bauhaus architecture, its stark loveliness begins, too soon, to bore. And it is so very easily corrupted.

Fingerprints on a beautifully carved wooden door are hardly noticeable, but consider the same on a severely modern table, in a white on white room. That's why so many modern neighborhoods are so ugly. They need to be cared for, cherished. And so often the people forced to live in them hate the place, the plainness. And thus the graffiti, the garbage thrown down out of windows . . . Perhaps we can just say, it wasn't a place anyone would choose to be in if they had another choice.

If the modest garden apartments in Jersey had said: "This is the best you can do," then the city's low-income housing projects in Waveside said, complacently and with utter confidence, "This is the best *we* can do *for you*. It is better than rat-infested firetraps in the South Bronx. Better than crumbling, unheated tenements in Harlem. Believe us."

They did not lie.

But neither did they tell the whole truth. If they had, then a rat or two or a little cold might have seemed more attractive to some of the people who would soon move into these new buildings to take up their lives. And Ruth and David Markowitz, after all, were not coming from a rat-infested tenement in the Bronx.

Seeing all they saw, they nevertheless reserved final judgment, the way an astronaut might, on first landing on a grim new planet. It was Sara who, after skipping the whole way, suddenly balked.

"Saraleh. Come. You'll play later . . ." Ruth cajoled, trying to pull her along. But she twisted away, her entire small body clenched against the idea.

"What's going on? What's the hold up?" Dave said, doubling back. "What the heck . . . ?"

Ruth pointed to Sara, shrugging. He nodded with sudden insight. Crouching low, he brought his eyes level with the child's, sharing her sight. The problem was immediately clear: there were ropes around the grass. For Sara, they are chest high, an impenetrable barrier. He reached out to touch them, surprised by their weight and coarse authority.

She will remember what he tells her then: "It's young grass, baby grass, soon as it gets thicker, stronger, they'll take away the ropes so you can play in it." And she'll always wonder if he knew the truth. And if so, whether he'd felt ashamed? Responsible? Let down? Had he been lying to her on purpose? Or, had Dave Markowitz, her father, been quite simply, quite honestly, deceived?

He smoothed back her light brown hair from her forehead. "Would you like your Daddy to carry you?" Not waiting for an answer, he lifted her. She threw her arms around his neck, grateful he had reduced the problem to something so small.

They entered the long, dim hall filled with the promising and not unpleasant smells of turpentine and newly cut wood. An elevator, shiny with chrome, deposited them efficiently on the top floor.

"I asked 'specially for this floor, because of the sea view," Dave explained, fumbling for the key, smiling anxiously at his wife.

Ruth hadn't seen the apartment. Typically, she'd let him rent it without her, really believing what she'd told him, what she was always telling him, "Whatever's good for you is good for me." Or perhaps it might have been just her way of avoiding responsibility for any decision, of putting the whole burden on his shoulders. This thought often tiptoed delicately and quickly through his mind, though he tried to stop it. When he couldn't, he gave himself a good talking to: "This is *your* responsibility. This is what *you* wanted and there's no reason to go on trying to pretend she'd wanted it too. No reason at all."

He took a deep breath then stepped gingerly over the threshold. "Now look at this living room, what a size!" he began, a salesman's octave of enthusiasm too high for him to sustain.

Ruth stepped in after him cautiously, tiptoeing almost like an intruder through the empty spaces. It was very clean, very spanking white and new. The windows faced the ocean and by looking carefully though the spaces of the brick towers, over the rooftops of decaying summer houses, she imagined she actually caught a glimpse of the green-gray sea.

Naomi Ragen

The view surprised and worried her. From that height, the
neighborhood's stark contrasts struck her all at once with a force
they did not possess at ground level. The dividing line was the
road in front of the projects: to the right stood the indistinguish-
ably solid brick buildings, massive and new; to the left, individual
two and three-story private homes with carved banisters and Vic-
torian gingerbread moldings, no two in the same stage of anarchic
decay. Then, and forever after, Ruth couldn't help feeling she
preferred the decay. There was something recognizably human in
their aging, exhausted slouch towards collapse; and in the massive
sameness of the projects something inhuman.

The shops, from what she could see, were rotting too. Many
had been boarded up and the rest—the bakery, grocery, pharmacy
and candy store—were painted in the gay fading pastels of a seedy
and abandoned summer resort. Ruth, brought up on Brooklyn's
Pitkin Avenue, didn't fault a place for being poor or shoddy. What
she couldn't forgive was that it looked so deserted. Lonely, she
thought, hugging herself against the view and turning to explore
the rest of the house.

Does it surprise us, then, that she nevertheless felt an
unexpected twinge of pleasure as she examined the inside the
house? It shouldn't. After all, it was still early in the day and the
light—not yet blocked out by tall shadows of buildings in the sun's
western movement across the sky—generously flooded the clean,
new rooms made larger by their emptiness.

"So?" Dave gave her a wide grin, but his eyes, unsmiling,
strained.

"Nice," she smiled.

He reached for her gratefully, pressing his cheek against
hers and leading her into a waltz through the empty living room:

"I'll be loving you always, always
With a love that's true, always
When the things you've planned

25

Need a helping hand
I will understand, always, always . . .

Not for just an hour, not for just a day,
not for just a year, but always

She rested against his shoulder, silently mouthing the words, allowing her doubts to be danced away.

They were all together. They were all well. It was enough for her.

For Dave, as usual, it was never enough. He ran around, telling stories, making jokes. He did the shopping, bringing back fresh, fragrant rye bread with tiny poppy seeds from the bakery and thin slices of sweet Meunster cheese and cold bottles of Coke from the grocery. He spread the baby's red blanket beneath them, giving an air of picnic-like frivolity and summertime grace to the act of eating on the floor without utensils.

"Comere kid," Dave crooked an arm around Jesse's neck, wrestling him close. "Listen. When the movers get here, pick out any room you want, fix it up beautiful, just like in Jersey. You'll bring all your new friends here, make parties . . ."

Jesse shrugged him off.

"I know, I know. What friends. But what do you think? What do you think? A good-lookin' kid like you with a head on his shoulders . . . A great pitcher . . . You'll have plenty."

"So what's the story with the movers, Dave?" Ruth interrupted.

"Ruth, you see I'm trying to talk to the kid . . . can't it just wait?"

Jesse shook his head, wandered off. The door slammed.

"They should have been here already," Ruth persisted, already regretting having asked. She lowered her voice, touching her husband's shoulder. "He's just a kid. He'll get over it. It's hard for kids to move. Don't eat your heart out, Dave."

He didn't answer her because it was none of her business and she was right, and he'd failed again. They should have been here already. He walked to the window and peered out into the distance. Imperceptibly, the light began to fade, casting long, dark shadows. A breeze, salty and cold from the unseen ocean, blew through the empty house.

"Dave, it's dark already . . ."

"What . . . ?" Her voice brought him back from some far place. "Let there be light! What's the big problem? Where are the light bulbs?"

"Gee, I don't remember. Did we bring them? I'm such a dummy. You'd think a person would remember that," she shook her head. "Light bulbs."

"I could've picked some up when I did the shopping if you would've mentioned it earlier . . ." he complained mildly, but seeing her face go all humble like a scolded child's, stopped. "So don't worry about it. I'll go next door and borrow. I'll call the movers too."

He soon returned, waving a bulb victoriously. "Great neighbors. Promise me you'll go in and say hello, Ruth. I'm telling you. Good people. Now, where do you want this?" His eyes met her's as they looked toward the socket high in the ceiling, both painfully aware of being short people.

"So I'll borrow a chair," he shrugged good-naturedly. Nothing was wrong. Everything was going to be just fine. Keep it up. Just keep it up.

She caught his arm. "It's not right to ask so many favors, to get so close with people right away."

He bowed his head, gathering patience. When he looked up, his eyes were wide with exasperation. "The big expert on how to get along with people . . . When are you going to learn? To have a few friends? To trust . . ."

"Pick me up, Dad," Jesse cut him off. "I'll screw it in."

Tall, but he weighs nothing, Dave thought, hoisting the

boy up to his shoulders easily, his own short arms muscled by years of manual labor. "Now you see what a good head he's got? We should send him to *The Sixty-Four Thousand Dollar Question!*"

The bare bulb glowed with a dirty, yellow light. The baby cried. "Truck broke down. They'll be here tomorrow," Dave whispered, embarrassed.

"You see? You see what you get when you start with friends! Aach! I had a bad feeling from the start . . . Why didn't you listen to me?"

"Ruth!" his arm shot up in warning.

On those rare occasions when David Markowitz got really angry, he could be frightening. Never remotely dangerous, or even really hurtful, he had nevertheless once and only once slapped her lightly across the face when she had kept him waiting out in the rain for her for over two hours. But it had scared her just the same. She looked at him, guilty and cautious, biting her tongue, and he seemed to calm down. "It could've happened with any company," he groused.

He had long ago accepted her indecisiveness, her dependence on him for everything. At one time, he'd even found in it something distinctly feminine, even charming. He'd never known much about women and had just assumed they were all like that. But the way he figured it, that gave him the right to make the decisions; if they were good, so they were good. And if they weren't, well, that was no one's business but his own. If you weren't willing to take responsibility, you had no right to second guess or criticize.

His own father had kissed his mother, his older brother Reuben, his sister Sylvia and himself goodbye in a little town in the Ukraine, then climbed into a rotting, horse-drawn carriage, which had taken him to the ship that sailed for America.

And then the family had waited.

He remembered his mother's face, the soft curly hair, the large, wondering eyes, the childish mouth which had stretched with time and disappointment into a thin, bitter line. He remembered her in the lamplight, the laborious scratch of her pen on paper, page after page, week after week, sending out letters. After two years, she'd paid a photographer to have their faces reproduced on a strong metal oval, which she'd sent to America with a good friend of the family.

Nothing happened.

And then there was the laundry—tons and tons filling the house, the yard, in big sacks; the steaming kettles, the harsh detergent fumes. There were his mother's white hands reddening, becoming harsh to his young skin. And then they, too, were on a boat.

His father stood waiting for them in Ellis Island, shockingly beardless and wearing a dapper new hat. He'd taken his wife's bundles solicitously and hugged her, there in front of everyone; a public act of intimacy that had made his pious mother cringe. He was still a strong, toweringly handsome man, not very different from his photograph in a Russian captain's uniform as undefeated boxing champion of his army unit. But his mother's eyes had never shed their disappointment, nor had her mouth relaxed again into the lost lines of their youth.

Dave remembered her, gentle in her dark, lustrous Sabbath clothes, her pious wig, ladling out the rich Sabbath food whose odors filled the small apartment. She had reached her goal, assuming once again the position of the respectable Jewish matron, never understanding that it was too late; that the traditional, averagely-pious Russian Jew she had struggled to rejoin no longer existed. That he now preferred Friday night card parties to heavy Sabbath dinners eaten by pious candlelight; bleached blondes to pious, dark wigs. Until he finally walked out and didn't come back. Dave Markowitz wasn't like his father. He was responsible, and he would provide.

"Marty came to the phone himself. He's sorry. He meant well. One of those things. Movers'll be here in the morning, first thing. I'll get the blanket from the trunk of the taxi. We'll sleep on the floor. It'll be fun! Right, Jesse, Saraleh? Like a sleep-out!"

"And we can tell scary stories," Jesse considered, forgetting he was never going to speak to his father again.

"And tell jokes, and tickle each other!" Sara shrieked. Dave covered his ears with his hands, grimaced in mock anguish. Then smiled: "What did I tell you, what did I say!?"

The icy living room floor seeped through the thin blanket, chilling Sara's back. She reached out for her father's warm hand. But he wasn't there.

"Daddy?" she whispered, no louder than her mother's soft breathing, lifting her head to search. But it was too dark to see. She got up carefully, treading carefully past her big brother's head, avoiding her mother's toes, padding softly from the living room through the long, dark hall.

Was that him? Her hands reached out but met only shadows dancing eerily on a cold, blank wall.

"Daddy!" her voice rose in panic. She had gone too far into the uncharted darkness, too far to turn back. She peeked through the door to the bedroom. There was the closet door. And behind it? Was it moving, opening? She lunged past it.

"DADDY!"

He'd been standing alone by the window, his hands in his pockets, studying the night. "Daddy," she whimpered, feeling his strong, solid arms curve around her, saving her.

"Vey . . . What are you doing up? What's . . . You're crying?" he asked, genuinely surprised as his lips met her salty, wet cheeks. She nodded, ashamed, relieved.

"Afraid," she admitted.

"Of what?"

"Of . . . of . . . (How could you name it? That thing. That terrifying thing that had no weight, no shape, no substance? That wasn't there at all?)"

"Tell your Daddy," he nuzzled her cheek, his breath warm.

"Come on now, sweetie." His voice was gentle and kind. She leaned into his shoulder with greater urgency.

"Of ... of ... (What lay hidden in heavy silences and strange whispers, looks exchanged) It's ... (in faces fading, disappearing in the distance. Trees without leaves. Ropes around grass.) It's what (most of all, the sudden choking sadness that caught you unaware, coiling itself around your heart). It's ... what's in the closet! Monsters!!" she finally blurted out, surprising herself at having found a way to make something so large fit inside one, small word.

He laughed low, his scratchy stubble grazing her cheek, his large hands warming her small, cold feet, and suddenly she also felt it was funny. There weren't any monsters. Not here, not now. But as he carried her back out to sleep, she couldn't help looking over his shoulder at the blackened window and wondering if they weren't out there, beating dark wings against the fragile glass, like insects, waiting to get in.

Chapter three

Ruth bent over the moving boxes, sending a puff of breath fiercely and deliberately towards her forehead. The tormenting wisps of hair that had been tickling her nose and striping her vision hovered for an instant before landing like some persistent, obnoxious fly, firmly back in place. Setting aside the wadded paper bundle (whose contents she could not begin to fathom since she had neglected to mark any of the moving boxes), she sat back on her heels. Using both hands, she smoothed back the hair from her eyes, sliding in a bobby pin just a fraction of an inch too high. Massaging her aching back, she once again leaned forward into the carton. Immediately, the unmistakable slide of the tickling, silken weight drooped down, blinding her once again.

She almost felt like crying.

A month had gone by and they were still not unpacked. Buttons were coming loose like baby teeth and piling up until she could locate the sewing box; mashed potatoes were off the menu until the masher could be located; and she had no idea where her good scissors had disappeared to. The only real progress she made, she thought with sadness and embarrassment, was on Sundays when Dave lent a hand.

She sat down on the floor, her back against the wall, awash in the familiar feeling of incompetence that had weighed down upon her since childhood. She unwrapped the bundle and smiled in surprise. It was an old picture album, the pages already yellowing, the photos gone sepia.

There was her brother Morris on her father's knee, a grave, unsmiling child looking dutifully into the camera; and there was her sister Saidie's husband, dead five years now, a serious young man in a dark skullcap and short beard standing before an ironing board in the fur shop, the heavy old-fashioned iron gripped in his hand. This infamous family picture brought a guilty smile to her lips. As the story went, while posing for it, the iron had burnt a hole in the expensive coat and her brother-in-law had been fired and had never held a steady job again.

And there was Saidie in a midi dress, in a picture taken before Ruth's birth, looking frivolously girlish, so unlike the somber, matronly woman who had taken Ruth in after her young mother's sudden death. It was a pity. She seemed like someone Ruth could have giggled with, even liked.

Ruth had been five years old when her mother died. She remembered the days of mourning: the delicate, beloved body in a cold, unmoving sleep above the bedcovers; the tiny army of candle-flames on the bedroom floor giving off their mysterious, sinister glow; the cawing of old women: "Poor, poor little *yosom*. Poor *kinderlech*," they had clacked, reaching out their wizened hands to caress her. Everyone had fussed over her, plying her with *rogelach* and little toys until she'd forgotten why they'd come and begun to be shyly pleased at all the attention.

Papa had stroked her head and wept quietly, the tears wetting his graying beard. "My precious jewel. My light," he had whispered, hugging her to his side, reluctant to have her wander, even for a moment, out of his sight. Sixty years old and grief-stricken, he had looked at his little girl with wonder and shock, as if amazed to still find her there. Morris and Saidie—children of his first wife—were fully grown and married. They hadn't approved of their father's rash, (indecent they called it amongst themselves) rush into the arms of a pretty, sickly twenty year-old straight off the boat from Poland so many years after their own mother's death. And when their half-sister Ruth was born, they'd looked at each other incredulously.

They weren't bad people, Morris and Saidie, she supposed. And they had been good to her in their plodding, dutiful way all these years. They had—she had at last been able to accept and almost forgive—meant well. Even when they argued Papa into letting her live with Saidie and her new husband, convincing him how selfishly wrong it would be to try and raise her himself.

And Ruth had hated it; hated the parting from her dear Papa, hated trading his soft indulgence for Saidie's hard, unbending rules. Instead of a candy or a toy every day, there had been elaborate table legs to dust, the kind that were full of deep, narrow crevices that pinched your fingers when you attempted a thorough onslaught. She never did a good job. A good *enough* job. She was a dusting failure, a pot-scrubbing incompetent, and a bad face-and-hand washer. A hopeless braider. And Saidie, all of nineteen years-old herself, recipient of the sage advice of a horde of old *bubbies* who lined the stoops and fire escapes of Pitkin Avenue and had no business more pressing than that of their neighbors, had shown no mercy. With their iron-fisted insistence goading her on, Saidie had taken away the plates with a martyr's sigh, washing them herself; gone over all the dusting with vigor; and stubbornly insisted on plaiting Ruth's hair well into high school, long after everyone else had cut theirs into sassy flappers' bobs. It had humiliated Ruth deeply.

She'd longed to have her mother back, her sweet smiling little momma. And Papa.

Dearest Papa.

Even now his image—merely a soft, indistinct shadow in the corner of her mind—knotted her throat in a grief that, she finally admitted, was never going to go away. Papa, sitting in the parlor during the long, slow Sabbath meals of roast chicken, *tzimmes*, and fresh baked challah bread, his soft black beard rinsed clean of the paint flecks that aged it during the week, his paint-stained work clothes replaced by the dark, festive satin waistcoat of a scholar. Seated on his lap, sharing the precious, golden circle of Sabbath candlelight, touching the large pages of the open *Talmud*, she had felt enveloped in an impregnable cocoon of contentment, security and joy. Sealed within the Sabbath peace, the world locked out for a few precious hours, she'd been allowed to become her true self: fearless, full of love, curiosity and quiet ambition. It was a feeling that had never quite returned to her.

Papa had grown old so quickly. Before she knew it, he too had left her forever. She had learned then not to oppose Saidie, but simply to retreat and retrench in the only territory where Saidie and Morris could not follow: her schoolwork.

Early on, Ruth had perceived Saidie's uncharacteristic shyness as she looked over Ruth's neat notebooks filled with mathematical equations and neatly printed English sentences; her awe at the sight of straight As on Ruth's report cards, the "outstandings" filling the spaces left for teachers' comments on conduct, work habits and deportment.

Brought up in the old country, Saidie and Morris had gone no further than the fifth grade in Polish grade schools, before being apprenticed to tradesmen in a virtual bondage. But as Ruth grew older, she found her sister's quiet respect take on a tinge of regret and finally a perverseness. School was all very well and good, she began to hear, but a trade, what of a trade? And then Morris would join in, evenings and weekends—the two of them singing in harmony that built to a resounding crescendo: "*WHAT ABOUT MAKING A LIVING!*" and less loudly, because they knew it involved expenses on their part: "What about finding a husband?"

Ruth had wanted to go to on to City College. It was free, she had explained to them, but their voices had taken on a new stridency, a mockery with a cruel and self-serving edge: What does a girl need college for? Learn-a-trade-earn-a-living, learn-a-trade-earn-a-living, they drummed into her head until she felt it would explode. After all, hadn't they been forced to? After all, didn't they have children of their own to support?, they reminded her with no intentional cruelty. She should feel a sense of responsibility. She should want, already, they prompted her when she was fifteen, to go out and be independent.

Her father long dead, her friends without her grades and thus her legitimate aspirations, she wearily dropped out of her academic program and took up commercial training. She became an excellent typist and stenographer.

After graduation, finding a good job had been easy. She became a secretary in the surgery department of a large hospital. The work had been challenging and the atmosphere—the sweet male homage by handsome young doctors to her lithe eighteen-year old body, silky reddish hair and shy, dark eyes—thrilling. She learned all the medical terminology easily, and by the end of July, they gave her a raise and a pat (more like a caress) on the back.

Dr. Geddes.

She closed her eyes. Young, blonde, blue-eyed, college-spoken. And Gentile. It was summer and the days had been long and light-filled, with plenty of time left over from lunch hours for walks in the park and little shopping trips to Macys and Gimbel's. His hands had been white and delicate, like instruments, when he took hers gently.

She opened her eyes. Even in her wildest dreams, she couldn't have imagined taking such a man home to meet Morris or Saidie. Fall came and the light faded earlier, and then it was winter. There had been no way to avoid it. She had to ask to be allowed to leave no later than 2 p.m. on Fridays in order to make it home in time for the Sabbath. Being Orthodox, it was forbidden for her to take the train home after sundown. It had been hard, embarrassing to ask, to explain. But the alternative—desecrating the holy day—was unthinkable. Unimaginable. With regret, they said they could not accommodate her "special religious needs."

Her next job had been with two Orthodox businessmen whose foreheads constantly glistening with sweat, which they wiped away with the back of their hands. Sour, humorless middle-aged men, they wore hats even in the office. She worked in a windowless little room, not often dusted, whose metal desks and filing cabinets screeched like nails scraped across a blackboard when moved, chilling her with goosebumps. They gave her twenty minutes for lunch and had her work late twice a week and half-days Sunday in exchange for giving her time off on Fridays, even though the office closed at noon anyway. Each day, she typed up the invoices, rolling in paper after paper to exactly the same spot, hundreds of them exactly the same, every day. And each morning, she would find hundreds more waiting for her.

Miserable skinflints. They gave religious people a bad name, those two.

She lifted the album, meaning to put it away, and a picture floated down. What? Could it be? That many years ago already? She looked at the sweet, laughing face of the lovely young girl, the shimmering swathe of sunlight down her silky reddish-brown hair, and at the dashing young man beside her with his exuberant smile and gay straw hat.

She closed her eyes a moment, remembering that hat.

It had been the latest thing that summer, charming and stylish, even a little reckless. The kind of hat that lasted only for a season, fading in the sun, or unraveling at the edges. An impractical hat that no man in her family would have ever dreamed of spending his hard-earned money on. Seeing it for the first time hanging on her sister's coat rack by the door, her heart had done a little dance.

She had been working at her second job for four years, getting so thin and pale that even Saidie and Morris had finally noticed and began to hold worried family conferences. Placing her in the center of the room, she would answer their interrogations with dull patience. Yes. Fine. No. Nothing. Tired, that's all. Late. Work tomorrow. Good night . . . Her litany. But then, coming home one evening, she had seen that hat.

The stranger was seated in the living room, next to Morris. She'd smoothed back her hair nervously and straightened her dress. He got up and extended his hand and she had hesitated—religious women didn't touch men, even in courtesy. Finally, not to give offense, she took it shyly. Morris' introduction filtered through in bits, like a bad telephone connection. A new man at the print shop. A neighbor. Joining us for dinner.

Throughout the hot, nervous meal, she'd felt alone with him. It was as if Morris, Saidie and her husband and their two children were soundless, invisible. His eyes laughed. His smile lit up the room. And he couldn't take his eyes off her.

She looked down into her food most of the time, staring at her mound of chopped liver, the bowl of yellow chicken soup and the bobbing, fat *kneidlech*. She was afraid to eat. Afraid the food couldn't navigate the huge knot in her throat or the incredible pounding of her heart that filled her whole upper body so that there couldn't possibly be room left over for a stomach.

Then, finally, it was afterwards. He got up to leave. He stood by the door, well built and darkly handsome, twirling his straw hat between his fingers. Would she like to take a walk on the boardwalk in Coney Island with him on Sunday? She hesitated—and his smile, the shine on his face, began to fade. Amazed at her unknown power, she nodded a quiet yes.

Watching it all from the kitchen, Saidie and Morris had beamed with relief.

Ruth dusted the picture carefully. She could almost smell that day: the salt water, suntan lotion, cotton candy, boardwalk *knishes*. He won prizes for her in all the booths—big and little teddy bears, a kewpie doll, sunglasses. It seemed as if he didn't know how to lose. His extravagance bowled her over, it was so unlike anything she'd ever experienced. And he was so confident; so sure he would win everything he had his heart set on. This time. Or the next time. And all it took was another penny, or nickel, or quarter or dollar . . .

"You should save your money, Dave," she told him. "I already have more than I can carry."

"Don't worry, Ruthie," he had smiled at her. "I'll help you carry the rest." And he had.

She smiled now, pushing the tormenting hair, once again, out of her eyes, scanning the still unopened boxes. For all she knew, the bears and dolls and plastic trophies were still in there, somewhere. All precious. All useless. Boxes, she thought. Full of things most of which we would never miss. How ironic it was that all the really important things in life, the things that really gave you lasting happiness, were never the things you struggled so hard to get. They were gifts: days without sickness or accidents or encounters with bad people. Days without misunderstandings or petty crimes—by you or against you, among the people you loved. And so what meaning did all these boxes have? And what was the point of accumulating even more things that would need still more boxes?

She was often philosophical. Her problem was that while the questions occurred to her easily and frequently, the answers never did. Of course, one needed things. But the vital things, the things that you couldn't get on without were mostly too boring and inexpensive to warrant longing: sewing needles, potato mashers, underwear, safety pins. And the things you longed for, the big, important things that brought you romance and excitement, most of the time, didn't last: pretty dresses got stained and faded, shiny new cars got dented and scratched, furniture buckled and sagged, and even a dream house, she imagined, must wind up feeling small and tacky after a few years, no matter how much you fixed it up.

How could longing and struggling for things that didn't last bring a lasting happiness? She often pondered this. The only conclusion she had ever come to was that the seeking, the longing, the struggle and that first moment of attainment sometimes made you happy. For a while, at least. Perhaps that's all there really was, she thought, those rare moments in-between all the rest. And the boxes and their contents were, in the final analysis just souvenirs really, reminders that you had once arrived and had a wonderful time. She kissed her fingertips, touching them to the old picture, thinking of Dave and regretting the anger of the morning.

Why, why, couldn't he just let things be?

What business was it of his, anyway, if she had friends or didn't have friends?

But he never let up. He had tried being funny and casual about it. He had tried cajoling, pleading, nagging. And now he had found a new tactic: sitting down by her side at breakfast, he had pushed away his cereal.

"I have no appetite. A small thing I ask you . . . What did I say to murder somebody? To commit armed robbery? Ruth, I beg of you, go into the neighbors' already. At least thank them for the help on moving day. Ruth . . ." and then he had done it, that final coup de grace which had left her without means of resistance. He had lowered his eyes and whispered: "I'm ashamed already to look them in the face. They'll think we're on a high horse. That we're better than everybody else."

That was the one argument that held any water for her, and that would never in a million years have occurred to her. That anyone might think that she, Ruth Markowitz, was a snob. That she held herself higher than someone—anyone—else.

It had been the same in Jersey. "Go into them. Make some friends," Dave had exhorted her until she had gone against her own instincts. Of course, disaster had followed.

41

Oh, those awful women! Those black-hearted hypocrites in their white aprons and pearl-button sweaters! Why, that little Mikey had even asked Sara to bring the new TV outside "because my Mom says I can't go into your Jew house." Imagine!

But Dave never wanted to believe people could be like that. Mikey was just a little kid, Dave said, excusing him. Probably his mom told him not to bother us, not to come in and make noise. He didn't see that it made a difference that his house was the only one for blocks with no berried wreath at Christmas, no multicolored lights, no crèche, no big bauble-laden, snowy pine tree visible in the living room. The only house around for blocks. He just refused to believe it. Couldn't comprehend it. In a way, she felt contempt for his resolute, willful ignorance, or was it simply saintliness? What other name could you give such an elaborate effort to avoid seeing the sordid truth laid out before your eyes? Yet in the end, it was had been Dave's idea to have Jesse's name legally changed from Markowitz to Marks, something she herself would never have considered. His explanation was ingenuous: "Life's hard enough without some clerk giving you a hard time every time you fill out a form. They don't even leave room for so many letters!"

It was the height of the war in Korea, all that stuff with the Rosenbergs. Being a Jew was bad enough. But a Jew with a Russian name on top of it . . . ?! What he really meant, but couldn't face, she understood, was simply that having the suffix "owitz" or "insky" trailing off the white forms, held a hard finger to your chest so that you couldn't breathe, couldn't move up with the regular Americans, the ones who were going somewhere fast. Still, to chop up, deform, your own father's name, your family name? It was one of the few times she had ever felt her respect for him dwindle.

But if she was honest with herself, (which at the moment she didn't really want to be) her lack of friends in Jersey had had little to do with her religion. There had been other women, kinder ones among her neighbors. She hadn't gotten close to them either, finding no common ground. She hated housework, hated cooking. She didn't go to beauty parlors and never read *Good Housekeeping* or *Ladies Home Journal*. She had never made popcorn balls or Jell-O with marshmallows. She didn't know and didn't want to know how to get shirts whiter, toilet train kids faster, keep linoleum shining and furniture dust free. She had no interest in the PTA, and of course, so much of her neighbors' lives were taken up with church activities. But Ruth was never one to fight against life. She was resigned, disenfranchised, tool-less to affect it in any way. She accepted this without bitterness. But this had not stopped her from seeing clearly that this was not the life she wanted; not the kind of people she desired as friends.

What did she want? She never gave it much thought anymore. Once it had been her father's encircling arms blocking out Saidie and Morris; then it had been good grades, clean notebooks, and hours to spend in the cool dark haven of the public library. As a young wife, she had thought she had everything: a man so handsome, so considerate, and the fulsome, overflowing joy of lying in his arms in their shared bed! She had never even imagined the roadmap to so strange and blissful a country. It had taken many years for her to even peek down and notice the mud the journey had left on her heels.

Then, all at once, unhappiness had just swooped down, vulture-like, from nowhere, carrying off bits and pieces. For one thing, she finally realized to her utter surprise, chagrin, and shame, she didn't like being home with small children.

If anyone had threatened them, if a flood or fire had pitted her life against theirs, she would, without a moment's hesitation, have gladly made the exchange. She was capable of deep, real motherly love. What she lacked was the dogged interest in following up the little details which transforms motherly love from an emotion to the rock-bed of a small child's whole existence. Boiling noodles to exactly the right consistency. Keeping track of undershirts and little socks so that there are always clean ones, always dry ones, no matter how many times a day it is necessary to change them. Keeping track of who did what to whom and meting out educational justice. Knowing when to let a child express himself by arranging cornflakes on the couch pillows and when to insist on keeping some semblance of order and cleanliness in a home.

At all these kinds of things, Ruth knew she was a dismal failure. She hated the oppressive, daily grind of the small, thankless tasks which keep a home from falling apart. It was not the work; she wasn't lazy or spoiled. She just hated the constant feeling of doing it all so badly.

In her mind's eye, she held guilty, secret rituals, exorcising herself of all responsibility, the equivalent of sneaking down to sit quietly on an empty beach during perfectly good working hours. And in these rituals, she was alone in deep silent waters, looking neither right nor left for weaker swimmers drowning, but taking slow, anarchistic strokes—joyously bereft of goals. And sometimes, in the early morning when everyone was still blessedly asleep, comfortable and well in their beds, she had the amazing vision of herself in a tailored blue wool suit, hair and nails shining, sitting behind the bright, clean surface of an oiled desk with a typewriter, telephone and dictation pad set out with simple orderliness before her.

"Come Saraleh. Come, I'll dress you. We'll go visit the nice people," she said without enthusiasm, catching Sara's arm as she danced around the room, finding herself dragged along, dancing behind her. What a kid! Ruth couldn't help smiling. She couldn't walk—she danced everywhere, pirouetting, banging into walls, scraping her knees, rubbing her elbows raw . . .

"Knock, knock," the child said suddenly, standing perfectly still.

"OK, come on now."

"Knock, knock!" she repeated insistently.

"Who's there?" Ruth said wearily.

"Boo."

"Boo-who?" Ruth said dutifully, "Now . . ."

"Boo-who-who?"

"Boo-who-who-who," Ruth gave in. "Now Sara . . . !"

"Boo-who-who-who-who?" Sara continued, delighted.

"SARA!!!!!"

"Please, Mommy! Just once more, please!!"

Ruth took a deep breath and closed her eyes: "Boo-who-who-who-who-who-who!!" she said slowly, with effort.

"Why, Mommy. Why are you crying?" Sara asked with great innocence.

"You little witch!" Ruth laughed. "Who taught you that one?"

"Daddy. Daddy knows lots of jokes."

"Your Daddy loves to laugh," Ruth told her, getting her dressed. When she was ready, Ruth checked on her sleeping baby, then held her daughter's squirming hand and walked rapidly down the long hall.

She felt better taking Sara along. Armed. There would be two against . . . she shrugged, feeling foolish. Against what? She knocked timidly, hoping not to be heard.

"Who is it?" a woman's voice demanded.

Ruth hesitated. The fear and suspicion in the tone put her off balance, so clearly did it mirror her own misgivings. And yet, it created a certain kinship too. "It's Mrs. Markowitz. From down the hall."

She was a very thin young woman with badly chapped, red-knuckled hands which she wiped nervously on a clean, but faded cotton housedress.

"Oh, Mrs. Markowitz. I'm sorry. I didn't . . . Please, please, come in," the woman said graciously. "Excuse this place," her hand swept in a wide arc, including in its apology the airless, sour smell, the threadbare rug and chipped wooden coffee table. But the table was dustless and the frayed couch pillows neatly arranged, Ruth noticed with respect.

From the depths of the dark hall a child's short, choking sobs wafted down to them. The woman turned towards it, her fingers becoming fists she plunged into her pockets. "'Scuse me, won't you?" she said stiffly, retreating into the bedroom. She emerged with a pallid, thin baby boy whose hair, like his mother's, was a faded, sunless blonde. The child's coughs turned into loud, gasping noises and his mother patted him, her bashful eyes narrowing in alarm.

Impulsively, Ruth caressed the child's thin little arm with its blue-veined, almost transparent skin and thought of Louis, plump and pink, napping in his crib. She intoned a silent prayer.

"It's asthma," the woman explained, again apologetic, concentrating, as if afraid to miss a cough.

"What does the doctor say?"

"That he needs dry air."

They looked at each other a moment in silence, aware of the living room windows facing the sea. Ruth searched her face for a trace of anger or irony, but found only a worried resignation.

"Those sea breezes must be the worst thing . . ." Ruth shook her head, then was appalled she'd spoken. It sounded like criticism. But the woman took no offense, nodding her agreement, intent on the coughing child, her eyebrows anxious, her face pleading.

She must be really very young, no more than twenty-five, Ruth guessed with compassion as the woman looked up and flashed a sudden, hopeful smile. "But we . . . we got . . . plans, my husband and me," she stood up with sudden energy, "Wait, please. I'll show them to you!" She lowered the baby gently onto the rug and disappeared into the hallway.

Sara rubbed her hand along the baby's pale cheek.

"No! Leave the baby be, honey," Ruth pulled her back.

"Oh, you don't have to worry, Mrs. Markowitz. That's not a catching thing, that asthma," the woman said carefully.

That her genuine concern for disturbing the child had been misinterpreted as self-interest made Ruth groan inwardly. But she felt helpless to set things right. In her experience, the more a person tried to talk others out of their misconceptions, the worse it got. So she advised herself to just shut up and at least not make it worse.

"Look!" Thick, glossy Chamber of Commerce pamphlets spilled out of large manila envelopes, covering the coffee table. Ruth thumbed through them politely at first, and then with real enjoyment. It was like basking in summer heat among healthy vacationers; a place where white houses on flat green lawns were inhabited by tanned young blondes in white shorts with nothing more urgent to do than water rosebushes. In such a place, Ruth thought, the woman's hair would grow really golden, the little boy's paleness darken into rosy health. She felt a sudden yearning to see it happen.

"They have jobs out there. Housing. Dirt-cheap. For a song. We just need a little nest egg, for moving, rent deposits, you know . . . And my husband Bill, they just let him go . . ." Her eyes looked off in the direction of the pale light streaming through the windows. They were tired eyes, Ruth thought, but eyes that had not yet given up.

"Well, where are my manners! Let me get you something— some cookies, a cup of coffee?"

"Oh no, no thank you very much. I've still got so much to do. Unpacking . . ."

"Oh, I know what that's like . . ."

"Place is such a mess. Can't seem to make a dent in it . . . And I left my baby asleep all by himself," Ruth got up quickly, trying to prevent the woman from troubling herself with extra work, yet anxious to avoid appearing insultingly eager to get away. "I just dropped by to thank you for the help. The light bulb and the phone call. You know, the movers came so late . . . We so much appreciate all you did."

The woman looked at her blankly.

"You know," Ruth repeated with heavier emphasis, wondering what in heaven's name she had done wrong now. "My husband. Oh!" Color flooded her face. "This is apartment 7H isn't it? My husband told me specially . . ."

"Seven A," the woman said softly. They stared at each other awkwardly, then suddenly both giggled.

"Glad you come by anyway," the woman held out her hand. "The name is Dundee. Dundee Williams. And if you do need anything, anything at all . . ."

Ruth grasped the work-roughened hand warmly. "Well, I'm real glad to have met you. And I wish you a lot of luck, going out West and all. Looks so nice out there," she smiled, surprised at how much she liked this woman in her old housecoat, liked and understood her as she had never liked or understood the PTA mothers in Jersey with their pleated skirts and pearl-button sweaters. She bent down, planting a swift kiss on the baby's white forehead, then edged away, saddened, as the coughing began once again.

"So how'd it go?" Dave asked later that night.

"Fine!" she said, being honest.

He studied her face a moment and then, satisfied, leaned back and relaxed.

Chapter four

"So what do you think now?" Dave bellowed, his arms flung wide enough to embrace everyone in sight.

"A bicycle!" Jesse walked around it for a while, giving it little unbelieving strokes, as if to make sure it wasn't about to disappear into thin air. "Gee, Dad, thanks!"

"And a Revlon doll," Sara shouted, frantically tearing open the box. But when she actually took it out and held it, so tall and with a spangly pink and silver dress and little diamond drop earrings and silver high heels, she stood absolutely still, sucking in her breath as if drowning in a huge tidal wave of joy.

"Oh, Daddy!" She ran to him, jumping up into his arms, squeezing his broad neck with her one free hand.

"Dave," Ruth's voice was deep, overwhelmed, as she draped the new fur coat around her shoulders. It wasn't mink, but still . . . a real fur coat!

His arms met around her back, caressing her through the thick, soft folds.

"Didn't I tell you I knew what I was doing? What did I tell you? What did I say?" He laughed.

Things were going well. He had a way with customers, not that it surprised him. He knew that from the store. But the tips! The way these city folks and tourists responded to a smile, a little decent service! He couldn't really afford all this, not exactly . . . but what the hell. The way things were going . . . well there was no telling how deep the mine was or how large the mother lode. Besides, he believed in celebrations; in not waiting for perfect moments, and this was about as good a time as any he had known in his life.

"To celebrate, I'm taking you all for a little ride."

"Aw, Dad, now? I wanted to take the bike out for a spin . . ."

Dave held up his hand. "Nothing's gonna help you, Jesse. Just get dressed and follow me."

In the gleaming yellow taxi, the off-duty sign on, he drove past the projects and the rotting hardware and grocery shops where old black men leaned back against peeling wooden shutters near displays of pomade and hairpins. He drove past respectable little wooden houses, Waldbaum's, a large white synagogue; past parks and schools until he entered a place where large private homes sparkling with huge picture windows were separated by tended lawns.

It was a place where houses seemed to live, but not people, Ruth thought, shuddering and hugging herself. She never liked these kinds of neighborhoods, all fancy shmancy. They made her feel inadequate and unfairly judged.

He parked the car, then ran around to open the door for her with a little bow. "Madame," he smiled, taking her hand with courtly grace and helping her out. Then he tucked her arm firmly though his, leading her through the gates and straight to the front door.

"Dave!! What are you doing?!" she protested, squirming to release herself. But before she could pull free, he had already pressed his thumb decisively onto the doorbell.

A voice—a bit alarmed, Dave thought with uneasy surprise, called out: "Who's there!?" Had he changed that much? He took off his cap, smoothing back his thinning hair. "Don't you recognize me, Rita? It's Dave."

The door opened stingily, the crack widening with caution until it finally framed an older woman. She wore an expensive black dress, the kind you'd wear to a catering hall or a hotel for a Bar Mitzvah, Ruth thought, with slight contempt. It was not a dress for the house in the middle of the day. The woman's sharply angled, ungenerous body discouraged anything as rash as a hug.

"David," the woman smiled tightly, her uncertain eyes wandering appraisingly from his cabby hat to Ruth's new fur coat. Then she exhaled.

"*Nu.* A real surprise. Come in, come in." She pecked at NuRuth's cheek and patted Sara and the baby with a little more enthusiasm.

"Reuben, you'll never guess!" she called over her shoulder up the stairs.

"Guess what?" An older man padded down the steps. The children looked at him, startled. Except for graying hair and a larger paunch, he could have been their father. Halfway down, he stopped, patting his pipe meditatively against his palm, staring at his younger brother. "Long time, Dave," he finally said.

"Yeah," Dave agreed, walking hesitantly halfway up the steps to meet him, shaking his hand with an ingratiating enthusiasm that made Jesse turn away his head in embarrassment.

"These are my kids, Reuben," Dave said eagerly, gesturing towards them, his voice suddenly hoarse.

"*Nu.* Time goes. Beautiful *kinderlech,* beautiful. So please, please, sit down, sit down." He led them through French doors newly painted in creamy white and gilt, into a room golden with sunshine and down-filled, yellow couches.

Sara sank blissfully into the soft luxury.

"Just watch the little feet, sweetheart." Rita said, her tone jovial, her eyes unfriendly.

Sara stared down at her toes with vague guilt.

"So many years to catch up, Dave. You look good. Right Rita, he looks good?"

"Very good," she nodded, bored.

"Couldn't be better," Dave agreed, rubbing his hands together, trying to have enough enthusiasm for all of them. "Just went into a new business a few months ago."

"What? You sold the candy store?"

"Yeah. Got tired of schlepping in cold bottles of seltzer at four in the morning. Instead I got this . . . these . . . taxis," he said, making it plural at the last minute.

"Yes? What? Taxis?" Reuben suddenly leaned forward.

"Well, it's actually only just the one at the moment. But with the way things are going . . ." Dave said eagerly, shrugging with a modest smile, like a man about to accept an award at a testimonial dinner. He explained his plan to Reuben, his hands reaching out and contracting, almost as if he were maneuvering around a boxing ring with a dangerous opponent. When he finished, he leaned back with nervous satisfaction and rubbed his neck, using the opportunity to take in and memorize every last piece of furniture in the room.

"Pretty quick return on a new investment," Reuben said calmly, taking out his pipe, tapping it and lighting up.

Dave smiled. This, he understood perfectly well, was not meant as a compliment, but an expression of Reuben's usual don't-think-you-can-be-smarter-than-your-big-brother-don't-even-try. Still, he smiled, because it was a beautiful day and his surroundings made him feel rich; because his wife was lovely in her expensive new coat, his gift, paid for by the return on his wise investment;

because his son was tall and handsome, his daughter pretty, his baby sweet. He smiled, because for once in his life his plans had worked out well and he had nothing to be ashamed of.

Reuben studied the smile, impressed. "Maybe you need a partner?"

Dave could think of many things to say, but only one stuck in his mind: Jackie Gleason's favorite line: "How sweet it is!"

"Just a thought," Reuben smiled uneasily.

"Right." Dave couldn't believe it! "So, how's your partner working out? What was his name again? The Pole?"

"Now Dave, let's not bring up that again," Reuben squirmed. "Five years we didn't speak. It's enough already."

"Sure, you're right. Bygones." Is there forgiveness in my heart? Dave asked himself, that my own brother preferred to take in a stranger to his business over his own flesh and blood? That he could have helped me and didn't? He searched Reuben's eyes. Yes, there was. That too, among many other things. He rubbed his hands together. "If you're serious, give me a ring. I'll think about it."

Rita brought out a small silver tray with cakes. "Take kids, but be careful with the little crumbs. And maybe you should wash your hands first."

Jesse drew his hand back, offended, but Sara stuffed her mouth full, shoving the cakes in whole before her aunt could change her mind. She was enjoying herself tremendously until she looked up and saw all eyes—including her aunt's—upon her.

"Be careful not to choke, darling," Rita said dryly.

Reuben suddenly got up. "I'll show you the house."

A really wealthy person, one with real taste and discernment, would have smiled at the offer—and at the house. It was all canned taste, bought by the pound. Department store Louis. But for Dave and Ruth and the children, it was like a fairyland. They followed him through what they perceived to be huge rooms, full of light and air and warm, polished objects: carousel horses and brass trays, and tables of dark wood. There were damask curtains and carpets your toes got lost in.

"This used to be Thelma's room."

"How is my niece? Still at that fancy Boston college?" Dave wanted to know.

Reuben cleared his throat uncomfortably. "That was years ago. Dropped out. Now she's in California. Her husband is a nuclear something. Makes a good living, bottom line, you know."

"Kids?"

Rita shrugged. "She has trouble with her tubes. I told her not to be in such a big hurry. What does she need it for? She's young yet, she should enjoy. But she wants babies, you know how it is. So, doctors, all the time doctors . . ." She shook her head at the foolishness of it all.

Sara stared at the four-poster bed dressed in lavender and white frills, looking as if any moment it would get up and dance. The furniture was all white and gold, bathed in a lavender glow from the sheer curtains. She longed to lay down in that bed, to bathe forever in the transforming glow of that lavender light.

The rest of the house flipped by them like the slick pages of a magazine, until their heads swum with undigested images of gold framed mirrors, gleaming copper pots, and crystal perfume atomizers. Even the water in the bathroom was better, Sara rejoiced, watching it bubble over her hand softly, instead of pelting it.

This—Sara thought, experiencing a conviction as powerful as any person undergoing a religious conversion—is what it means to be happy.

"And here's the garden," Reuben said, opening the patio doors.

"Sara!" Ruth cried out, mortified.

"It's all right. Leave her, leave her," Reuben chuckled magnanimously as the child rolled over and over, laughing, on the lush green lawn, breathing in the sweet fragrance of the tender grass, of safety, of privacy, of ownership . . .

"Look at her, look at her!" Rita shook her head, disapprovingly.

Dave watched the child, a smile frozen on his face, his heart aching.

"While you're in the visiting mood," Reuben interrupted, sending his wife a withering look, "go see Sylvia. She lives ten minutes from here, with the Gelts. Multimillionaires. She always complains how you don't keep in touch."

"So, how is my sister?"

Reuben shrugged. "Sylvia's all right."

"How good can it be for a childless widow?" Rita interjected, shaking her head.

"It could be a lot worse," Reuben said sharply. "Fifteen years she's been alone, you know," the critical, accusatory edge in his voice sharpened.

Dave shifted uncomfortably. He hadn't come to his brother-in-law's funeral, hadn't even paid a *shiva* call . . . If he hadn't spoken to his brother Reuben in five years, he hadn't spoken to Sylvia in twenty.

"Not that I'm really in touch with her all that much either," Reuben softened his tone hurriedly, by no means interested in assuming the thankless and tiresome role of family peacemaker.

Rita took Ruth's hand, looking reproachfully at Dave. "Don't be strangers. I . . . we . . . never wanted this . . . not talking . . ."

"Shh . . . forgotten already," Reuben cut her short with an irritated and authoritative clap. "You live close by?"

Ruth shot Dave an anxious look.

"Not far, not far. But we plan to move soon. This is not a bad neighborhood," he looked around appraisingly, ". . . and seeing how it's near the family. If something comes up, you know, five bedrooms . . ."

Ruth swallowed hard.

". . . Something good, not just anything. Something like

yours, you know? What do you say, Ruth? Five be enough? You know, one for guests. It's good to have an extra room. For guests."

Ruth's eyes pleaded as she pulled him gently towards the door.

Just one more stop, Dave said as he started the car. He flew past florists and elegant boutiques to the next township where huge parks bordered each other and houses could only be glimpsed in the distance, behind hedges and gates, like palaces, and the silence was uninterrupted except for the endless rustle of clean wind through treetops and flowers.

He pulled up along the curb and stopped. Over the hedges, at the end of a winding road flanked by poplars and solid old oaks, they glimpsed the Gelt's estate.

"Makes Uncle Reuben's look like the servants' quarters," Jesse hooted.

Dave grabbed him around the neck, playfully squeezing. "Yeah," his eyes sparkled. "Yeah."

"How do people get that rich anyway, Dad?"

Dave released him. "Any damn fool can make money in America, unless you're a dope like Morris . . ."

"Dave!" Ruth warned.

". . . sitting on your can and watching it spread for thirty years. Afraid to make a move, to pee too long in case the boss should look at you funny . . ."

"There's more to life than making money, Dave. Morris is a good father and husband . . ." She looked up sharply. "Dave, this isn't about Passover, is it?"

"Well, honey . . . we don't have to talk about it right now. But actually I did think we could stay home one year. That I could sit at the head of my own table. Read my own Haggadah . . ."

"You'll break your teeth over the Hebrew," she laughed.

"So, I could say it in English. Where's it written it's a crime to use English?"

"Listen. Between everyone we're talking to and not talking to, we've got hardly anyone left! I want the children to feel they have some close family."

He didn't answer her, getting back into the taxi and gripping the steering wheel, looking out at the big house nearby, the smiling lines around his mouth sagging, hardening into uncharacteristic bitterness.

Ruth climbed in next to him. "I'm sorry I said anything. You have nothing to regret. You were such a good son."

A good son, a responsible son, Dave thought, turning the key in the ignition. And his mother had clung to him like a life raft in a raging sea. He'd been the only one to take her part. Reuben had said that since the old lady had fought with the old man for twenty years trying to get him back into a skullcap and side curls he couldn't understand why she wanted him back when he decided to leave. And Sylvia, who had introduced her father to the buxom, aging blonde who became his second wife after he divorced their mother, had said (and they were the last words she ever said to her brother Dave) that their father deserved better than an old greenhorn.

He had sided with his mother, but it was his father he understood.

You had to forget about the synagogue. You had to keep the store open, take the cab out Saturdays, holidays. You even had to change your name so it wouldn't point a finger at your chest and back you up against a brick wall. And in exchange for playing it by the rules (rules his mother hadn't and his wife didn't, wouldn't, understand) you were promised the jackpot. Reuben had played and won. Sylvia had played and won. And now, he thought, driving past the house behind the hedges, now, it was his turn.

Chapter five

To her great surprise, Ruth found herself happier than she had been for a long time. Life in the housing projects, she realized, was like the life she had loved as a child in the large apartment houses in Brownsville that were always alive with warm voices and familiar faces. In New Jersey, each little house had had its own gate, its own lock. And the streets had been as deserted as graveyards. Here, she felt she knew everyone and they her. There was no need for pretense. The furniture was worn, the clothes mended and unfashionable, the hairstyles devised over the bathroom sink. But if you needed a cup of sugar, you could knock on any door. She viewed each door a little like she did the cover of a novel. Beyond each was a separate world, a story.

In 7E were the Cohens. Despite their Jewish name, Ruth soon discovered, they were devout Catholic churchgoers, except for the father, a grumpy Jewish alcoholic disowned by his family, including his brother the doctor. He kept his refrigerator locked with a chain so that his three teenagers, Mary, Willy, and Andrew, wouldn't eat up his drinking money. Mrs. Mary Cohen, a handsome, heavy-set woman, seemed an older version of those good, red-cheeked Catholic schoolgirls in their plaid skirts. Ruth had great respect for Mrs. Cohen and was mortified that a Jewish man should be giving her so much trouble. They spent time together, trading immigrant stories, teaching each other about religion. And Mary, a pretty teenager, often babysat.

The two MacDonald sisters were in 7B. A widow and a spinster, their thick Scottish accent charming, if hard to understand, their home smelled of spicy cookies and freshly ironed linen. Both were in their late sixties, with beautiful rosy complexions and silvery white hair and a way of speaking which Ruth found incredibly encouraging. Just a nice, sunny day was enough to set their cheeks beaming, their eyes alight. Often, they showed up at her door with hand-knitted doll clothes for Sara and warm booties for Louis.

The Cramers, a childless old couple who kept parakeets in open cages, were in 7C. Sometimes they would leave their door ajar and you could see how they kissed the birds and allowed them to peck food from their mouths. Mr. Cramer, a retired postal worker, walked around in an apron and never left the house by himself except early each Sunday morning. Even in the bitterest weather, he could be seen jogging along the beach for miles, red-faced and near collapse. The unkind rumor was that he chanced the cold, the risk of being attacked by dogs or vagrants and even a heart attack for the sheer pleasure of getting away from Mrs. Cramer, at least for a few hours. The old couple often invited Sara in, letting her play with the birds, teaching her how to hold her finger so they would fly to her.

Mrs. Robinson was the first Black neighbor on the floor. The day she moved in, some neighbors grouped in the hall talking, creating a low unpleasant buzz. But when they saw her get off the elevator—a plump, grandmotherly woman with horn-rimmed glasses, the air cleared. Later they learned she had raised a family of nine alone, and now had taken in a grandson with a heart condition. She supported herself by sewing and mending and soon became custodian of the floor's broken zippers and unhemmed pants.

They all liked each other. They felt at home.

Then, without warning, things began to change.

Dark scrawls of breasts with darkly penciled nipples appeared on the staircase walls; and on other floors the strong smell of cheap cooking vegetables filled the hallways. The elevator's only window was smeared with spit and an army of small Black boys guarded the main entrance with sticks, barring Sara's way or challenging her to pee down the elevator shaft, until their mother appeared with menacing wooden switches and herded them home.

The original flow of tenants—respectable blue collar workers, retirees, struggling small businessmen—was joined by a trickle, and then a steady stream, and finally a deluge of large welfare families from the Bronx, Harlem, and Puerto Rico, turning the original tenants into castaways, helplessly stranded on a rocky promontory in the center of a vast ocean not of their choosing.

There was prejudice against the newcomers—yes. But mostly, fear and resentment. The first tenants had come from the decaying core of the city's heartland, neighborhoods in Brooklyn, the Bronx and Queens, places where the owners of small, family-owned grocery stores had been bloodied and robbed; where it had become an act of courage or foolishness to walk out of the house after dark. They'd come because they honestly believed in the benevolence of the great city who had offered them these new homes by the sea with rents they could afford with dignity. They'd believed that the projects had been built for them, to right a wrong, to protect and care for them. And now they felt the great swell of horror at their betrayal; without their knowledge or consent, the festering inner core they had fled had been brought to them.

Most of all, they felt ashamed. How had it happened that they'd fallen so low, without even having felt the wind at their back, or the precipice, or the one silent step forward that had brought them down?

Only Sara took the change in stride easily. She watched with admiration the older Black girls in their amazing games of double-Dutch jump rope, trying to join in, tangling her feet until she was hooted, and mocked and pushed out of the way. She tried to talk to the beautiful, dark-eyed Puerto Rican girls with their shining braids, or the sweet, fat, dark-skinned babies that crawled naked through the halls. Mostly, she wound up smiling helplessly when they answered her in the rapid staccato language she couldn't understand.

Used to the safe, child-friendly streets of Jersey, she was constantly pushing to go outside. Ruth, afraid, kept holding back. "Later," she would say. "Later, I'll take you to the park." But then she would forget, or get caught up in housework or making dinner. Often, Sara snuck out by herself, holding her breath in delight and shivering with pleasurable adventurousness. Ruth, at her wits' end, compromised. She could go by herself if she stood near the benches so that Ruth could look out the window and check on her.

Sara tried. She'd sit for a while, closing her eyes and feeling the sunlight kiss her face, breathing in the new mown grass. She would dance along the bench, or walk like a tightrope walker, one foot in front of the other, balancing along the backrest. She felt hopeful and expectant, waiting for parades to begin, music to start, and usually she was not disappointed. Something always happened.

"Wanna play?" She was a plump white girl, a little older than herself, someone Sara had never seen before. She didn't look Sara in the face, her eyes fixed on the doll in Sara's lap.

She had taken her gift outside for the first time, after what seemed like weeks of begging that had finally resulted in her mother's reluctant approval. After days of just watching it, as if it were a picture, and days gradually gaining the courage to actually play with it, she had grown bored, her solitary delight proving too lonely a pleasure. She craved the envy and admiration that could only be found in the eyes of her peers. Now, in this stranger's covetous eyes, she found exactly what she had been longing for: a confirmation of her good fortune.

The girl lunged, grabbing the doll and holding it high over her head. "Wanna play house? I'll be the mommy."

Sara's stomach plunged, her heart beating wildly. This was not fun.

"Give it back!" she shouted.

"Aw, keep yer bloomers on, whydontcha?" The girl turned it around and upside-down, examining it slowly from all sides, but always out of Sara's reach. "I had one like this here but my brother peed on it, and my pop made me throw it inna garbage. You gotta brother?"

Sarah nodded anxiously, watching the strange fingers wrinkle the precious silver and pink fabric. She looked up, a little desperately, straining to see her mother's face at the window.

"He tries to smash your face, right?"

"My Daddy doesn't let," she answered, relieved somehow at just the thought of her father.

"Jeez, my Pop don't do nothin. Just sits there drinkin' beer: Wha, wha, youse fuck'in kids, cancha lock yer damn holes shut," she mimicked with pleasure, laughing, her eyes shifting craftily, surveying the area. "Why was ya lookin' upstairs?"

"'Cause my Mamma's up there. She'll be coming down to get me in a minute."

The child's face clouded over, sullen. "I wasn't doin' nothin," she insisted, her tone petulant and wronged. "You can have it back. You think I need this? Jeez, I got better stuff then this here. I got a whole room full. Dollhouses, baby dolls, rocking horses . . ." Her eyes suddenly brightened with a new thought.

"Wanna come to my house? We can play," she smiled sweetly. "We can be mommies, and feed our babies. I have this tea set. C'mon!" She didn't wait for an answer, holding the doll securely, walking away. She didn't hurry, but walked deliberately, calmly. If she had run, Sara would have felt the violation, cried or run home. But watching her walk away like that, her back so calm, made Sara think that perhaps, after all, they were only playing.

Down long flights of stairs, past benches and fenced-in concrete playgrounds, they walked. Sara had never been so far away from home before. In a way, it was thrilling to look around, to explore. Almost as if she had crossed over an invisible barrier and was suddenly free. She skipped, danced in circles, turned somersaults, feeling almost grateful to the girl for having taken her along.

But then her feet began to drag. She grew tired of the long staircases, the dreary scenery. For no matter how far they walked, nothing ever changed. It was all the same, the same: tall, ugly buildings the color of dried blood and endless ropes around the grass.

This surprised and appalled her. For she had expected—as in any magic kingdom—that somewhere she would pass through the door and it would all be transformed. There would be tall trees again, whose fallen leaves would turn the sidewalks into oceans of crackling gold, crimson, and brown. And tender grass that you could roll and roll and roll in . . .

She thought of her friend Mikey, wondering what he was doing now. Catching bees in jars? Picking hard, sweet pears from the tree?

At last, the girl turned into a building. "Is this your house?" Sara called after her, relieved. But she didn't answer; she just kept on walking. Sara ran to catch up. But as soon as she entered the dim hall, she felt her body tingle with regret. It was not its strangeness which revolted her, as much as its eerie familiarity: If this, which seemed so much like home, was so far from home, then how would she ever find her own door again? She leapt up the staircase, forgetting her horror of the dark, panic-stricken that she would lose sight of the one person who could lead her back to where they'd started.

She caught up to her on the fifth landing. The girl turned to her slowly. She smiled. With relief, Sara smiled back.

"Knock, knock," the girl said.

Sara smiled some more, confused. "Who's there?"

"Knock, knock," the girl repeated, this time banging Sara's forehead with her closed fist. "Anything in there? You want your doll back?"

"I want to go home," Sara said, rubbing her forehead. Was this a new game? She felt the first stirrings of fear.

"Then you godda do like I say. I ain't gonna hurt you," the girl whispered, looking straight into Sara's dilating eyes. "I'm just . . ." She giggled, and the sound was so ugly, Sara thought, not happy at all, but low and menacing.

"I don't want to play anymore. I want to GO HOME!"

She felt herself pressed back against the cold wall. Harsh, insistent fingers pressed into the secret places of her body, places she had not been fully aware of until now.

"No!!" she pushed out against the intrusion, the heavy, insistent body and felt the angry fingers withdraw, becoming fists that fell on her head, stomach and legs. A dream, she thought, with a hard edge. A confusion. That was when she understood for the first time what it meant to be alone. That was the root of her fear, more than the blows, the pain. The idea that she was open now on all sides, with no parent or sibling or friend to shield her. She tried to make fists, to kick, and amazingly, the blows fell on her less often. She turned and fled down the stairs, fingering her throbbing bruises. To be home!! To have the locked door of her own home in front of her! Her mother and father and brother on all sides! She would never, ever ask for anything more! She got up to the front door of the building, then stopped, appalled.

Her doll. Sara couldn't even recall the exact moment when,

incredibly and unfathomably, its existence had faded from her mind. A new feeling, deeper than anger, shot fresh strength into her weary body as she bounded once again up the stairs. In the darkness her foot kicked something. She heard a dull clatter down the steps. When she bent to look, two bright blue eyes stared back at her from a plastic head on which a single curl still twined. She sat down on the steps, beyond tears, feeling she'd gained a knowledge for which she was not yet ready.

Outside, she wandered aimlessly, hopelessly, led from building to building by a familiar window, or a bench she thought she recognized. But when she drew closer, she'd lose courage. The inside . . . the hall. The darkness! What if it were the wrong building? If she knocked on the door of 7F and a dangerous stranger opened the door instead of her mother? Terrified at the idea, she walked on, holding her breath with fear past groups of Black teenagers who loitered around the benches. But they did not even turn to look at her. They spoke to each other in low voices, sometimes breaking out into songs with mournful falsetto harmonies, like singers on the radio.

"Why, honey, you lost?"

She looked up, frightened by the Black stranger who bent over her. But then she recognized her: Mrs. Robinson!

She nodded, letting the sudden, scalding tears fall.

"Now, don't you cry child, hear? 'Cause I'm fixing to take you straight home to your mama." She offered her large, soft hand. Gratefully, Sara slipped hers inside.

Chapter six

Dave padded into the bathroom, closing the door softly behind him to keep the running water and the light from disturbing his sleeping children. He splashed icy water into his eyes to pry them open and then examined himself in the mirror. He was always a little surprised and disappointed at his reflection. He thought of himself as a young man, a happy man, not at all the person who stared back at him each morning—paunchy, exhausted and going grey. He slapped himself in the face with good-natured open palms. Humming softly, he patted a few wispy strands into an optimistic wave over his balding scalp.

> *"Brill cream a little dab'ill do ya,*
> *Brill cream you'll look so debonair.*
> *Brill cream a little dab'ill do ya!*
> *She'll love to get her fingers in your hair."*

He pulled aside the jungle-like tangle of wet laundry which blocked the view from the window, hoping to catch a glimpse of the sea. It was actually a nice view when the incinerator smoke wasn't rising from the basement and condensing in grey ash on the glass, as it was now. Some laundry fell to the floor, entangling with rubber ducks and battleships. He stooped patiently, putting the toys in a neat row and rehanging the laundry more securely than his wife had done.

In the dim hall, the heavy odor of baby powder and warm blankets enveloped and cheered him. He looked in on the kids. Louis had thrown off the covers again. How long had the kid been like that? Dave worried, tucking the blanket into the bottom of the crib mattress securely, army-style. The one useful thing he had learned in World War II. Sara's head was, as usual, under the pillow. He waited anxiously for the reassuring rise and fall of her chest. It was foolish, he told himself. She was, after all, in kindergarten, a strapping, healthy kid long past the stage when sudden, unexplained disasters happened in the night. He wasn't afraid, really. Just responsible. They were his babies.

He would have liked to look in on Jesse too, but the boy's door was, as usual, closed tight and it would not have been respectful to open it. Six months and he was still mad—at moving, leaving his friends, his bike, his Little League games and who knows what else—Dave sighed, then suddenly brightened. Next year, when Jesse was Bar Mitzvah, he'd write it on the cab door: Markowitz and Sons, Inc.

Maybe then the boy would understand.

Nearing the kitchen, he heard the faint scraping of a spoon and knew he had failed again and Ruth would be there and they would have the same argument they had every morning: "Now why'd you have to get up so early? I could've poured myself a few Wheaties," he'd grouse, and she—her beautiful face scrubbed pink with Ivory soap like one of the kids—would scold him back: "You don't take care of yourself! A man needs a warm breakfast." And he would murmur, trying to sound annoyed, something about killing herself waking up at five every morning, trying to hide how much it meant to him. Then he would eat the awful stuff—which would either be overcooked and mushy or as grainy as sand but never prepared the way it was meant to be, all the while conscious of her face filling with pleasure each time he took another spoonful. And when he'd scraped the last of it from the bottom of the bowl, he knew he'd have no choice but to smack his lips and ask for another bowl.

He watched uneasily as she pulled her worn bathrobe around her, giving the cord an extra tight yank. Whenever Ruth was serious, dead serious, she buttoned up or yanked closed, kind of pulling herself together. He leaned across the table, patting her on the shoulder.

"What's up doll?"

She flinched. "It's Jesse."

He looked into his bowl.

"You don't want to know!"

"What kinda thing is that to say?" his voice rose indignantly, annoyed at his own utter transparency. It was just too early. He'd have to carry it around with him all day, like an indigestible meal.

"He came home with another bloody nose yesterday."

He felt the cereal thick and gluey on the roof of his mouth, the dryness of the blackened toast.

"He hates the teachers and sits in his room all day sulking. He has no friends . . ."

"Why can't he at least try to make friends?" he interrupted, feeling the rise of acid from his quickening ulcers. "There *must* be *some* nice kids . . ."

She studied him carefully, puzzled. "You know it's a bad school, Dave. A bad neighborhood. I'm afraid."

He stared at her, sudden understanding dawning in his eyes. "Something happened?"

"Last week. One of the girls from the ninth grade was going to the bathroom . . . They think it was a boy from twelfth grade. Mrs. Cohen told me."

He shut his eyes a moment, exhaling deeply. "So what can we do? Is there anyplace else we can send him?"

"You're not going to like this, Dave. But there's a private Hebrew Day School in Far Rockaway. It's not far," she rushed on. "He could get there by bus."

"Ruth!" But then he shrugged. Father and husband. Provider. "Private. So, how much?" When she hesitated, he realized that everything that had gone before had simply been a buildup.

"A couple of hundred, but they give out scholarships!" Her voice was pleading, apologetic and implacable.

It was like being hit over the head. He tried not to show he was reeling. "So find out about it for next year."

"You mean it!? We don't have the money . . ."

"Money, what's money?" he said gaily. "By next year, who knows? Someone might forget a bundle in the back seat."

He would just have to work a little harder, that's all.

The warmth of her soft lips lingered on his as he sped through the deserted streets into the dark daybreak. He peered at the rows of silent houses rising slowly out of the shadows, turning lavender, then silver in the coming light. He thought of the families that would soon be getting up together, gathering around the kitchen table. Like Robert Young, the fathers would joke with their kids, making sure they brushed their teeth and drank their milk, patting them on the behind and tousling their hair.

With a sudden ache, he thought of Louis waking, standing in his crib, his baby cheeks already hardening into something less fragile and full. Only on Sundays did he ever see his baby son awake. He considered that. Never, except for Sundays, and even then, not every Sunday. They grew up before you had a chance. With Jesse and Sara it had been the same. How was it possible? He had always planned to be just like Robert Young, the wise father in his favorite TV show, *Father Knows Best.* Successful and friendly and always there.

"*Nu,* so what? So what do you want? The life of Riley?" He

berated himself mockingly, mimicking his brother-i
strident, nasal whine. "Why don't you get a goo(
Why don't you work for somebody forever for notl
good enough for you?"

"Naw, Morris. It's not good enough for me," h~ ..nispered
to his grinning reflection. He slid his palms with pleasure around
the steering wheel, feeling his control of the powerful machine.
Shouldn't make fun of Morris. He wasn't a bad guy. Maybe one
day he'd be generous to Ruth's brother. Take him out from under
his blessed union, his foreman Weinstein, so he could pee without
permission. He chuckled, imagining prying Morris loose from his
union benefits, his pension, his little chair in front of the printing
press . . .

When he got to Brooklyn, he stepped on the gas. Brooklyn.
It was too full of old buildings, old people and bitter memories.
His parents had been dead for so many years, but their fights still
went on in his head. And in his nostrils, the odor of billowing dust
from rose-patterned pillows beaten on hot fire escapes continued to
mingle forever with the melting tar of tenement rooftops.

He glanced at the bums who leaned against the old buildings, blending in with the cast-off tires and armchairs and heaps
of paper. Creeps in torn rags looking as if the Depression had
never ended. He had no sympathy for them. None. The greatness
of America was that if you really wanted to, if you worked your
can off, you could not only get out of Brooklyn, but get Brooklyn
out of you. Money was the best detergent. With enough, even
memories could be sanitized, all the ugliness and pain scrubbed
out, leaving behind just the pleasant, greeting card glow of benign
nostalgia. If he had a credo, that was it.

Whatever you wanted to say, even the projects were better
than Brooklyn; those ugly tenements defaced by grafitti, those
filthy, dangerous staircases. He didn't agree with Ruth, who preferred the personality of those old brownstones to the project's
repetitious (heartless, she called it) landscape of ugly bricks piled

up like a fortress against anything personal, anything human, Ruth complained. It was like a prison.

He didn't feel that way. But he understood. Being part of it, having your rent subsidized, was demeaning, and the system wanted you to feel trapped, as if you'd lost your right to choices, however trivial. The housing inspectors could walk right into your apartment to see if you had roaches that needed killing, or walls that needed painting. He tried to imagine the thousands of cans of paint piled up in warehouses somewhere, all the same institutional shade of white, just waiting to be trucked out and shoved into people's lives.

He didn't think there was anything really wrong with that. It was as it should be. After all, a grown man who can't make enough money loses his right to demand or to decide. He thought of Reuben in his big house, his idle wife in a party dress on a Sunday afternoon; of Sara rolling on the fragrant lawn of her uncle's big backyard.

Something inside him—something solid and motionless and as firm as the earth—suddenly shifted. I don't know anymore, he realized. All those things that had been so clear, suddenly weren't. The idea that they'd have to struggle for a while, and that that was OK. That he'd be fine . . . just fine . . .

He wasn't. He was so tired: of getting up early, of battling the traffic . . . and the cops: Everytime you made a move, they whipped out the little book: no left turns, no right turns, no U-turns, no parking, no standing. There'd been six hundred and ninety eight cabs called off the road just the other day. Faulty meters, they said. And then all those rumors . . . Quill from the transit workers wanted to ban all auto traffic in Manhattan, all parking in Manhattan and Queens. They didn't let a man live . . . But it wasn't just that. That, he could take.

It was Sara sitting by the window looking out into the street, afraid to go outside by herself anymore. It was Jesse in that school, his nose bloodied. A spasm of pain contracted his stomach, flushing hot acid through his bowels. What could he do about any of that? And there was no question he had to do something, that it was, after all, his responsibility.

As he crossed the bridge into Manhattan, the heaviness seemed to lift from his soul, the weariness replaced by a sudden energy. Manhattan. As always, it flowed through him like a drug. The store windows filled with expensive leather bags, tweed coats and hats; the thick steaks decorated with sprigs of parsley bathed in the florescent glow of fancy restaurants; even the way New Yorkers walked, throwing themselves recklessly headlong into the new day.

It was a city of treasure-hunters and gamblers, he thought, the pulsing excitement of their quest almost palpable, a vibration of their collective strivings and hopes. He had thrown in his lot with them, come what may, his fingers as long and clever as the next guy's reaching for the brass ring.

Impulsively, he made a sudden turn, heading towards Wall Street. There they were, all those men who had grabbed the ring before him; the *alrightniks*, pouring onto the sidewalks and up the elevator banks of office towers. The men who owned these streets and guarded them, keeping out the riff-raff. He felt no resentment, only admiration. There was so much wealth there, you could almost touch it, he thought, marveling, almost taste it—sour and nutty—like some liqueur. He saw it in the way men stopped on corners to read the paper, kneeling over shoeshine boys like princes. He saw it in the cut of their clothing, the starched collars of their shirts. But mostly, he saw it in the smooth whiteness of their clean fingers.

These guys had figured it out, he thought admiringly. Money needed to work for you, not you for money. He knew that. Heck, everybody knew that, except maybe Morris. Only shmucks slaved for a little paycheck, or dragged out icy bottles at two in the morning (or drove cabs). What was the secret? How did you find room for your feet on these crowded streets?

It was then Dave noticed him. Small, neat-looking. Too

short, really, to belong to Wall Street, where all the men were tall, young college boys, six-footers (or so Dave imagined. They were the only ones he saw). That's why he looked again. This guy was even shorter than himself, but with a certain firm brace to his shoulders that made his chest reach out importantly. He pulled gleaming white cuffs out of his expensive black wool coat, flashing the gold of cufflinks. About the same age, too. A little guy, on Wall Street. A man who smiled at himself in the mirror in the morning, washing his face with expensive soap and drying it on monogrammed towels. Prosperous. A man who had what he needed, and could be generous to the ones he loved, Dave mused. He was so absorbed in speculation that it took him a while to realize that the guy was standing on the pavement looking right at him; waving him down.

There was something arrogant about the way he raised his bent knuckle, a gesture so supercilious and overconfident it could have felt like an insult had Dave been looking for insults. He wasn't. He was only too happy to stop, open up the cab door and let him in.

He wanted to go to the airport, but first to stop at his hotel. Dave was thrilled. The airport was a real fare. "If I make real good time, you think you could give me a good tip on the market?" Dave joked, his eyes serious. He watched with fascination as the guy took out a silver cigarette case, opened it, and leisurely tapped down the tobacco before answering.

"How much do you want to invest, friend?"

"Oh, I don't know . . ." he shrugged sheepishly, then caught the little, mocking smile that sprang to the guy's lips. He inhaled deeply. "Mind if I ask you something, Mister?"

"Not at all."

"I don't suppose you know how much a cab is worth today, with the medallion, I mean, do you?"

He shrugged. "Couldn't actually say for sure . . . Two thousand?"

Dave leaned back, avenged. "Guess again. Twelve thousand bucks."

"You don't say?" he said calmly.

"That's right, mister. Took me seven years to earn that kind of money. And I'm still paying off loans. Mind if I ask you something else, Mister?"

"Not at all."

"On Wall Street, how long does it take to earn twelve thousand dollars?" He didn't wait for an answer. "And I bet you don't have to get up at five, either, do you, Mister? I guess you eat breakfast with your kids every morning, then put on a nice, warm coat, go up to one of these offices where it's clean, and someone hands you good hot coffee too. Then you make a few calls, home by five, six at the latest. Help the kids with their homework . . ." he mused, dreaming. "I wanna tell you something, Mister. Something I just figured out. I'm gonna sell this thing and get into a decent business. A business where I can eat breakfast with my kids."

The guy leaned forward with new respect on his face, Dave saw, his satisfaction almost overcoming his shock at having said such a thing and having actually half-meant it. And that, really, was all Dave remembered clearly later on when remembering exact details became so crucially important. That and the calm movement of the guy's lips under his moustache. That long ride to the airport was not accurate, in the way of photographs or recordings. It was impressionistic, like a painting, whose color and shape stayed with Dave for a long time: the strong black curve of confidence in the remembered tone of voice, with no hint of ingratiating humor—exactly as Dave had always imagined rich people spoke; the conservative browns and greys of his language, drawn across a large abstract canvas, brightened with just a bold hint of red in the success stories he shared so offhandedly.

One story especially stayed with Dave: The shoestore owner who had sold his business, invested his money, then retired to

Florida. And every month he got a check. For the rest of his life. Not a whole lot of money—four, five hundred a month. In a white envelope. Without worries, regular.

If the story had been about gold mines, millions, instant wealth, rags to riches, it would have washed over David Markowitz like a fairy tale. But that shoestore owner . . . Dave could just see him bending over rows of smelly feet, running back and forth to fetch and carry for tough-nosed old ladies who would drive him crazy and then walk out without buying a thing. And that check. Every month. Like a salary from God.

It was security.

And then, although Dave didn't recall that part, they must have gotten to the airport. "Would've liked to talk to you more," Dave remembered him saying, or something like that, when he handed over the fare and an impressive tip. Only the next part was etched clearly on his mind: How the man's clean, manicured fingers had reached into the pocket of his silk-lined coat and taken out an embossed business card which he pressed into Dave's work calloused palm, his smooth fingers recoiling slightly from the contact. "Vincent Hesse, Investment Advisor."

Chapter seven

In Uncle Morris's apartment the homemade wine exploded, showering the rug. Seeing it, Sara relaxed, less terrified of spilling the dark red wine on Aunt Harriet's brilliant white tablecloth. She was surrounded by adults who pinched her cheek and looked her over with wary smiles. They seemed to know all about her, but she only vaguely remembered them. She felt sorry for her father who fidgeted uncomfortably with a black skullcap, laughing too loud, slapping too many backs. Only her mother seemed to be enjoying herself. The light of the candles melted away the fine lines that had lately begun to crack the smooth surface of her skin and she smiled and winked girlishly at her relatives.

Uncle Morris stood up, holding a silver goblet of wine towards heaven and all the voices suddenly softened, as everyone looked up expectantly. But the words he spoke Sara did not understand and the wine dribbled down his chin onto his white shirt. Everyone began to drink. Her cousins teased her about getting grape juice instead of wine.

"That's enough wine, Jesse. You'll get sick," Ruth scolded as he poured himself another cup.

"I'll be Bar Mitzvah soon. I'm a man," he ignored her, filling his glass with determined eyes.

"Leave him, leave him," came a chorus of voices, Dave's the loudest.

"He'll throw up, or get *shikker*," Aunt Harriet prophesized.

"At least mix it with a little water," Ruth pleaded.

"The Rabbi said four cups, filled to the top, otherwise there's no *mitzvah*," Jesse replied calmly.

"That's what you get for sending him for Bar Mitzvah lessons!" Dave bellowed. "Drink up kid. Get in all the *mitzvahs* you can!"

Uncle Morris looked at his brother-in-law disapprovingly. The whole subject of rabbis and *mitzvahs*, to his thinking, did not warrant this kind of levity. But then Dave was known as the *shegetz* of the family, so what could you expect? He sighed, deciding to let it pass. "Time to wash!" he announced.

Everyone poured water from a large copper cup over their hands into a washbasin. Morris dunked some parsley into bitterly salty water and passed it around the table. Sara, her stomach already rumbling in anticipation, bit into it eagerly. She spit it out, gasping, then looked down, shamefaced, as her cousins laughed.

"Enough!" Morris warned. "Silence! A little respect!" He picked up the plate of *matzot*, removing the satin cover.

"Haw lachmaw anya di achloo avahatana be'ara di mitzraim.
Kol dicphin yasay ve'yachool, kol ditrich yasay ve'yifsach.
Hashatah hacha lashana ha' baah b' arah d'Yisrael.
Hashatah avday, lashanah haba'ah b'nai chorin."

"I think we should say it again in English. For the kids," Dave said apologetically.

Morris frowned, then shrugged. "So you do it."

Dave looked around him, uncertain but pleased. "This,"

he pointed to the *matzot*, "is the bread of affliction that our forefathers ate in Egypt. All who are in want, sit and eat with us. All who are in need, stay and be satisfied. This year we are here, next year may we be in Israel. This year we are slaves. Next year may we be free men."

"Now one of the kids has to ask The Four Questions! Jesse?"

Jesse looked down, shaking his head.

"*Nu.* It'll be good practice for the Bar Mitzvah . . ."

"He started late, Morris. His Hebrew's not so good," Ruth interceded, seeing Jesse's face cloud dangerously.

"A Bar Mitzvah boy who can't read Hebrew? So how will you read the *haftorah*?"

"A *shandah*," Harriet clucked.

"I'll know it!" Jesse replied, too loudly.

"Don't get excited, be a nice boy," Harriet warned. "I told you. He's getting *shikker*."

"I'll read the questions," Ruth said shyly. "Just like when I was a little girl in my father's house. Remember Morris? *Ma nishtanah halaylah hazeh, micol halalos, micol halalos . . . .*" The room grew quiet as she read the words with uncharacteristic confidence and pleasure.

Then, finally, after they had burned their lips and the inside of their cheeks and tongues with freshly grated horseradish that made their eyes smart, and ingested unconscionable quantities of colon-clogging *matzos*, the food came: hot chicken soup with *matzah* balls, boiled chicken, sweet carrots, potato kugel. They ate and ate, feeling the torture was over, the fun about to begin. Morris, in his own home, feeling magnanimous and hospitable, leaned back comfortably.

"So Dave, how's business?"

"Couldn't be better, Morris."

"It's risky. You should get a good job, move back to Brooklyn. The commuting out to Rockaway is terrible. Even the subway is double fare it's so far out."

Dave shrugged. "I couldn't do what you do, Morris, live in Brooklyn, work in the same job for twenty years. See the same people every day until they bury me."

"When I retire, I get a union pension on top of Social Security. You got some kind of insurance?" Morris bristled.

"I don't believe in it. They're all crooks, those insurance guys. You pay in and pay in but then, to get them to shell out, that's another story. A man has to make his own insurance," he tapped his chest, "have his own business. You can never make it on a weekly paycheck."

"There's nothing wrong with being a worker," Morris's piqued voice rose. "Save a little, watch it, put some away for the kids . . ."

"It depends on what you want . . ." Dave said squirming, trying to end the conversation peacefully.

"And what you want is to live with the *shvartzes* out there in the slums!?" Morris challenged, the wine finally hitting the jackpot.

Dave shrugged off Ruth's restraining hand, the blood boiling up into his face. "I'd rather have that temporary," he said, beginning softly, but growing louder and more insistent with every word, "than some stinking, roach-infested, rent-controlled apartment in Brooklyn permanent!"

The dishes suddenly stopped in mid-clatter, and voices lowered, making his seem even louder. "And some gold-plated watch from a fat-ass boss like your Weinstein when I've got one foot in the grave! You never had a good idea in your life, Morris. That's why you're just a worker and will never be a boss. To be a worker you didn't have to come to America!"

"Dave, please!" Ruth begged, laying her hand over his. He looked up, suddenly aware of the shocked, disapproving stares. He swallowed, managing a faint, apologetic smile.

"Look . . . it's not important. It doesn't mean anything. You might even be right, Morris. Who knows?"

Morris didn't seemed to hear him at all standing motionless as if struck by a sudden illness that made his body shiver, his skin transparent. He avoided Dave's eyes, staring at the rug until Harriet touched his arm and whispered: "*Sha, sha.* It's Seder night. Family. Go. Finish." He sat down heavily. "In my own house!? To be insulted at my own Seder table . . . !?"

"He didn't mean it, Morris! It's nothing! Don't make a *tzimmes.* Go, go finish!" A chorus of voices urged him.

"Yeah, Morris. Sorry. You know, I don't mean anything by it," Dave began, already regretting opening his mouth.

"Aach, please. It's family! Forgotten already," another relative chimed in.

"The *afikomen*," Ruth said quietly. "Morris. The children."

A friendly moan went around the table. The older cousins smirked and Sara suddenly remembered the game. One piece of *matzah* was hidden and until it was found, the Seder could not continue. She should have searched for it earlier and then any toy she wanted would have been hers as ransom. But now it was too late.

"It's mine!" Jesse announced, holding the prize high above his head. Shouts of adult laughter and childish disappointment went up. "I want a . . ." he surveyed the faces around him, calculating, "a fishing rod . . . and a record player . . ."

"Oh, you hear that? A real businessman!" a cousin mocked.

Jesse reddened, then smiled. "You want to finish this thing," he waved it tantalizingly, "and go to sleep?"

"Yeah. Better give him what he wants," Aunt Harriet agreed. "It's late already."

Morris nodded. "All right. A fishing rod. After *yontiff.*"

"I'll take care of it, Morris," Dave offered.

Morris pointedly ignored him.

"Time for Elijah," someone said, and an older cousin went to open the door. Everyone stood up silently staring at the large silver goblet in the middle of the table. A slight breeze made the candles flicker.

"There's less," Aunt Harriet whispered. "Look, it's been tasted!"

"Yes," Ruth agreed. "A drop less."

"Who drank?" Sara tugged at her mother's skirt.

"Elijah the Prophet. He comes Seder night in a flaming chariot to announce that finally the Messiah will come. Next year we will all meet in Jerusalem."

A chorus of "God Willing" and "Amen" rang out, along with laughter.

Were they making fun of her? Was it like Santa Claus who never came? Sara wondered. She saw the wine glisten in the cup and reached out to drink from the same place where the angel's flaming lips had rested. It was cold, and a little damp. But the wine went down her throat like fire.

Chapter eight

"Dad?" Jesse whispered loudly, hoping his father was already awake, but not at all guilty about getting him out of bed if he wasn't. A promise—even if no one remembered it but himself—was still a promise. He listened for the soft shuffle of feet or a low moan and blankets rustling, but heard only his parents' syncopated breathing flowing without interruption from behind the closed bedroom door.

Damn! Now what?

He hesitated, his hand fidgeting with the doorknob, but pulled away. They would be lying there together. It had never bothered him before, but lately he had developed a squeamish delicacy about his parents' bodies, lowering his eyes if his mother's loose bathrobe accidentally parted, feeling queasy and unnatural coming upon his father after a shower. Only recently had he realized his mother was actually a woman with breasts and . . . (No! That was as far as it went . . .). He fought equally hard against the vision of his father's bulge straining against his pajamas, frightened and ashamed of these strange new visions, this unwanted knowledge.

So, he stood there, unmoving, paralyzed by the unseen vision of what lay on the other side of his parents' bedroom door, not knowing what to do next, until the solution suddenly dawned on him.

"Sara! Get up!" He shook her rudely, until she swam up from the depths of sleep, her eyelids fluttering, struggling to dive back under . . . "Come on! For once in your life, do me a favor!"

"What . . . ?"she whimpered.

He shoved his hand quickly over her mouth. "Shhh. Just be quiet, will you? Nobody is doing nothing to you, OK?"

She pried the bony lock from her lips. Recognizing it was only Jesse, her terror transformed into fury.

"Le'me alone!!" Her eyes were hot slits.

Go ask a face like that for a favor. His heart sank. "Listen Sar," he began hopelessly, his voice measured and cajoling, "can you just go into Daddy's room and tell him that it's time to get up if we're going fishing, okay?"

"Fishing?" She sat up.

"Come on! I'll do you something good. I swear. I'll . . . I'll," his imagination faltered. She was a strange little creature to him. A girl. "I'll let you watch *Queen for a Day* and *Mighty Mouse*—that is, if the Dodgers aren't playing . . ." Watching the spark of interest in her eyes fade, he rushed on recklessly. "You can come too!"

"Fishing?"

"That is, if you want," he hedged, filled with immediate regret. That was all he needed. Sara tagging along! Then something else occurred to him, and he smiled. "Sure you can. Just do like I tell you, all right? Go in and wake up Daddy." He laughed silently, watching her throw off the covers and rush past him into the hall straight into his parents' bedroom. He heard muffled groans, and soon his father showed up, sleepy and disheveled.

"You didn't forget, Dad, did you?"

". . . What?"

"Fishing. Remember what you said last Sunday?" Jesse read the answer in the twinge of startled recognition that widened his father's eyes.

"What do you think I am, huh!? Forgot? Who forgot! A promise is a promise is a promise, right?"

Jesse followed his father's reluctant gaze towards the darkened windows. Outside, trees bent in a harsh wind.

"Looks pretty cold," Dave began doubtfully. "I thought for sure, after Passover, it would be nice weather already . . ."

"But it ain't raining. Remember you said cold is nothing. You said the fish bite better in the cold when the bay is empty . . ."

"Awright, awright," he said, holding up his palms in surrender. "I said, so I said. Eat a good breakfast and then let's get this show on the road."

Jesse struggled into his warm woolen socks. They were too small, he realized with pride. Way too small. He could feel his father's happiness each time he grew an inch, his young shoulders inching up past his dad's. It had been so long since they'd been on their own somewhere. There was always somebody else hanging around: his mother, Sara, the baby, the cab . . . There were so many things he wanted to talk about man to man. Things he didn't want his mother or sister to hear. He wasn't sure he'd have the guts to ask straight out. But he thought that, maybe, if they were alone his father might ask the right questions, like he used to, years ago.

Behind the counter in the candy store, in those years before Sara had come along and put the knot between them, slackening their bond, he and his father had been like two ends of a seesaw, balanced, reciprocal parts of one whole, sensitive to the other's slightest mood change.

Sometimes he felt his father pulling hard, trying to make things come tight and smooth again between them. But so often Sara was always there, in the middle, making it impossible.

"What, in this weather?" he heard his mother say. There was

the usual rise and fall of voices: his father's deep, sincere bass, his mother's hesitant soprano that soon faltered and fell silent, allowing his father's voice to go on alone with convincing assurance.

He was too excited to eat, but his father's uncompromising gaze beat him back into his chair, and he understood that this was the one thing his father had conceded to his mother. The stuff was awful! Sticky and scorched and tasteless like everything else his mother cooked. So he stirred it around with the spoon, trying to reduce the amount by getting some of it to stick to the sides of the bowl, so as not to hurt her feelings. Out of the corner of his eye, he studied his father: the face rugged with stubble, the happy, expectant eyes, the red flannel shirt.

He loved that shirt. It was his father's "work" shirt, which meant that he put it on for hammering, oiling and fixing— everything except going to work. It was the shirt that meant he was home with them. But the thing he loved most were his father's boots: heavy rubber with fifteen manly metal clasps, disaster-ready, wading-into-danger boots. He even forgave his father the embar- rassingly baggy woolen pants because of the boots. He longed for a pair just like them instead of the flimsy kiddy galoshes he struggled to pull over his own shoes. Sometimes, secretly, he'd try on his father's boots. But as tall as he was, they were still way, way too big.

But this morning, even that didn't bother him. It was all OK. They were going fishing. Him and his dad. He was happy. He found the pails and the new rod, bought by Uncle Morris (who had tried to talk him out of it and into an American Savings Bond). Jesse held it reverently.

"Ready?" his father said, standing by the door. Jesse nodded, brushing past him out the door, a feeling of strange unease making him quicken his movements.

"Daddy!!" Sara suddenly wailed.

"Dad, come on! The elevator's here already!" he said urgently.

Dave hesitated, picking up the child who was by now in tears. "Let it go Jess. Just a minute, okay?"

Jesse watched the door drop back into place and the machine slide down, lost to him.

"Jess, you wanna come here a second?"

He saw his sister sitting on his father's lap, her hands possessively around his neck.

"Did you tell her she could come?" his mother accused.

"I said . . . that is . . . we had this deal . . . about television . . ."

"Fibber!"

"You want to come, Saraleh," Jesse heard his father say caressingly. His heart sank.

Sara nodded solemnly.

"Everything," Ruth's voice rang out with great conviction, "everything I give in to. But not this time. Not in this weather."

Jesse's heart rose. It was what he'd counted on! His mother to the rescue, like those times long ago when she had swooped down on his tormentors in Brooklyn alleyways.

Sara's sobs rose.

Dave looked from one to the other, astonished to be at the center of so much unhappiness when he had sought just the opposite—to sacrifice himself to keep them happy, giving up his precious hours of Sunday morning sleep, his warm bed, his wife's soft, pliant body . . .

"We'll bundle her up good, Ruth. Kid's gonna be so disappointed," he appealed to her in a whisper, touching her shoulder. She stiffened, but he just left it there until she finally weakened, going a little hunched.

By the time Sara had finished dressing and eating, the streets were beginning to grow light. A bitter wind made their coats flap like the wingspread of hovering birds. The rising sun and the bitter cold turned their faces ruddy.

When they got to the bay, the best places had already been taken by silent, solitary men, who hunched over old poles, staring into the swirling, dark waters like figures in a wax museum.

"Aw, shoot. Bet all the good fish are gone already. She always ruins everything!" Jesse swore.

"There's plenty left for us, Jess. Just leave the kid alone," Dave warned, giving him a playful kick in the rear. Jesse felt the nudge with deep humiliation, giving his sister a look of pure malevolence. She shrank back, hiding behind her father.

Oblivious, Dave took out the can of worms. "Now this is what you gotta do," he explained cheerfully. "First, you slice up the worms, that way you get more bait out of it. And a worm isn't like a person. You cut up a person, he dies. But a worm, he just keeps on going."

"You can live without arms or legs," Jesse argued.

"Yeah, but I mean his brain, or his heart. You take that away from a person and what you got left don't matter. But you see, God gave everything its pluses and minuses. A worm, see, it's the lowest of the low. It's got to crawl on its belly in the dirt, but it never has to worry about a broken heart."

Yeah, worms, Jesse thought, watching his sister. But she didn't seem squeamish about it, cutting them up with glee and sticking them, wriggling, on the hooks.

"You mean kid," he whispered, "hurting those cute little worms. How'd you like to get sliced up?" He brought the knife close to her and she lurched right into it, startled, letting it graze her arm. She screamed.

Dave grabbed her, examining the long, shallow scratch, his lips compressing. With great effort, he stopped himself from giving his son the *zetz* he had coming. Instead he smacked his own thigh.

"Why do you have to make me so mad, huh? I get up early, I take you out, try to be nice to you! Now be good kids or I'll never ... all this fighting ..." He took a deep breath, and then sighed. "Look, we're gonna have fun, right? Take the pole and throw it back like this—of course you have to be careful to look and see nobody's behind you. You could take someone's eye out, know what I mean?"

They watched their father's old red pole swing, the silver line arcing through the air, then disappearing soundlessly into the water. Infected with his enthusiasm, Jesse and Sara imitated him eagerly. It was magical, watching the hook sink beneath the waters, on its way to search for hidden treasures in the ugly brown liquid. No one spoke, each holding carefully onto their line, waiting for the thrilling tug. Slowly, the bruised scars of the sky faded, healed by the rising sun.

"Hey, Dad!" Jesse shouted. His rod was visibly bending.

"Wouldja look at that! Wow! *Nu*, so roll it in, come on!"

"How?"

"A fish!" Sara jumped up and down, her line dancing with her.

"Hold on to it, Jesse! Now, slow, roll it in. Careful. NO! Not like that! It's too fast! Too fast you'll lose it!! . . . Wait until they swallow the hook good."

The rod bent almost double, snapping and struggling in the air.

"DAD!!" Jesse implored.

"Don't let them know you're scared. Or it'll just cut loose and run."

The rod seemed to quiet down for a moment, then all at once the line began unraveling furiously. "Stop it! Hold on to the line! Reel it in!"

Jesse reeled furiously with all his strength, the line jerking with spasmodic resistance.

"It's almost here! Almost at the surface! You've got it!!"

Then suddenly the line began to reel in easily, swiftly. The weight was gone.

"Ach. I should have taken over!"

"I did everything you told me!" Jesse shot back, near tears.

"Sure you did, kid. I know, I know . . . don't get me wrong. You did swell. Damn!" Then his face brightened: "OK. So what happened? That was just the baby. Now let's go back in and get the big, fat daddy, OK?"

Jesse followed his father's gaze and saw that his eyes betrayed him. They were unsure, defeated, nothing like his words! And yet, his eyes never looked down, but straight ahead, beyond the dark waters, above the twinkling human lights, up, up to some shimmering yet painfully distant vision that seemed to sear him with its unattainable beauty.

It was then it occurred to him that he might confide in his father.

"Dad?" he whispered. His father turned to him, and in a moment he saw the uncertainty fade, replaced by the familiar, too cheerful fatherly grin.

Jesse hesitated. It was not the face he wanted to tell, yet it was the face that was waiting to hear, after all.

"Dad," he repeated, not knowing at which point to begin. "I've got into a bit of trouble at school."

"Yeah?" Dave said slowly, waiting.

"Well, it all started the first day. This jerk I've got for social studies . . ."

"Who, the teacher's a jerk?

"Yeah. The teacher."

"Oh," Dave shrugged, amused.

"Anyhow, he's giving us this textbook crap about the Four Freedoms, Bill of Rights . . . So I kind of raised my hand and told him about the bosses and the workers, and the way people are being hounded for no good reason . . . I told him about Paul Robeson." Fellow traveler, Jesse thought. That's what Dunleavy had called him, and the class had hooted. And he had been called a Jew-Commie-Cut-Prick by the micks ever since. And Dunleavy had written: "Try vocational" on all his tests and papers, never giving him more than a C minus, though he knew he deserved at least a B.

"I didn't mean any big deal." (Actually, he had given quite a good speech, very heartfelt, a defense of all the good, hardworking and honest people, the workers of the world, against all the dark forces of exploitation, hatred and oppression. Just the basic stuff his father had been telling him all his life.) "All I said was how come McCarthy's still around if we're the land of the free? I mean, I didn't think it was any big deal. The teacher's been out to get me ever since." He looked at his father hopefully, waiting to be reassured—even praised—then stopped, aghast. His father's face, swollen and red, seemed ready to explode.

"YOU CAN'T TALK LIKE THAT IN SCHOOL!" Dave shouted, then took a deep breath. "You can't . . . you see, kid," he said, trying for a measure of control. "It's my fault. I should've explained it to you better. And it was all true. Back in the '20s, the '30s, everybody knew that it was the big bosses, the monopolies, that were killing us. I mean . . . I mean . . . you had to walk down the street looking down at the pavement because your soles were so thin that if you stepped on a rock or a piece of glass your feet would start to bleed, and then the shoes—the only damn pair you had—would be ruined. And if you wanted to work, you needed shoes; you needed to work twelve, fifteen hours a day. You couldn't pick your head up, couldn't ask for better light, for more air because the minute you opened your mouth there were ten guys out in the street waiting for the boss to crook his little finger and toss you out on your behind.

"But then, you see, came the war, and the big bosses were the ones making munitions for our boys at the front. They were the ones helping us to win against Hitler. And then . . . then . . . you couldn't talk anymore about workers and bosses. It was all mixed up, see? I was mixed up. But I decided, that whatever happened, I was going to be a boss, not a worker, and that no one was ever going to throw me out on my ass any day they felt like it. You have to play the game, Jesse. Play it whatever way you have to in order to win. Throw overboard whatever stands in your way. And that means graduating high school with decent grades."

And for a few brief moments, David Markowitz thought of his own father. Jacob Markowitz had known how to play the game. He'd shaved off his beard, gotten rid of his skullcap, worked late seven days a week. He'd let the prayer books, the fringed garments, the cubed *teffilin* boxes yellow and gather dust.

Dave's mother, though, had never learned, clinging to her long-sleeved dresses, her wigs, her meticulously *kashered* chickens, her worn synagogue pew. She had cajoled and cried and screamed, trying to pull her husband back from the edge of the New World and inevitably, she had lost him. She'd never understood that the American Dream was a god more powerful, more jealous and cunning than the one her ancestors had worshipped. Every day it demanded new sacrifices in exchange for irresistible rewards. It held you in its lush arms and kissed you, beguiling you with unspoken promises until you forgot where you had come from, or that your name had ever been Markowitz and not Marks.

It wasn't just about money. It was fitting in seamlessly. Being a regular guy. An American. It was being part of—like Truman said—"the greatest strength, the greatest power the world has ever known." This, after being bonded to a people who had never been able to protect their own bones. Money itself was beside the point; anybody could make money in America, unless you were a real dope, like Morris. Or like Max, the union organizer, his dear friend, riddled with bullets two days after the first strike. Or cousin Elya, deported to Russia for "un-American activities." The fool.

"Son," he said, wanting to sum it all up, but failing, because as he tried to formulate the words, he couldn't believe how ashamed he felt to say them. "Son," he finally said. "Think whatever you want. But learn to keep your mouth shut."

Jesse looked at him, his eyes moist, realizing for the first time how short his father was. He re-baited his hook, flinging the rod back angrily over his head then sharply forwards until it fell like a blow into the water. No one spoke. Nothing happened. After an hour of fruitless waiting, Jesse's feet began to tingle, and soon they burned with the cold. At first, he walked around quietly, secretly trying to increase the warm flow of blood to his freezing feet. He cupped his red hands, blowing on them with warm breath, hoping his father wouldn't notice; feeling guilty and angry with himself for his weakness. But the colder he grew, the more he threw his father secret glances, wondering when he would look up and notice. But Dave was oblivious to everything but the line, pulling it out with dogged hope, rebaiting it, flinging it back in, waiting . . . waiting . . .

Jesse glanced at his sister, resentful and envious of the calm, unmoving arch of her small back as she sat uncomplainingly on a carton, her red hands loyally clasping the line. Suddenly, she jumped up, reeling in her line until a small golden blowfish swung puffing in the air.

Sara stared with horror as the creature gasped frantically for air, the hook tearing into its delicate mouth as it struggled to escape. With a wild sob, she dropped the line.

"Ho! A little blowfish! That's not worth anything!" Jesse jeered.

"Quit it!" Dave shouted, gathering his little girl into his arms, his body suddenly stiffening under the silent reproach of her icy hands around his neck. As their foreheads touched, his knees trembled. She was burning up with fever.

Jesse walked over to the pail, peering in then poking the still moving blowfish with a contemptuous finger. "We should throw it back in. It's not good for anything."

Sara's sobs rose. Dave's hand shot out, catching his son fiercely on his cheek and part of his nose. They rushed home in silence, Jesse following behind his father and sister, his vision, clouded with tears, blurring their two figures into one

*   *   *

Black monster waves. Sara watched them forming out in the distance; watched the way they heaved back then rose upwards like the jaws of a pitiless beast. But they were still far away from her, she realized, looking at them in fascination from over her shoulder. They were not a danger really. Too far. But slowly, she could see them inching their way closer. NO!! NO!! They were almost there!! At her heels!! And then they were not waves at all, not water at all, but something harder, with an awful, incomprehensible bite of crushing weight.

It was then she understood that she was about to do something terrible. Something for which she would never be forgiven, not by her dear mother or dear father or anyone else she loved or who loved her. They would not love her anymore because of the black, unmentionable horror she was about to commit. They would take away their love and their protection, because it was a very, very bad thing and she was going to do it . . . NO!! She had done it!! And the huge, bony thing was coming for her, arching over her . . . !

She screamed.

But it was not the dark bony thing. It was firm and smooth and smelled of toothpaste and warm pajamas. The soft scratch of stubble grazed her cheek, and she felt the firm, cool flesh on her own hot skin. Then the arms lifted her and the black thing retreated.

"Saraleh, sha, sha. It's all right, all right. A dream, that's all. A bad dream. You want Daddy to stay with you, tell you a story? A nice story about Peter Rabbit or the Three Pigs?"

She didn't answer, letting him rock her, feeling the unnamable joy of being safe in his strong, cherishing arms. He was so cool and she was so hot. She shivered faintly, deliciously against him, still feeling the black thing close. She did not want a story, but to hear distinctly, perfectly, the rhythmic intake of his breath and the soft, even thumping of his heart. But she understood how much he loved to tell about the Three Pigs and did not want to offend him.

"Three Pigs," she murmured and was immediately rewarded by his smile. But then she was very sorry because there was the wolf pounding at the door, trying desperately to get in. A big, bad, black wolf.

"No more, Daddy!"

"You feel better now?"

She nodded, lying, trying to please him.

"Now you go to sleep, and I'll tell you what—I'll give you all my money and then you can buy yourself something terrific tomorrow? What do you say? OK? He held out his wallet to her, and pulled out ten dollars. "Here. For you. Now you just think about what you can buy with so much money and you'll have beautiful dreams? OK, sweetheart, Daddy's girl?"

She nodded, grasping the bill in her hot palm and closing her eyes. She saw him walk out and close the door.

Later, in her dreams, she heard their voices. First her mother's: "Why did you give it to her?" And then her father's "Felt bad. Where could she have put it?"

Half waking, she saw him get down on his hands and knees and search beneath her bed. "A lousy ten bucks," she heard him say, his voice breaking, like a wave. Then she felt her palm pried open, the cool night air kissing the spot where the money had been.

Chapter nine

All that dark, rainy, cold April morning, a morning that seemed to promise winter would last forever, Dave kept slugging away at himself: "Shouldn't have gotten mad! Shouldn't have hit the kid! Why'd I hit him?" he asked himself again and again, as if expecting an answer.

Imagine, giving that jerk Dunleavy a lecture on Communist philosophy! With the House Un-American Activities Committee still going full blast, despite having lost a little steam (Sir! Have you no shame?!). Hadn't they murdered the Rosenbergs in cold blood just last year? Trumped up garbage—why even the Supreme Court had been in on it, allowed it!

Now the kid had screwed himself up in school good . . . Jeez. He shook his head. Education was the key. Sure it was going to be Markowitz and Sons. But he wasn't going to be a cabby for goodness sake! (Should've explained that to him, didn't do a good job!) He was going to be an expensive lawyer or a C.P.A. A money manager. College-spoken, educated. Full of booksmart ideas they'd argue about on the weekends, when he came home in his college-letter sweater. He'd never have to struggle, to wear himself out, to grovel, to prove anything. He'd have respect handed to him on a silver platter. He was American-born. He had it coming.

The harder Dave worked at trying to forgive himself, the more his guts coiled and twisted in an agony of confusion and regret and heartbreaking pride over the image of the kid standing alone in front of the whole class defending Paul Robeson. His mind wandered to those Sundays in Brooklyn when Jesse had been barely two, an only child, a holy terror, carrying seltzer bottles up and back across the kitchen table while Ruth, horrified, had ineffectually begged him to stop. And he, Dave, had sat in the background, laughing until the tears ran down his cheeks, finally grabbing the kid and hoisting him up, upside-down, over his shoulder. And the only thing that had quieted him down, keeping his little feet from kicking like pistons, was that magic word: "record", which to Jesse, had been synonymous with "Robeson."

He remembered sitting on the old sofa, Jesse's head resting against his chest, his little fat feet miraculously motionless along his thighs, listening to all the old Russian work songs, songs of oppressed laborers rising with dignity. Listening to Robeson had been like looking at a centuries-old redwood, its girth immense, its roots as thick as arms reaching down to the center of the world. It was a voice as deep and honest and dependable as country earth. He wondered how the kid remembered. Hadn't played Robeson in ages . . . Might even have gotten rid of those records (although he *knew* he hadn't, and never would . . .).

Then towards the end of the long day, too weary to defend himself anymore, his mind went back again to the moment when his hand had struck out at the pale, cold face, the young bitter mouth, the disappointed eyes. And then suddenly, too, the image of himself prying open Sara's hand to take back the money. Ten bucks, he thought. Ten lousy bucks. But without them, there wouldn't have been money to put gas in the tank.

Shouldn't have done it, he berated himself. Should have
. . . should have hugged him, about Robeson. Should have told
him how proud . . . His ten fingers flinched on the steering wheel.
Here I am, he thought morosely, driving down the road to hell.
Surprise. It really *was* paved with good intentions. By four he felt
drained. He touched his coat pocket for the necklace and bracelet
of red glass beads he'd bought Sara, the record player for Jesse,
all on credit. He was anxious to see their faces as he gave them
the gifts, to erase the day before. He turned on his "off duty"
sign, and headed home.

It was pouring and almost as dark as midnight as he took
the cab down Eighth Avenue. This part of Manhattan always
looks as if a bomb has just hit it, he thought, depressed by the
ugliness, the crumbling brick walls, the decaying garbage-filled
lots. He tried to ignore it, already imagining himself standing in
front of the kids with his peace offerings so that he almost didn't
see the fare waving him down with all his might. Checking if the
off-duty sign was really on, Dave drove past him. But then, glanc-
ing in the rear-view mirror, he saw the guy pull his lapels a little
tighter around his neck as the rain pelted his dripping head and
soaked jacket. With a sigh, Dave slowed to a stop. The man ran
to catch up, throwing himself into the back seat.

"Brooklyn Jewish Hospital."

Something about the way his body stretched taut against
the back seat, a certain quiver in his voice, made Dave uneasy.
"Somebody sick?"

"Look, just shut up and drive, okay?"

A conversation stopper, that. Dave swallowed. But there
was nothing to do about it now. There he was in the back seat,
after all. He pressed on the gas.

"Look, my off-duty sign was on. I'm doing you a favor,
Mac."

"Yeah. Sorry."

"I'll take you as far as the bridge."

"Yeah. That far, huh? And how much you gonna charge me?"

"Twenty cents. Okay?"

"It's gonna cost a lot more. You, that is."

It was then Dave felt the cold metal tremble at the side of his head. He thought of grabbing the gun away, bashing the guy's head against the window. Forty-two years of trying, working, loving, dreaming—flashed through his head. Was it all about to be extinguished by a stranger looking for a little easy cash, probably not even enough to buy a better jacket? He looked down at the record player, the red beaded jewelry. "OK, OK. Don't do anything stupid. Here it is."

A cold metal chill moved along the back of his neck, sending chills down his spine, of anger even more than fear; a fury that the world harbored such indecency. And when the creep said: "Thanks, sucker. Guess you should've kept driving," he couldn't say he was surprised at how bad it made him feel. But what did surprise him was the heaviness of the metal as it smashed into his temple just after he gave him the day's take and just before he could tell him to go to hell.

Chapter ten

"I'll be loving you, always, always.
With a love that's true, always.
When the things you've planned need a helping hand,
I will understand always, always,"

Dave sang softly, pressing her small dark head into his shoulder.

It was birthdays and Chanukahs and anniversaries and graduation days and holidays; it was a month of Sundays rolled into one glorious afternoon. Everything shone (even years later they'd remember it, that glow, in their father's and husband's face) Dave beaming royally as he dispensed the largesse of a rich and happy man.

That was the way it was, the day he sold the taxi and invested half the money with a new, mysterious friend, a sort of fairy godfather who had popped up from nowhere to save them, like the good angels in black and white Thirties films with Bing Crosby. And every month, like clockwork, a fat dividend check would arrive. And in bed at night, Dave's arms would meet around Ruth's back as he caressed her hotly through her worn nightgown, his heart thudding with happiness, smothering her own measured beats.

It was the old Dave, the Dave she knew; not the man who had come home from the hospital with stitches in his head, who had lain in bed for weeks staring at the wall.

He had bounced back from the mugging with all the resiliency of a crushed paper fan. She had never seen him that way. He'd been a stranger who'd burrowed close in the night like a terrified, comfort-seeking child, who'd admitted with shame: "I just can't do it anymore."

Then, out of nowhere, Hesse had appeared: a man who remembered their birthdays and anniversaries, who took cabs from his home in Manhattan to visit them in the projects, who had made things all right again. Better than all right.

She blessed him for redeeming her husband.

With the second check, Dave had bought an old Buick and taken them all to the country, to the old farm hotel which really did still exist, although the scales were gone. They'd sat in the sun in old, handmade Adirondack chairs and watched the moon rise, pale gold amidst a million silver stars. They'd held hands like teenagers, Ruth speaking softly about buying a house or opening up a dry cleaning store with the rest of the money, and Dave listening quietly, patting her little hand, his face indulgent and happy in the moonlight. And under the silver glow, a million crickets had rubbed their legs together, rioting in song.

And the children in their old sand-dusted suits had wound their way down to the lake, barefoot in the cool, morning dew. Amid the encircling green willows that guarded their perfect peace like sentinels, Jesse showed off his dives, while Dave taught Sara how to swim and held the baby on his shoulders, gently crouching until the tips of Louis's toes touched the calm surface and the child squealed with joy.

What Dave enjoyed most, though, was telling Ruth the details of his investment, the company stock that had not yet gone public, the chemical plant with the million-dollar patents, and (again!) about how much Hesse thought of him, what a great, regular guy he was, and how smart, and how many plans he had . . . until Ruth (always too soon!) grew sleepy or disinterested or somehow uncomfortable and he was forced to stop.

But Jesse listened. Sitting at his father's feet, he would drink in every word, asking a million questions. How do you go public? How many shares? What kind of patents, exactly, were they? What kind of chemicals? And Dave, beginning with enthusiasm, explained it all with patient pride until he found he didn't know the answers. And then he would lean back, exhausted and a bit annoyed and confused, blustering good-naturedly about slowing down, and wasn't that something about the Brooklyn Bums actually winning the series? And against the Yankees, no less!

And then, at the beginning of November, the check failed to arrive. Instead, the phone rang.

"*Shabbes*. Don't pick it up," Ruth warned, not sure it wasn't a dream.

Giving her head a conciliatory pat, he jumped out of bed to get the call. And when he returned, she saw through a fog of sleep that he was getting dressed.

"Where are you going?" She sat up, alarmed.

I don't need a fight now, he shrugged. Let her understand: *Shabbes* or no *Shabbes*. "It's Hesse and it's important. He says he's sorry to get me up, to bother us. I have to meet him in Brooklyn in an hour."

She stiffened. Unless someone was dying or having a baby in the back seat, driving on Saturday had no earthly justification in Ruth's book, he knew. He didn't waste his breath begging for absolution. Urgent, Hesse had said. And the money was late. He tucked his good shirt into his good pants then leaned over and planted a small kiss on her creased forehead.

"I'll be back as soon as I can."

Traffic was light and as he sped through the quiet streets and over the bridge, he tried to calm his nerves by spending his money once again. When his shares went public, the first thing he'd do was buy the house. Near Reuben. That was final. Let the kids grow up near family. And Ruth would get used to it, even though it was quieter than Pitkin Avenue. He chuckled, then grew sober with remorse at his disparaging thought: And where did you grow up, friend? On Park and Fifth?

One question lingered irritatingly in his mind along with his discomfort at the awkward leave-taking, and, to a lesser extent, having to drive into the city on Saturday. As he hunted for the address Hesse had given him, he felt his body grow heavy with apprehension. Why today? Why here? Why not in the regular place on a weekday? Or at least at Hesse's house in Manhattan?

He hated this part of Brooklyn on weekdays, let alone when it was half-deserted on the weekends. There was something horrific about crowded streets suddenly fallen silent, emptied of all life. There. Building 1019. He looked uneasily down the dark, deserted hallway. Office 209B. There was no sign on the opaque glass door, no indication of who or what was behind it. He knocked, feeling small chills run up his arms and chest. From behind an old, scratched metal desk, Hesse smiled at him. Relieved beyond words to find him there, Dave smiled back.

*   *   *

"At least you're back early," Ruth called out, hearing the door open. She was bent over Louis, fastening his diaper pin and pulling up his rubber pants. Only when she finished did she look up and see her husband.

"Dave?" she said a little too loudly, questioning not his presence but the reality of the change in him. The car! A smash-up! She could think of no other explanation. "Comere, comere," she said to him, instinctively lowering her voice to the kind of whisper that one uses around the victim of a sudden, harsh accident. "Come sit down. Are you hurt?" she led him to a chair.

"Daddy!" Sara jumped into his lap, but she too pulled back, looking at his pale face, appalled.

He kissed the top of her head, and gently pushed her off. "Go play now. Mommy and Daddy have to talk," he said kindly. She crept off his lap and looked at her parents, afraid.

"Dave, what is it already!?" her tone had risen, becoming slightly hysterical.

"I'm all right . . . Just . . ." He got up and weaved towards the bedrooms. He knocked on Jesse's door, then hearing the music from the record player, knocked again, almost desperate.

"Jesse," he put his hand on his son's shoulder, resting the burden of his weight against him for a moment until he regained his balance, "I want you to take Sara down to the beach. Pick shells with her for a little while. Do me a favor."

Jesse was just about to say "damn" when he noticed something in his father's face that made him think better of it.

It was only when the children had gone that he finally raised his eyes to face her. For one panicked moment he thought wildly of escaping, of running away and never coming back. But if he was going to do that, he'd have to do it right now, because in a few moments it would be too late; he'd have to carry that look in her eyes around with him forever, no matter where he went.

He took a deep breath. "Ruth, the business is finished. We're wiped out. Everything is lost."

Her hand went instinctively over her mouth, as if she feared what might come out. She looked at him helplessly, waiting.

"The company lost its patent. Some stupid technicality. They have to stop working immediately."

"But the factory, the equipment, it can be sold. There has to be something left!" she pleaded, as he had pleaded with Hesse.

"Nothing. There were debts, see. Hesse lost everything too." He buried his face in his hands and trembled.

"Dave, Dave. It isn't the end of the world. What's the matter with you?" She shook him gently, then harder. "Dave! Please! Stop!"

He looked at her thinking: My dear wife. My dear, dear wife.

"Oh is it the end of the world? Is it? It's only money, right?" She laughed a short, bitter laugh. "Thank God we've still got the other five thousand . . ." Something in his face startled her. A darkness, like a shadow.

It was then that what had really happened suddenly bore down on her with a hard physical impact that made her reel. She groped towards the couch and sat down heavily, not looking at him, but listening to his breathing and her own. Later, she was not sure how much later, she asked, "Everything?" the way a child asks, hoping to be called foolish, to be laughed at and comforted.

"You see, honey, you see," he begged, "I thought, such a good deal. Twice as much invested could earn us twice as much. I didn't know . . . I thought . . ."

She felt something shatter—an idea, a view of their life together—and thought: all the King's horses, and all the King's men . . . He hadn't asked her. He had taken the rest of the money—all of it—without so much as discussing it with her. As if she didn't exist, as if anything she might have had to say was irrelevant. Like a child, she thought. First my father handing me over to Saidie, then Morris arranging my future, and now Dave. Dave too. And I hadn't known, hadn't realized, all these years, what he really thought of me . . . the contempt. "You thought," she said quietly, not looking up.

With a strange detachment, she watched him sit down next to her and throw back his head. His mouth opened but no sound came out. A part of her cried for him, but most of her was indifferent, shutting him out, separating his grief from her own. And then she heard the sickening small sobs struggling up from deep within his chest. She watched him and a blankness came over her, erasing what had been so definite just a moment before. The fight left her. The will to overcome.

"Stop it!!" she cried out.

Then, seeing that he could not, she wanted to take his head between her hands, to kiss the soft vulnerable flesh so close beneath his thinning hair. She wanted to . . . Instead, she looked at him the way one might look at a stranger who has thrown up on a bus, with discomfort and a little grudging pity.

She ran her fingers through her hair, smoothing it back with dignity. She tucked her blouse into her skirt, took off her damp apron and hung it neatly on the door hook. And then, in a movement which she would always feel changed the course of her destiny, her husband's and children's lives, a movement for which, rightly or wrongly, she would never forgive herself, she turned her back on him and walked slowly out the front door.

He watched her go. His eyes were desolate.

Chapter eleven

For the next three days, he went over it obsessively. A hundred, maybe a thousand times. Waking, sleeping. It was like a television show that kept starting from the beginning and never got past the station break. Something was unresolved. There was a piece missing, but what it was, God help him, he couldn't figure out. At first he thought maybe it was that business with the office again. But Hesse had explained all that: the regular offices were closed weekends and his apartment was much further from Rockaway. It made sense. So why did he see that red light flicking on each time he thought about that Saturday morning with Hesse in the dingy Brooklyn office? The shock, sure. But he was getting over that. Some you win, some you lose. Hadn't Reuben lost his pants the first time he went into business? He had made plenty of bad deals he wasn't talking about now. If it hadn't been for his wife's money bailing him out . . . As for Morris and his advice. Let him be a big shot with his stinking job, his stinking pension. If you never went into the kitchen, you never broke dishes.

So what was it?

The answer came to him gradually, in flashes, like words written white on black. At first you can only see the black incomprehensible shapes in between the letters. Then, out of nowhere, the white words appear. And once you see them, you can never unsee them. They are there every time you look, mocking your blindness, your stupidity.

On the third day, taking the subway into the city to look for work, he went over it again. The small, unfamiliar room littered with dead flies and dusty old paper cups. Hesse's hand on his shoulder pressing him gently into a chair. The grave eyes that looked directly at his without wavering, without avoidance. Dave felt that same rush of admiration for Hesse's calm, businesslike acceptance of defeat. He himself had been such a coward, unable to look at Ruth's eyes at all, terrified of exposing himself, or seeing her pain. But Hesse had looked at him without a flicker. As if he was used to it. *As if he had done it before.*

He sat back hard in the plastic seat, unseeing, letting station after station roll by, losing track of time. He pressed his nails into his palms, tearing away at the callused flesh until it began to bleed. Only then was he satisfied, seeing the blood ooze out, wishing there was more of it, wishing he could smash something soft and fleshy and see the streets stained with it. His blood or Hesse's. What did it matter?

It took about twenty minutes to find a pay phone that worked. He dialed carefully and when the stiff recorded female voice said "disconnected," he put the phone down and tried again, this time catching the "this phone has been . . ." In Hesse's office, they said he had taken a short vacation.

It took forty-five minutes to reach the upper West Side. He was amazed at how clear his head felt. He could pick out every detail around him: the slivers of glass in the smashed side window of the car ahead of him. The perfect cutting edge of skyscrapers against a high, indifferent sky. He was, he thought, like a drowning man going down for the last time who sees the water with other-worldly clarity, not as a blurry mass, but as individual drops piled one upon the other.

He noticed and was impressed once again by the doorman and the large potted palms, the clean old marble squares in Hesse's lobby. He waited for an opportunity to go in unnoticed, then sneaked quietly up the stairs. Hesse's door. Hesse's bell. He pressed the buzzer; not knowing really what he would say when Hesse's friendly, open face appeared at the door. He began to feel a little foolish after all.

When there was no answer, he knocked and waited for footsteps. He wondered out loud if they were deaf or something in there. Then he tapped on the door with his wedding ring. Gently at first, adding one knuckle at a time to make the sound a little louder until, before he knew it, he was banging on it with a clenched fist. He would have continued indefinitely, not knowing what else to do, if one of the neighbors hadn't opened the door to tell him what he had known all along.

"You're wasting your time," the thin, well-dressed older woman said not unkindly (perhaps even with a touch of pity, he winced). "He moved out three days ago."

So Dave went home. In the mornings, he would just sit around the house, his eyes, with despair, following Ruth everywhere. He tried to help, washing dishes, cooking, doing the laundry. At night he drove a cab for a big fleet in Manhattan. The midnight to seven a.m. shift. Through Harlem. Through Brooklyn. The only job available.

At first he tried lawyers (at fifty dollars a shot) who listened quietly as he described once again what they had agreed upon— he and Hesse—explaining the whole business as carefully as it had been explained to him, laying out the signed documents, the promissory notes. Sometimes, as he searched the faces of these men, men who had been to college, who wore suits and had brokers and a house in the suburbs, he imagined he saw a trace of irony, a smirk . . . But in reality, they all remained totally, professionally expressionless as they told him the same thing: the signed agreement was a worthless legal document. A fake. All he had, really, was Hesse's receipt and all he could do was find Hesse and bring him to court, get him to admit the verbal agreement that had been breached, the guarantees. But if he was out of the State, they were out of luck. Fraud was not an extraditable offence in New York, or any place else in the country.

So then, reasonably, he tried to find out where Hesse was. A private investigator (two hundred dollars, plus expenses, all borrowed money) told him the following:

Item One: Vincent Hesse, a.k.a. Bernard Ratsin, a.k.a. Bernard Cooper, a.k.a. Carl Bernard, a.k.a. Arnold Shawn had plied his trade on a variety of people, mostly middle class, mostly elderly, mostly female. He was under indictment in Florida for having sold one Ella Engles, at the time 64 years old, title to land under swamp water in lieu of her life savings. There were several women in Illinois and Kentucky, middle-aged widows, who had sued him for breach of promise and for the return of thousands of dollars worth of jewelry and cash. In California, Hesse had been recently indicted for extracting 19,000 dollars from a Grace Pernell, having promised to buy shares in a chemical company that was about to go public. The indictment had been dropped when Pernell died of injuries sustained in a fall from the fifteenth floor of the office tower of Laine-Rebbers (suspected suicide) where she'd worked as a secretary for thirty-five years. With no inheritance, no relative could be found willing to undertake the legal expenses of pursuing the charges.

Item Two: In his youth, the subject had worked briefly in Hollywood as a bit player in several melodramas.

Item Three: Ratsin/Hesse was last seen in New York

City, on September 28, at a Greyhound Bus Station. His destination couldn't be traced.

Dave took the report home. He hid it under his old shirts. And then he took to his bed. For three days, he couldn't eat, didn't sleep. For three days, he lay in bed and thought. Ruth hovered over him, bringing him chicken soup, begging him to see a doctor. But he just shook his head, turning his face to the wall. For three days, he thought, until finally, brutally, he had flayed himself of that layer of self-love that insulates every human being from the utter despair inherent in the act of living.

A Ponzi game. And he had been the mark. The vision of what had really happened, his own role in the scenario, sent him spinning into the center of a maelstrom. Like the winds of a tornado, the terrible downward spiral succeeded in stripping him naked of his last shred of dignity, flinging him bruised and helpless thousands of miles from where he had started; too far to ever find his way back again.

Ruth hugged him. She kissed him. She tried to comfort him. She begged him to cheer up, to forgive her. She brought him food, insisted he eat, refusing to understand that he just wasn't there anymore. It was a shell she shook and nurtured. His entire insides seemed to be burning away as if someone had spilled hydrochloric acid on them. His body became his enemy, an entrapment, his insides burning and twisting with hatred and despair. Slowly, he began to disintegrate, to fail to accommodate the flow of life that had coursed through him with such energy and hope throughout his whole existence on earth.

He burned, burned.

Then, sometimes, the burning would come out in words, in a monstrous lapping flame. "I'll tell you what I need!" he'd sometimes admit to Ruth in a rasping whisper. "Not soup. Not medicines. Not kisses. I need to find him. To find that bastard. To put a bullet through his head!"

"Dave!" Such talk terrified her.

"You think I couldn't do it? That I'm too soft, huh! Well, let me tell you the old Dave is finished! I'm a new man now. I could break his neck with my bare hands."

She'd turn away from him, unable to stand it. What more? What else could she say or do? She wanted to escape: to leave him, the kids, the constant talk about Hesse; to be a young girl again, working as a medical secretary with handsome bachelor doctors who were always pleasant and made such easy small talk! Sometimes, she was terrified that he would become a criminal. It was as if that devil, Hesse, had not only taken his money but his soul.

And then, one clear day two months later, David Markowitz saw Hesse again. At first he couldn't believe his eyes, feeling like a parched and dying wanderer in the desert who sees a gushing waterfall. But as he drove closer, he saw the proud little chest thrust forwards, the shiny patent leather shoes tapping the ground impatiently. He saw those smooth, manicured fingernails, the diamond pinkie ring . . . He was just standing there, out in the open, in front of the Diplomat Hotel, like nothing had happened. Could it be possible? Out there in the street with other human beings like . . . like . . . he was one of them? Like he had nothing to hide? He saw Hesse lift his hand and realized with panic that he was about to hail a cab. He would be gone in a second, disappearing into the flow, like garbage going down the incinerator chute.

Dave swerved quickly and heard the angry honks well up all around him. He ignored them, pulling up to the curb and jumping out of the cab, running as if his life depended on it. He tapped Hesse gently on the shoulder, needing to feel the good, solid flesh beneath his hand, afraid Hesse would turn out to be liquid, a vapor that would slide through his fingers. Hesse turned slowly, the mild surprise frozen on his face widening into shock.

Dave grasped him firmly around the wrist. "You sonofa-bitch, you lousy sonofabitch!" he said with quiet menace.

"Hey Dave, what's up!?" But there was real fear behind the smile.

He saw Hesse struggling to change faces, to find the right one, like an actor in rehearsals. But that didn't work with Dave Markowitz twice. Dave Markowitz was a shmuck. A loser. A mark. But at least he learned. His large, rough hands squeezed the other's small one. He thought how strange it was that he had once viewed those small clean hands with envy, even feeling a certain disgust towards his own. But now, staring at his work callused fingers, he felt grateful for the work he had done in his life that had given him those broad, strong fingers; the good, honest work that was paying him back now like an ally. He had the strength. Hesse was captured.

That was how he viewed it, so that when Hesse began to cry: "Let go of me!" to shout and attract the attentions of passersby, Dave was not even embarrassed. He felt like a sheriff at High Noon. He knew what he had to do. He walked a few blocks, dragging Hesse behind him. He felt himself bursting with release, with a feeling of magnificent deliverance; like winning a lottery that will change your whole life, or seeing yourself speed down a finish line first.

"Officer. I want you to arrest this man!"

The cop looked up, pushing back his hat brim slightly, taking in the situation. Dave saw his eyes pause at his own cabby hat with its faded, slightly frayed and dirty tweed, then travel downwards to where his rough hands wound tightly around the other man's small, clean one. He saw the cop's eyes take in Hesse's good cashmere coat, his shiny shoes, the small diamond ring.

"I think you better take your hands offa him, Mac. Don't you?" the cop said mildly, tapping his heavy stick on the ground.

"He's crazy!" Hesse kept repeating with assurance and calm derision.

For one panicked moment, Dave thought: He's going to

weasel out of it. He's going to walk away. He turned to the cop, his eyes begging.

"I'm making a citizen's arrest. This man robbed me! I've been looking for him for months!"

It might have been Dave's eyes, or the way he wasn't going to budge, or perhaps Hesse had overplayed his hand with his superior calm in front of the big Irish cop, but finally the cop said: "OK Mac, I'll take him in to book him if you want to file a complaint. But if you're lyin', you could get yourself locked up, see. Pressing false charges, see. You wanna take the chance?"

Dave hardly heard. He only saw Hesse disappear with the cop into the station house. He followed behind them, almost too happy to walk straight. He filed the forms.

"Tomorrow morning is a preliminary hearing. Get your ass down here, buster. And you'd better not've made a monkey outta me," the cop called after him.

"Just grabbed him right off the street! Made a citizen's arrest!" Dave repeated the story for the umpteenth time.

Jesse, sitting at his father's feet, made a fist and punched a couch pillow: Wham! His eyes widening with satisfaction and relief. But the truth was, he wasn't quite sure. There had been something wild, almost savage in his father's joy. He felt an odd queasiness.

"You should've seen that cop give me the eye. I tell you!"

Jesse watched his father's hands rub against each other with impatience, dissatisfied, as if the words were not enough, as if he wanted to conjure up the magic of the moment for them, wanted to transport them all by some alchemy to the exact place and time of his triumph. "I tell ya, he just couldn't believe it, such a thing. Thought I was the crook!"

He looked at Jesse and the boy caught the glance gratefully, realizing that the source of his own unease was not doubting his father's great triumph, but rather at the nagging sensation that he had been eavesdropping. It was a feeling difficult to shake, for in the last months his entire knowledge of Hesse had been gleaned from muffled sentences leaking through closed doors; single, disjointed phrases thrown across the kitchen or living room; anguished animal sounds hidden deep within the night. They had never told him what had happened. Never acknowledged it. Oh, he could understand wanting to keep it from Sara and Louis. But he deeply resented being lumped together with them in the despicable category of "the kids." Like a detective, he had pieced together the vague and fragmented story of Hesse and his father, letting it scrape his insides raw with the fine, deep, precise pain of a scalpel. He had cauterized the wound with a white-hot fury that was directed mostly at Hesse, but also at his parents, especially his father. He'd tried to stop his anger, wanting to analyze, to find excuses, but always the searing pain stopped him, preventing forgiveness of any kind. And now, for the first time, he felt the undissembling directness in his father's glance, free of guilt, which did not say, "What is this kid doing here?" but rather "You and me, Jess. We can handle it, together!"

So later, when he heard his mother's soft doubtful mutters, he knew himself bonded to his father, at one with him against all timid, sickening equivocations that aimed to pull down his unquestionable victory. Laid flat, his father had pulled himself back to the center of the ring, and like one of those bloodied old boxers in a Garfield movie, had flailed out against the odds, splitting the soft rotten underbelly of corruption. His mother's soft entreaties, her warnings: "Dave we're not out of the woods yet!"; her "What if he gets a smart lawyer who can twist things around?"; or, more ominously, "What if he's spent the money?" filled Jesse with the same fierce, impotent rage he saw reflected on his father's face.

"You're never going to be satisfied. Made a mistake once, that means the rest of my life . . . You're just never going to trust me . . . never!"

"Dave, it's not that! You know I ... I ... just don't want you to get your hopes ..."

Jesse saw his father pivot to face his mother with a contained violence that shocked him. "HOW MANY MORNINGS DID I GET UP TO DRAG IN THOSE BOTTLES TO THE CANDY STORE? HOW MANY!!!! There wasn't even a dog—you hear!—not a dog out in the streets. But I got up, two, three in the morning. How many times did I go out in the dark to drive people all over town? Getting stiffed, getting robbed, getting tickets!? For that money, for my wife and kids ... Does he think he can con me, that I'm a shmuck, a greener? Ponzi games! Who does he think I am ... that I'll go away quietly ... ?" he screamed in uncontrollable rage, like a wounded animal.

"Dave, not in front of the kids!" she implored.

His father's answer was swift and satisfying. "Jesse is no kid. I have nothing to be ashamed of. He's my son, he understands." He put his arm roughly around the boy. "I'm telling you, I put him behind bars. Now he'll give me back what he owes me. We have courts of law! We have judges, justice in America! Even if the judge doesn't want to believe me, all he has to do is look at the guy's record. Just to look!" Dave's voice rang deep and bell-like, filling the room until there was no room for anything as petty and wretched as doubt.

The Brooklyn courtroom was overcrowded, overheated. It smelled of harsh floor wax, old coats, and people with bad teeth. The pews were filled as Dave, Ruth, and Jesse walked in with their lawyer. They could already see Hesse sitting up front, leaning over to whisper to the man beside him, a man with soft, smooth hands and a gold ring. A man that could have been Hesse's brother.

"Markowitz versus Hesse!" the bailiff's voice said finally.

Dave walked briskly forward, hat in hand, towards the judge whose black robes and crisp white collar made him look vague and unreal, like a picture of a judge.

Dave jumped up: "Your honor, I'd just like to say that this man," he pointed to Hesse, "this man has taken the food from my children's m . . ."

"What the hell is this?" the judge exclaimed, looking around, amazed, at the bailiff, the lawyers, smashing the gavel down. "Silence! Would you please instruct your client that another outburst of that nature will get him into jail for contempt."

Dave felt his face grow hot. He let his lawyer pull him back down into his seat and heard his bored whisper. "Look, this is just a preliminary. No point in getting riled up. Save it for the trial. OK?"

Dave's lawyer spoke. Dave tried to understand him. He wasn't angry enough, Dave thought. All those big words. He wasn't telling the story the way it was. Yeah, there were promissory notes. Yeah there wasn't any collateral. But you've gotta tell the judge how he did it. His face. His smile. The handshakes. The little gifts. The way he looked into your eyes and said: "Trust me, believe me." All the stories . . . Tell him about the chemical plant, and the patent, and the promises . . . !

"OK, John," the judged motioned to Hesse's lawyer. "What do you have to say?"

John, he called him, Dave heard, shocked. By his first name, he called him. And Hesse's lawyer got up and smiled at the judge. He talked a few minutes. He put Hesse on the stand. A business deal. Exhibit A, Exhibit B. A business deal. Mr. Markowitz knew the risks. Disgruntled partner. Vindictive. Baseless. Partnership, and Hesse had taken his lumps like a man, and he, Dave Markowitz, was sour grapes, unbusinesslike. Vindictive. *Vindictive!!*

Dave watched his own lawyer rise, noticing for the first time the rumpled suit. The lawyer protested. He presented in evidence Hesse's past record. The judge glanced at it briefly, and then looked up at Hesse's lawyer with a sardonic smile.

"Quite a businessman you've got there, John." Then he looked with the same expression at Dave: "You're a cabby, I understand, Mr. Markowitz. A New York cabby. Mr. Markowitz, from my experience, a New York cabby knows what's what. You took the notes. You signed them. You handed over your money willingly. I don't know what kind of crooked deal you two had planned, but it seems to me you both got what you deserved. Case dismissed. Bailiff. Next case please."

"What," Dave looked at his lawyer, puzzled. He looked back at Ruth's sad face, at Jesse's appalled one. "That's it?!! That's it? Yeah, well, we'll see about that."

He jumped over the desk and ran to Hesse, grabbing his shoulders and shaking him. He shook off the restraining hands that were reaching out to stop him from every corner of the room. He felt his fists crack bone and pierce flesh and land squarely and heavily into Hesse's soft middle. He had the strength of a goring bull. No one could stop him. But when he saw the blood spurt up and out of Hesse's nose and mouth, his eyes begin to blacken and swell, he dropped his arms helplessly, letting himself be dragged away. Blood money. But blood was not money. It was not an even exchange.

Chapter twelve

There were only two more people in front of her. Ruth shifted her weight from her right leg to her left, easing the discomfort from the long wait. At least she could do this for him, stand and let him sit. Let him sit. Rest. He needed rest. Maybe here, afterwards, they would take good care of him, make sure that he ate the right foods. It was quiet here, no kids running around.

"Next!" It was the kind of arrogant voice she hated most. "Medical insurance?" Ruth studied the nurse's flawlessly white cap with its sharp edges and answered softly, with deep shame: "Welfare." But the nurse said she couldn't hear and made her repeat it again, loudly, so that everyone behind her in line looked up.

"Not here. Welfare is down the hall, two turns to the right. Next!"

"Another line?"

The nurse stopped shuffling her papers for a moment and stared at her. "Down the hall, Missus."

Ruth took the forms humbly and walked back to where Dave sat waiting. "It's not the right place. I'll go . . . I'll be right back . . ."

"Let me go. You stood so much already."

But she pushed him gently back into the seat. He did not resist her. Three hours later, after he had already changed into hospital pajamas that made him look like a prisoner, and been placed in a room crowded with five other men, they said goodbye. "I'll be back tomorrow before the operation. They told me you go in at four o'clock."

He smoothed her cheek with his thumb. "What are you so worried?!" With tremendous effort, he flashed her one of his old smiles. "So what's the big deal? You heard the doctor. Minor stuff. I'll be out and good as new. Lousy ulcers! Only one thing worse: lousy bleeding ulcers. Can I say goodbye to the kids?"

"Jesse already took the baby home. He couldn't wait anymore. They don't let kids come up. But Sara wouldn't go. She's waiting downstairs."

"So sneak her up the stairs. I'll wait for you."

"Dave?"

"You'll be OK?"

"Huh?"

"You'll be OK?"

"Sure, sure. Stop with the long face already! Go, honey. Bring Sara up. Kiss Jesse and Louis for me. Tell them I'll be home before they know it. We'll buy them something, huh?"

"Sure, Dave." She drew him to her for a moment, too conscious of passing strangers to do more than just peck his cheek and whisper: "Tomorrow."

"What are you worrying? I'll buy the paper, stretch out in bed. Like in a hotel. Breakfast in bed. Like in the movies, right?"

"Right." She smiled back, her eyes blurring for a moment. "I'll get your daughter."

*   *   *

Sara heard her mother's too quick steps, the frightened turning to check if any officious white-coated enforcer of hospital rules might be on their trail.

"Saraleh, I'm going to get Daddy. You stay here a minute."

Alone on the dark stairs, the child trembled. But it was too late. Her mother was already gone. But then there was a shaft of light and he was standing there, a thin stranger in an unfamiliar striped robe. She could not understand, neither then nor later, how she actually got to him. It was as if the space between them suddenly evaporated from the heat of her joy. Her small arms strained vainly to encircle him, kneading him, wanting to find the muscles beneath the thin flesh.

She pressed her mouth into the unfamiliar cotton of his robe, tasting and smelling, searching for the odor that had come to her as a comfort so many times in the night. But it had been robbed from him, overpowered and rendered sterile. He was theirs.

Daddy, daddy.

Buried in his arms, still the terror hovered near, entering with the coolness that crept between them at the slightest shifting of their bodies. It was like being encased in a soap bubble, she thought. All around them, it was luminous and exquisite, but so fragile she was afraid to breathe. She felt filled with a sudden urgency, a desire to plead with him, to utter sacred vows, promises never do it again, no never (whatever she had done to bring him here, to separate them)! If only he would come home!

Daddy, please. One more chance. Just one more.

And then she felt anger. He had promised her something, and it hadn't come true. She wanted to tell him that. To warn him that she was older now; that she understood that he hadn't spoken the truth. For she had seen them take away the ropes when the grass was thick and strong, only to replace them with a long, steel chain that looped for miles around the earth. Chains around the grass. And now he, too, was chained off, theirs, to be approached guiltily, behind turned backs.

She needed to tell him this, and that she forgave him. And that she loved him and didn't want him to be here anymore. But the words wouldn't come. Already, she felt her mother pulling her gently away.

They had to go! He had to go—back to them!—before they were caught.

She clung on desperately, all words dammed in her throat, unable to dislodge a single one. "Daddy!" she finally called out, foolishly, knowing it would not tell him a single thing.

But she was wrong.

He understood her perfectly, pulling her towards him with some of his old stubborn strength, giving her one last hug as willful, as desperate and as terrified as her own.

Then, slowly, as if in a dream, she felt his arms slipping away.

And then, he was gone.

Chapter thirteen

Ruth didn't like leaving Sara and Louis the next day, imposing on the neighbors. Yes, and seeing Louis cry. He had been left with strangers so few times in his life and was so miserable and frightened. But the Cramers had been so kind about it, and Mrs. Cohen had promised to check in on them. A hospital was no place for small children, especially since they wouldn't even let them come upstairs to see Dave anyway. Dave would be so disappointed, she knew, that she hadn't brought them. But she didn't like all that sneaking around up back staircases. He'd be home soon enough anyway.

The screech and sway of the subway car hurled her from side to side. She grabbed on to Jesse, steadying herself. He was already five feet seven iches and growing so fast that his pants were always a little too short, no matter how fast she let them down. Dave had been so worried he'd be a shrimp like himself. She smiled. No danger of that, although with two short parents it was a miracle. A blessing, she thought, from God.

They rode in silence. She did not press him, respecting the

strangeness that had crept into their relationship in the past few months, the mutual shyness in the way they saw each other. She wished she could tell him now that it was a comfort to her to have him next to her, so quiet and manly. A shoulder to lean on. She knew Dave felt the same.

How happy Dave would be to see him! Of all the children (although he had never betrayed himself in word or deed) Jesse meant the most to him. Maybe even more than she did. It didn't bother her anymore. You couldn't compete with a man's love for his first-born son. Only a fool would resent it, and a maniac try to change it.

Dave had done a good job hiding it. Sara would never suspect and Louis was too little to notice. So good, in fact, that the one person who had the least idea of all was Jesse himself. It was as if Dave was training him to win a race, riding him hard, expecting so much from him. And Jesse was like a young racehorse, full of pride and spirit, believing he was smarter than everybody else—classmates, teachers. Not that his marks helped make his case. Cs, Ds . . . If he was a kid who didn't like books, well, you could understand. But a kid who hates school and spends his life reading? His afternoons taking home books from the library? And yet, he had flunked math twice and she had had to talk to his English, history and social studies teachers. In New Jersey, his teachers had had only good things to say about him. But here, they didn't care, didn't appreciate . . . A good teacher could make gold out of him. Why, she mourned again, the old bitter mourning, didn't he have a good teacher?

It was Dave's fault too. While he defended the teachers, lecturing his son, berating him for his obstinacy, she could tell (and so could Jesse, she had no doubt) it was simply lip service. He also thought the teachers were idiots and that his son had nothing to learn from them. But he never sided openly with Jesse. He sided with him the way he loved him: behind his back.

She wasn't worried about the operation, not really. Just the pain. The doctor had made such fun of her, making her feel childish, foolish for even asking if Dave would come out of it all right. "An operation on bleeding ulcers is not, Madame, brain surgery." He had looked down at her over his reading glasses, which had made his face look severe and amused. Well, he couldn't help looking down on her. She was so short. She didn't take it the wrong way, getting insulted or anything. The opposite! The doctor was being very kind to make her feel so dumb for worrying, for encouraging her to stop. And since she wasn't paying him, she'd felt no right to ask him too many questions, to demand anything, but only to be grateful. She didn't even know his name.

"Mom, I was thinking . . ."

She smiled at his quizzical face, his sweet cracking voice on the verge of turning forever deeper into a man's voice.

"We should bring something. Flowers or candy."

She thought of her thin wallet, of buying groceries for the week . . . But this was no time to be practical. When they got out of the subway, they bought five roses. She counted out the money slowly and tried not to think about tomorrow as she saw her son hold them proudly, carefully. In the elevator up to the ward, she saw his eyes darting, comparing his bouquet with those held by other people.

When the elevator stopped, he hurried out ahead of her, looking for the room number Ruth had remembered from the day before. She was surprised when she saw him hesitate at the threshold. She caught up, slightly breathless, ready to tease him at his sudden shyness, but stopped. In one corner an old man was snoring loudly, while in another several strangers turned around to stare at them. The only other bed in the room was stripped to the dark gray stripes of the mattress and the dull metal frame. It smelled strongly of newly applied disinfectant.

"But where?" Ruth whispered. "Maybe they switched rooms after the operation? There were a lot more people here yesterday."

"Ma, you just screwed up the room number." He said it

so surely, she almost believed him. It would have been just like her.

Jesse ran down the corridors, stopping nurses, looking into rooms. Finally, a nurse asked them who they were looking for. When Ruth told her, she looked them over queerly, and led them into a waiting room. "Please wait inside for the doctor. He'll be there in a few minutes." And as an afterthought, biting her lip: "I think it would be best if the boy waited outside."

"You stay here, Jesse. I'm just . . . I'll be . . . right inside."

"But . . . !"

"Please. The nurse said. Please."

He slumped into a chair.

She opened the door and found herself in a wood-paneled study. She looked around, admiring the dustless shine of the polished mahogany desk, the sparkling glass doors on the bookcase. She reached out timidly, picking up a large glass paperweight and turning it over, watching snowflakes fall peacefully on top of the Empire State Building. She remembered finding such a toy once in her father's generous pockets. And for just a moment, she ached for a father's hand.

She waited and waited, beginning to be bored and nervous. She tried reading the titles on the spines of the neatly arranged books, but gave up. Then, finally, she heard the door open and voices in the distance: "Glenn, glad I caught you. About the game this Saturday. Lynn has some kind of benefit for the museum." She heard the other man's sounds of polite distress and then footsteps coming towards her. The door closed with a loud sigh.

"I'm Dr. Glenn Gleason, head of the Department of Internal Surgery."

She heard him pause and wondered if she was supposed to say something like "How proud your mother must be!" or "How wonderful for you!" to acknowledge the value of the information. But he wasn't looking at her, which convinced her not to interrupt.

She thought he might hold out his hand and nervously wiped her sweaty palm across her coat sleeve. But he didn't. He just continued in his firm voice that made her feel he must be smart and right, whatever he said.

"I'm sorry to tell you Mrs. Berkowitz . . ."

She was startled, then ashamed for him. But she held back her corrections, hoping there would be more mistakes and that the voice would leave more holes, yawning gaps through which she and her children could escape.

"Your husband passed away two hours ago."

"Dave? Dave Markowitz?"

He looked down, shuffling papers, confused. "Markowitz? Yes. I'm terribly sorry. Markowitz," he repeated.

"What?" she said harshly, stupidly.

"For the mistake, and of course, for your loss," he shifted uncomfortably.

She looked at him, appalled. She was so stupid, that's why she didn't understand, when he was trying so hard to make it clear. It was all clear now, wasn't it?

"Why? From what? He didn't even have his operation yet. Four they told me. In the afternoon, they told me. But now it's still morning. It wasn't dangerous, they told me . . ."

"Mrs. Ber . . . Markowitz, your husband's operation was rescheduled by the surgeon in charge. We tried to call you but no one answered. There were serious, unexpected complications. I doubt if the medical terminology would mean much to you. We tried our best. My condolences. You'll have to speak to the office about arrangements . . ."

"I want to speak to his doctor," she felt the hysteria rising and fought to control it.

"Who?" he shuffled the papers some more, searching for details.

She suddenly realized that they had never told her the surgeon's name. "I don't know," she said.

"Yes, here it is. Dr. Wilson. Uhm, I don't know if he's here. Would you like me to page him? Can you tell me what it is you wanted to know?"

To know!! Ruth thought. She thought of so many questions she would like to ask that doctor, the one who had been so contemptuous of her fears; who had told her not to worry. And suddenly she forgot what it was she had wanted to know and a great spasm of pain, a feeling of being utterly drained, made her body hollow.

"Perhaps you'd like me to bring in your son now?"

My son! She remembered, glad, then terrified. Nodding yes, she watched the doctor rise like a figure in a dream whose very motion is suspect. Nothing was fixed, real. It all floated like bits of soap masquerading as snow, fake turbulence in a fake world. It was only when the door opened and she saw Jesse step over the threshold with those flowers in his hand that the vagueness congealed into something solid and real. She had never been so proud of him, his height, his handsome face and body; never so glad that she had once given birth and had a son who now stood taller than herself. He went to her awkwardly, shifting the roses, which were already wilting from the tenseness of his grip.

That was what suddenly broke her heart in two.

"Your mother has something to tell you, son," the doctor said professionally.

Yes, there was something to tell him. She would remember in a minute. Then the spasm, the ache went through her again.

"Jesse, Daddy's gone."

His face looked annoyed, then puzzled, then angry. "Gone?" he said. "Gone where?"

How funny, she thought, startled, wanting almost to laugh. "Passed away," she told him, and then wanted, meant, to hold him. But instead, she found herself being held. She held his hand as if he was a little boy again weeping in the alleyways of Brownsville, waiting to be rescued. She held his hand as if he was her father.

"Come, *tateleh*."

Behind them, medicine carts and voices rumbled with indifference, like subway cars careening heedless in the dark.

Chapter fourteen

There would be no place for her here, next to him, she noticed. It was a bargain plot, arranged by Morris through his union, reserved for members of a club to which Dave had never belonged: The Conquerors Club, the sign said. Rosicrucians? Knights of Columbus? She didn't know, and didn't want to ask.

All she wanted, as she stood there getting more and more confused, was to wake up; to feel that unconscious comfort that seeps into nightmares, revealing their smoky core. Ah, the relief! Just a dream, all the hard complications, the razor-edged difficulties at once softened, resolved; life suddenly simple again.

She waited for that moment.

Instead, she saw them lift him. The box rocked gently, like a boat coming into harbor. To her horror, she felt a sudden, deep rage. She wanted to run to him, to pry open the lid, to shake him, to scream: How dare you do this to me? How dare you leave me like this, a widow with three small children!? She closed her eyes, trembling with the effort of sanity, imagining the soft earth with horror and envy and finally, calm acceptance. Rest. He needed that.

Dave!!

Don't leave me. Don't leave me here alone. My love. My husband. My children's father.

My dear friend.

"*Kal Malay Rachamim,*" her lips moved with the words. "*Hatzur Tamim Poalo . . .*" The Rock, His work is perfect, for all His ways are judgment; a God of faithfulness and no iniquity, just and upright is He. The Rock, perfect in all His work; who could say to him what are You working?

I could say it to Him, thought Ruth, and He would have nothing to say for Himself. She bowed her head, defiant, yet already defeated. Who had the strength to fight God? Besides, He is off somewhere. On vacation. The clods of earth fell over the coffin, thudding, dark. It was the way they covered garbage, she thought. Even old prayer books got placed in attics, protected from the rain.

Her heart, wrung with faith, ached. "He rules on earth and on high; He causes death and restores to life; He brings down to the grave and raises up again. The Rock, perfect in every deed; who could say to Him, what are You doing?"

Yes, she had to believe this. For what else was there?

She brushed back her hair as it escaped from the fancy hat Rita had hurriedly lent her, appalled that she had thought to cover her head with only a simple scarf. Its unfamiliar weight, its theatrical (she thought) veil made her wince with embarrassment. But she had thought it better to listen to Rita, not trusting her own judgment.

She reached out for Jesse, taking his hand in hers, patting it. But the moment Jesse's shoulder brushed hers she couldn't stop herself from resting her full weight against him. She felt him tense but was helpless to straighten herself until she felt his unmistakable stagger. He was still, despite his height, a little boy. She straightened her back, ashamed.

"Show us, God, loving-kindness," she prayed, able to cry now, feeling the full burden of her responsibility. "Just in all Your ways. O Rock, slow to anger and full of compassion, spare and have pity upon parents and children." She enfolded her son's hand, the long, awkward fingers of an adolescent boy and caressed them. She wondered again if she should she have brought Sara. Everyone had convinced her that a six year-old had no place at a funeral. But what would she be able to tell the child, she wondered, that would be as definite and irrevocable as this box being lowered into the ground? How would she explain it without sounding as if she was making it up and thus had control over the telling, the beginning and the end?

And what was the beginning? Ruth thought helplessly. A dream in a boy's head on the boat ride from Russia? Hesse? The gene of some unknown ancestor? Or was it, quite simply, a scenario in the unfathomable mind of God? And was this, then, the end? Or only the imagination failing, despair, the part in the tale where the teller himself gives up or dies. And what was left then, was the middle in all its confusion and injustice; the middle, which had to be seen to be believed.

This solid box, already obscured by layers of earth, would have told the child everything she needed to know, she realized. And as they threw the last spadefuls of earth over it, she was pierced by the knowledge that these well-meaning but foolish people had robbed her daughter forever of the only sight that would have eventually brought her some measure of understanding and comfort. And she, by abdicating control to them, had allowed it to happen.

"Yours, O Lord, is forgiveness and compassion. Whether a man live one year or a thousand years, what does he gain? He will be as though he had never been. We know, God, that Your judgment is just and it is not ours to brood over the standard of Your judgment. You are just, O God."

Yes. She must accept this. But she could not accept that

this dead man was her husband. Not yet. Nor her own terrible crimes against those she loved.

"God has given. God has taken. Blessed be the name of God."

She saw the men surround Jesse. Some like Morris, out of piety, and some like Reuben, out of simple bossiness, draping the child with the fringed prayer shawl that was too long and too broad for his narrow shoulders.

She saw Jesse tremble with rage, but stop short of shrugging it off. She saw how his eyes wandered from man to man, finally resting on the man newly-covered in earth. He pulled the striped wool prayer shawl close around him.

Morris held out a prayer book. Ruth wondered if her son would take it, or if he would scream, rejecting their canned lamentations, their ritualized mourning. I could find myself in that scream, she thought, amazed. It would create a place to rest all the horror, the injustice, the ugliness now wandering homelessly, forbidden to enter the calm beauty of prayers written in tranquility.

But the boy took the prayer book, comfortable among the men, wanting to prove himself worthy to remain. He read where Morris's insistent finger moved down the page, dutifully reciting the prayer of a son for a dead father, his tongue tripping over the unfamiliar words as Morris whispered corrections in his ear.

"*Yisgadal V'yiskadash Shmei Rabbah . . .*"

Morris took the prayer shawl off the boy's shoulders, folding it neatly; his eyes catching the mound of freshly turned earth. "Big ideas," he thought with irony, but not without compassion, wiping cold tears from his eyes. "A big hole in the ground."

Then he gripped the boy's hand firmly, turning him away from the grave. "Come son," he said. "It's enough." He tried to sound fatherly and was surprised at the cold, pedantic firmness of his words. The boy shrugged him off, staring with unblinking defiance until, appalled, Morris looked away, feeling the yeasty rise of resentment bubble up amidst the warmth of his compassion.

Jesse watched him go, then turning back toward the grave, he slammed his fist into the palm of his hand so hard Ruth heard the dull thud of his bones against his flesh. She knelt, tearing out the grass and throwing it back towards the grave, as was the custom. Then she put her arm around Jesse and she, and her son, and all the men and women who had gathered there walked away, stopping only to wash the uncleanness, the touch of death from their hands.

> *He shall make death vanish forever,*
> *and my Lord, Who is merciful even*
> *in stern justice, shall wipe away*
> *the tears from all faces . . .*

Chapter fifteen

Ten days after the funeral, Ruth sat in front of the big picture window at Reuben's house, studying the patchy winter lawn and the faded blue of the sky. The faint sunlight streaming through the glass penetrated her clothing, going straight through to the marrow of her bones. She leaned back enjoying it, wondering and guilty over the heat and calm she had not expected to feel again.

It was a small thing, really, something she was embarrassed to even think about, that seemingly permanent shiver that ran along her bones; the feeling that her body was somehow open now on all sides, vulnerable and separate. She had felt it first after leaving Dave's body behind at the hospital. Then, she had considered it just a spasm, a chill born of circumstances, objective and treatable: Button the top button, put on warmer gloves. The real cold had begun later, at home in bed. It was having so much room, being able to spread out and roll over; never coming up against anything to stop you, to hold you still and warm and firm, and knowing it was not for just a day or a week or a year . . .

She felt flushed, almost blushing, as if the mere awareness of her body was a subtle form of disloyalty. And yet she didn't move away, because with the warmth came a kind of quickening, something akin to strength.

Now, she thought. I can do it. I can go home.

They had stayed at Reuben's for the *shiva,* the traditional seven days of mourning. Dave's family and hers had come and gone, sitting in circles around her, talking in low tones, discussing the weather and politics and the stock market. They had asked her sly, prying questions about the future, clucking over the children with that obscene, hidden mixture of horror and unconscious relief people cannot help feeling over someone else's tragedy. And she had sat beneath them on a low stool in a ritually-torn dress, forced to listen.

Reuben and his wife had been kind. Nice. Sorry. One part of her recognized and appreciated this. But mostly, she looked at them like strangers: Where had they been years ago when they took in outsiders for partners? When they'd sent Dave away with empty hands? When their help could have meant a different life for them all? Now, she thought, who needs you? Let someone else stay here and watch you play the good family. I don't want to be your audience anymore.

It would be a small victory.

When she asked Reuben to drive them home, she saw him hesitate. "Stay a few more days," he urged, and Ruth hoped, but could not be sure, he was sincere.

Maybe that was the worst part. Not trusting anyone anymore.

It was as if a curtain had been drawn aside, allowing her a glimpse into a world so unlike any she'd ever imagined, that her very view of reality had been changed forever. For if a human being could do something like that—pretend friendship, then rob another man, a man with three young children, a good, kind man who had worked so hard, so honestly for his money . . .

If a man could do that . . . ? What was Hesse spending that
money on—money distilled from the sweat of a thousand cold,
dark mornings when, rising at dawn, a man had left his wife and
family to wash and dress and go to work? Hotels in Florida? A
good dinner? And did he feel good there, basking in the sun? And
did the food taste good to him as he chewed and swallowed it,
with no aftertaste of the dead man whom he had crushed and
squeezed dry?

If a husband could talk the wife who loved him into giving
away their life savings; no, could take it behind her back and give
it away without her knowledge or consent . . . then, anything was
possible. She thought of her children. For their sake she must do
it. Be on her guard. Never trust. Never love again, not completely.
Never.

"It's nice of you, Reuben, really, to offer. But I think it's
better for the children if we go home," she lied, in the full knowledge that her children were fine, better off with Reuben's charity
than with her own proud incompetence. It was she who would
be better off at home in the dingy apartment in the housing
projects, out from under the stares of Dave's snotty sister and
sister-in-law, whose disapproval beat down on her like the harsh
light of a police lamp shone into the face of a suspect as he
is grilled by detectives. Silently, the relatives probed her crime,
disbelieving her show of innocence. But the crime she felt guilty
of, was not the one for which she's been indicted.

For them, Ruth's crime has always been that she isn't stylish
enough. Modern enough. Most of all, she's too religious. Fanatic,
they whisper behind her back. What they mean is that she lights
candles Friday night and knows how to make the blessing over
them in Hebrew. They themselves don't know any Hebrew,
and Sabbath candles are but a faint and distant memory in the
Long Island mansions, and in the suburbs of Pennsylvania. Such
things are embarrassing. Uncomfortable (they won't admit dangerous. Even after Julius and Ethel Rosenberg, and the House

Un-American Activities Committee when Jew became synonymous with Communist, which was synonymous with traitor. After all, it was only a few years after Hitler. They were careful to disassociate themselves with Jew, Communist, traitor, religion, candles, Hebrew, blessings. These things had nothing to do with them, with any good American.) For them, Ruth will never be quite American enough to satisfy their implacable standards, the standards of first-generation Americans deathly anxious to cause no inconvenience, to arouse no contempt. And part of that—or perhaps in addition—was the fact that she never kept a neat home. Didn't even own dishtowels and had inefficient, outdated appliances . . .

Her crimes were endless.

Even to her own family, to Morris and Harriet, who went to the synagogue and kept a charity jar full of quarters and did not hold her religion against her, she was a dismal failure. Forgetting their role, they had long come to believe that their sister had committed an act of wanton recklessness with her marriage—for she'd joined herself to a dreamer, a man who hadn't had a steady job, or a union to buy him a plot or help with the gravestone or provide insurance for the family he'd left behind. And now, being dead, his failure—and hers—was clear and irredeemable. Even the little they'd scraped by with between dreams was gone, the family left penniless, and a burden upon hard-working, dues-paying, union employees . . .

Enveloped in pervasive shame of unclear origin, and of a general nature, was it any wonder Ruth plotted her escape?

Reuben did as she asked.

But standing before the door to their apartment, studying the scraped red metal, the doorknob covered with greasy fingerprints, she closed her eyes and panicked. Paint fumes from a newly rented apartment wafted through the halls, transporting her back to her own moving day a little over a year before with its sawdust and newly-cut wood; to Dave fumbling, hopeful, for the key, dragging her dancing through the bare, unknown rooms.

"Ma," Jesse shifted the suitcase he had insisted on carrying, rebuffing Reuben's offers of help. The handle cut deeply into his young flesh.

She opened her eyes. Now, her hand on the knob, she had no illusions about what lay on the other side of the red metal: the silent, slightly seedy reality that would never change. Nothing frightening, all familiar, and yet more ghastly, really, than finding a ghost. She tried to focus, putting Louis down and rummaging through her bag for the keys, hoping she hadn't done anything markedly stupid like losing them. What if they were lost? Her fingers dove with panic into the sticky underworld of pocketbook debris. Unthinkable! There would be no way of getting in, and they'd be forced to call Reuben again and to remain in the hallway. Fatherless, homeless.

"Ma!" Jesse's voice unexpectedly hit a man's deep note and Ruth looked at him startled, and oddly comforted.

"It's in there, Jesse," she said, handing him her purse.

He found the key and opened the door. The acrid smell of the room hit her like a furnace blast.

"Ma, I'm hungry," Sara said.

"Ungry," Louis echoed, tugging at Ruth's skirt.

She felt the children's soft, heavy bodies leaning against her and for the first time she understood: however radically her life had been transformed, nothing had really changed. The floor would still have to be mopped, the pots scrubbed. Bread needed to be spread with peanut butter and jelly; packages would have to be carried and Louis wiped after he went to the bathroom. And, she realized with terror, the rent would still have to be paid. Yes, the rent.

She felt a sense of annihilation, as if each thing in itself was so tremendous it could not be accomplished, let alone the sum of all things.

"Gimme me some money, Ma, and I'll go get somethin' to eat," Jesse offered. "I'll get this show on the road."

She looked up at him. He was so much like his father. Maybe this was how God intended to save her. For surely, someone, something, must save her.

She counted out her money.

There was the hundred Morris had pressed into her hand (God bless him.) A fortune for Morris. But at least—his father's son—he would enjoy the dividends of a *mitzvah,* a good deed, however burdensome. Reuben's fifty; the twenties the other relatives must have slipped inside when she wasn't looking. And that, she thought desperately, was that. There was no savings account. No insurance, because insurance salesmen, as Dave had so often insisted, were all crooks. Something inside her rumbled like laughter.

Painfully, she peeled off five dollars. "Let me write you a grocery list."

"I'm not a baby," he argued, cutting her off. "I know what to get."

He left before she had a chance to say anything. Secretly, she was glad. In the kitchen, she cleared off the table from week-old crumbs, sponging the stale puddles off the counters. She rinsed the tea kettle and set the water boiling for coffee, gaining comfort from each small accomplishment.

"Alle fini," Louis called from the bathroom, and she thought: Dave is right. He's old enough to wipe himself. Then she stopped, appalled to have thought of her dead husband—sacred now—in connection with such a thing.

Nothing exists apart from him, she suddenly realized. He's a part of everything I have, everything I think, everything I remember. And even in the lifetime of things yet to come, I'll know what he would have thought, or said or felt.

"Alle fini!" Louis called again, his voice more insistent, bordering on tears.

"Mommy's coming! Mommy's almost there!" she called back, terrified he would cry. No one, she thought, must cry.

When Jesse returned, they gathered around him in the kitchen watching as he unpacked Devil Dogs, a bottle of Royal Cola, a bag of potato chips, and a Wonder bread.

Ruth looked over the items, speechless. "On this you spend my money?! This you call food shopping?"

"I like it," he answered sullenly.

She sat down as her legs grew weak. A giggle rose to her throat, then a laugh that exploded from her chest, shaking her body and sending tears rolling down her cheeks. The children looked on uncertainly.

"My savior," she murmured, unwrapping a cream cake and licking the gooey vanilla cream from its center. The children smiled, feasting on potato chips, chocolate cake and warm soda that burst from the bottle like a geyser, splattering the kitchen wall.

Later on, the neighbors came by with a straw basket filled with food. Ruth touched each one and felt the returning warmth of their cheeks and hands buoying her up.

"And if you need anything . . . If we can help you with the kids . . . anything," Mrs. Cohen nodded encouragement.

"Please, Ruth, feel free to ask," Dundee Williams implored, her pale baby in her arms, his delicate skin blue-veined, almost transparent.

"For goodness sake, don't be bashful a moment about it," one of the elderly Scottish sisters insisted kindly.

"How . . . ?" Mrs. Cramer began delicately, "did it happen?"

Ruth saw them shuffle their feet in embarrassment and wanted to answer quickly to spare them. But the more she tried to think of a way to express clearly and sensibly what had taken place, the more she realized that she really didn't know.

Had he fallen ill or had he made himself sick? Had the operation been a "safe" one, as the doctors had promised and his death a result of blatant incompetence? Or had something unavoidable gone wrong, even as the best doctors tried to save him? Or had God simply turned His back on them, with or without a reason?

"I don't know," she finally whispered, as if to herself and saw their faces fill with pity and surprise.

"Can we do anything, anything at all?" Dundee Williams pleaded.

Ruth began the polite reflex of shrugging off their help, but something stopped her. "If you could lend me some potatoes, until tomorrow," she asked humbly, "I could make a little supper."

"Oh, come to me! I'll make you a good supper!" Mrs. Cramer insisted.

"No, thank you very much. Kids are tired, you know. But if I could just have a few potatoes . . ." she heard her voice take on a new tone—humble, yet wheedling and impressive.

"Of course, of course!! Don't even mention it!" they said in a chorus, appalled she might have misinterpreted their stunned pity for reluctance.

"Honey," Mrs. Robinson put a kind arm around Ruth's shoulders, saving her from any confusion, "you just lost your man, the good Lord help us. Can't nobody do nothing 'bout that. But what I mean to tell you, what we all mean to say, is that you're not alone. Understand, honey?"

Ruth nodded, unable to speak, a sharp stab of love taking her breath away.

The potatoes were new and white beneath the dirty peels, she noted with pleasure as she grated them. She felt an inexplicable sadness as she watched the solid knob dissolve into a formless mass. Perhaps if I had been stronger, she mourned, watching the nicks on her fingers tinge the formless mass pink, perhaps I could have saved him. Pressed up against life's merciless sharpness, she wondered now what it was that would keep her from dissolving. What was the answer? Someone, she told herself, will have to step in. Even now, out there, somewhere, they must be planning her rescue.

A poor widow with three small children.

She turned the phrase over in her mind, mesmerized by its power, appalled and attracted, almost enthralled by its solid edges, its weighted presence.

A poor widow with three small children!

You couldn't ignore that. *No sirree.* She looked at the crumpled yellow cellophane paper and the straw from the neighbor's almost empty basket. Bless them! They'd be there for the cups of sugar, the odd cup of milk. Morris would do what his conscience and his religion dictated. He would struggle to be generous and invariably fail. He had growing daughters of his own who would need orthodontia, expensive vitamins, college educations, dowries, weddings . . . About Dave's family, who had money, Reuben and his sister, she had no illusions. They would disappear the same way they had suddenly surfaced. Even as they'd walked away from the grave wiping their tears they'd already begun to shy away from her, to give excuses, she thought bitterly. The poor relation, she thought, already feeling superior to them, happy to be rid of them.

She will never admit the truth to herself: that she too was at fault. That she never played the game. Never invited them over. Never accepted their invitations. That she was shy in the rudest possible way, and now, needing them desperately, she knew that she'd burnt her bridges. It was so much easier that way: A poor widow, with three small children! And they, the husband's family, who don't call, don't visit . . . To finally be so clearly in the right after all the years of being in the wrong. But no one will accuse her now. Whatever her crimes, she has finally earned absolution.

A Poor Widow. With Three Small Children.

Widow's and Survivor's benefits. From Social Security. How much? Enough for rent, food, clothing? How much? she wonders, adding her last two eggs to the batter, and pouring the oil into a frying pan. Waiting for it to sizzle, she turns around and glances at the ragged sofa, the public housing white paint on the dirty walls, the windows dusty with incinerator smoke. How did they say it on TV? "Ruth Markowitz, this is your life?"

Her skirt was tugged. There was noise in the bedroom. Sara and Jesse, fighting. Again.

"Hungry, Mommy. Hungry," Louis tugged, a little desperate, his face flushed from sleep, his eyes worried.

She looked down. He thinks I can help him, she suddenly realized with wonder. He thinks I'm in charge. The provider. The final address for all needs, all complaints, all lack. Me, Ruth Markowitz, the youngest child, the dependent, who always had someone to care for her. Her stomach rumbled with panic as the child's wails rose.

She lifted him, wiping his tears. "Hungry? Poor little *tateleh*, poor little sweetheart. Mommy makes you something yummy, in a minute, OK?"

This, she realized, was the answer: to think about the next minute, the next half hour. She could almost smell the potato pancakes frying, see them heaped with sugar on the plate. The kids would love them. They'd be satisfied and go to bed full. And then tomorrow for breakfast, there was still the jar of jelly from the straw basket, and the white bread Jesse had bought. As for lunch, that was far away. Eons away. There was no point in thinking about it now.

Chapter sixteen

Something permanent happens when you are a small child whose father or mother dies. Your life is not crushed—for there is tremendous resilience and irrepressible joy in a child—as much as it is transformed. You are thrust from the splendid simplicity of peanut butter and jelly sandwiches into the complexity of mourning. Most of all, you are forced into contact with the world of the spirit, with the idea that body and soul can be disconnected. And once you know that, even cornflakes in a bowl can never be the same again.

And then too, you learn that adult lesson of aching and longing and being denied; of begging some unknown power to please, please make it all a mistake. And you grow up with that unrequited longing, that unanswered prayer, and your view of life can never go back to what it was when you held your good father's or mother's hand and watched the Merry-Go-Round dance its way singing past the brass ring . . .

But Sara was to be extremely lucky. Although nothing in those dark days could have ever foretold it, something else would come along, so unexpected, so warmly beautiful, that she would once again begin to blossom and grow. But this was some time later and not as magical, or even unusual, as people might suppose.

All that summer and fall, Sara sat by the window. Oh, to be sure there were breaks for doll-playing, for television watching, for food-scavenging (meals, balanced on a plate, protein-vegetable-carbohydrate were beyond her mother's skills or imagination. "Do you want a little corn?" Ruth would ask her). But the distilled essence of her days, that which she would remember as her childhood, was looking out of the window, imprisoned. Until of course, she was finally rescued.

Picture her there, her elbows on the sill, her face intent and serious, her imagination fed by producers of Hollywood depression movies and cheap game shows. She watches the Black teenage boys grouped around the projects' wooden benches, studying their legs flung wide, their elbows draped possessively across the arm-rests. She strains to hear their songs, melodies with no beginning and no end. She does not understand that they too are dreamers, dreaming themselves out of Rockaway and poverty, into Motown, slick suits and national fame. Unaware, their gathering threatens her, for they seem to lie in wait, impassable sentinels, blocking her path. It is they who own the streets, the playgrounds, the elevators, the stairways.

But from the seventh floor even the biggest Black boys with the nylon stockings wound around their heads (for ringworm, her mother says) looked like dolls. You could watch them running after each other and hitting each other (she never actually saw them do this, but imagined it nevertheless within their power), and they couldn't see or touch you. She loved to rest her hand over the radiator and feel the hot steam rising, warming her face like a caress. If I was outside, would they beat me? she often mused, drowsy, warm, and safe. Would their big hands hit my face, my chest and legs? It was delicious to let your mind wander out there and then snatch it back, safe and warm behind the window. The lovely, lovely window.

"Why don't you go outside and play? Look how pale you are!" her mother's litany would begin each day, at least once a day. She had learned to ignore it, reading the answer in the fearful pinched crevice between her mother's eyebrows, which contradicted the words, begging her not to go.

But it was not the Black teenagers she was looking for as she sat there, lulled by the warmth of the rising steam, the soft light that filtered through the incinerator smoke, curling its way around the dark red bricks. They were simply part of the landscape. She thought of herself as a lighthouse keeper, a watchman on guard, a sailor on the topmost rigging, scouting for land. It was her duty to be there when the magic moment happened, as it surely must, for no other explanation made any sense.

She scouted the men passing by, searching for those of a certain height, a certain weight, a certain walk. So many men passed each day. She followed each with hope until he turned right instead of left or left instead of right, or drew close enough to prove too tall or too short, too thin or two heavy. And each disappointment chipped away at her hope, reducing it, but never actually killing it. Like a plant cut to the ground, the roots sent up foolish new growth that twined around the facts, embellishing them, giving them something akin to beauty.

Hadn't they told the Little Princess that her father was dead? Hadn't they taken away all her beautiful clothes and toys and given her only scraps of food to eat? Hadn't Shirley stamped her stubborn little foot and shaken her pretty curls refusing to believe, sneaking away from that awful school and waiting by the train station where soldiers were coming back from the war? And hadn't she found her father lying on a stretcher with a bloody bandage around his head? And then, hadn't Shirley smiled and said: "It wasn't true. Oh, I knew it wasn't true!!" And everyone told her she was a brave little girl, a good little girl for not believing, for waiting . . .

So Sara sat there, looking beyond the red, eyeless brick buildings, out to the small houses by the sea; houses—her father had once explained—which used to be filled with the summering rich who'd built them. Houses with chimneys, porches and rocking chairs; places that seemed to have faces that welcomed you home, not like her own. She would have loved to live there instead. But the people who did—the old Black men with hair like steel wool, the heavy Black women, the hordes of shiny-faced little boys— made it impossible. These were their streets. Here too, she believed she had no permission to pass by unmolested.

From the seventh story of her prison tower, she surveyed her enchanted kingdom like one of those spellbound princesses in the fairy stories she adored. One day, a fairy godmother would find her, giving her golden wings to soar above it, a magic wand to drip fairy dust down upon it, transforming it all into something manageable and benign. This is her plan. Until then, she allows nothing to distract her from her post, her vigil, and her watch. Nothing but food and television—the fuzzy grey-white picture, the indoor antenna one needed to cajole and massage into producing clearer visions. It was a way out of the projects. A place you could fly to safely without moving your body through dangerous obstacles.

Her favorite show was *Queen for a Day*.

"Now don't be shy. You just tell our studio audience your story." A heavy, middle-aged woman ran her hand nervously through mildly disheveled hair. Sara noticed the hair especially because it looked like her mother's. It was the only show on TV where women had hair like that and were too fat. The woman looked at her sadly. The man who asked the questions was a regular TV person with nice clothes, neat shiny hair, and a little smile. He asked the woman how many children she had and when she told him six, he staggered back as if flabbergasted and repeated it, shaking his head, and then began to clap and the people you couldn't see clapped with him. Sara shifted impatiently, waiting for the main thing, the part that would decide if the woman had a chance or not. Now, finally, he got to it.

"And what would you like if you were Queen for a Day?"

The woman stopped smiling so much, as she had when the people clapped for her six children. Her face became serious, even mean. Her Jimmy, she explained, was hit by a car two years ago and was now confined to bed. What she wanted was a small TV to put in his room so he could have something to do all day.

Sara considered. Her story was better than the woman's who wanted a new washing machine because her family played football all the time, or the woman who wanted an airplane ticket to visit her sick father. If he was dying, the father, well then maybe, but like this . . . You always had a better chance with a crippled kid, she'd learned, or somebody dying. And also if you asked for something small and cheap that most people had.

There were three more candidates. If no one had a sicker kid, she was in. Sara waited impatiently for the laughing and clapping to be over. No, that was no good—tires for the car. Boring. But then the last one: a motorized wheelchair so little Debby could get around after her operation which had left her completely paralyzed and not just sick. Paralyzed, Sara considered, impressed, wiggling her fingers and toes.

Now the time had come. The time to choose. It would be hard. The screen went white and instead of people a small arrow appeared, lying on its side. As each woman stood up, the arrow moved forward, propelled by the clapping of unseen hands. Magically, like a thermometer measuring the fever of enthusiasm for each misery, the needle moved.

The clapping was not sad, but joyful, almost like cheering at a baseball game, and Sara felt that she did love the women with their sad, mean faces and heavy bodies and the magic hands that thundered approval for each. She felt her own hands tingle with pain as she joined in the clapping, which surged wildly for the woman who wanted a small TV and then for the woman who wanted a motorized wheelchair for little Debby. Then the two women stood side by side and the people were asked to choose.

The small-TV-woman looked into the camera with a humble smile. You weren't supposed to do that, to smile. If you smiled, it really didn't mean that much to you, what you were asking for. The other woman looked as if she would never smile again; as if her life would be ruined or she would pass out. It was the same kind of power her mother had, Sara thought, when she spoke humbly to people and said: "I am a poor widow with three children and I can't . . . afford to buy such a big chicken . . . pay for a seat in the synagogue on Yom Kippur . . . pay any higher rent . . ."

Yes. And as the motorized-wheelchair-woman stared into the camera the needle went as far as it could go. Now she would not only get the wheelchair, but finely styled pumps, exciting jewelry by Sara Coventry, exquisite fashions from Hollywood and a new washer and dryer . . . at least.

Sara tried to picture her mother up there with the lovely, sparkling crown, the long velvet robe draped around her shoulders, the flowers in her hands and all the people clapping for her. And what could she ask for, Sara often wondered, so that the people would clap for her? Well, a new TV for one thing, for her poor, fatherless daughter. And maybe, a place to live with a backyard . . . but that was too much. They'd never clap enough to get anyone a new house. And even the TV . . . Well, being fatherless wasn't that sad, she thought. But maybe if her brother Jesse was paralyzed, her mother could ask for special medicine for him, to make him move his legs and arms just a little, but not enough to be able to break her toys anymore, or beat her up, or change the TV channel . . .

When she tired of daydreaming and adjusting the television

154

antenna to make the fuzzy grey images recognizable, Sara looked through magazines the neighbors had given her. She began a scrapbook, cutting out her favorite pictures. She called it a "Family Album." For her grandmother she chose a picture of a smiling white-haired lady, who sat knitting in a rocking chair, her heavy, motherly arms covered in a shawl. The woman wore gold-framed half-glasses, which she peered over kindly. At her feet, small, happy children played; a cat drank from a saucer of milk. Red and white checked curtains framed a window that looked out onto green trees and grass. In an ad for milk she found a young mother with smooth dark hair who wore a crisp, clean shirtwaist and a white apron with no spots even though she was in the middle of baking. With one hand she offered a plate of chocolate chip cookies while with the other she held a white china pitcher, from which she poured milk into tall, clean glasses for two small, clean, smiling children. Everyone looked so healthy, so rosy and happy. Sara cut it out. This would be the picture of her mother, herself and Louis.

The rest of the magazine's contents did not really interest her. Only the ads seemed to define that ineffable state of happiness she longed for. Her feelings, vague and unfocussed, came to the shiny color pictures like a shy seeker of truth. From them she learned what she hoped to know about life. Real lives—her own, her mother and brothers'—gave her no clues. She was convinced that her own family was fundamentally, hopelessly, shamefully mistaken, their error as obvious as it was simple: They simply didn't know how to buy the right things.

For it was only through merchandise that one could reach salvation, that state of happiness she knew was promised to each living being—even the sad, fat women on *Queen for a Day*. Her own unhappiness, therefore, was temporary and correctable. The moment she acquired those things necessary to make her look like the children in her first grade reader, and in the advertisements, she too might smile beatifically. Oh, to be Dick and Jane!! To live in a small house on a green, safe, quiet street and wear clean shorts! To have curly, short blonde hair and a mother standing by the door in a clean white apron and a father in a white shirt and tie, his suit jacket flung over his shoulder as he returned by railroad from his well-paying city job!

At night, dreaming, scenes would flash back to Sara in the darkness: Daddy pacing up and back in the living room, his voice unfamiliar in its bitterness: "That *mamzer* . . . let him die, let him rot in hell . . . that Hesse"; her mother standing by with a pinched face, wringing her hands, saying over and over: "So what can we do, what can we do?" not expecting an answer. Her father sitting on the couch in the living room, his face hidden by outstretched hands, and then the heartbreaking lift of his head, his lips drawn back over his teeth—so far back you could see his gold tooth, so far back it could almost have been a wide and joyous grin if not for that shocking and impossible sound from deep inside, a sound that cut through her like a hot knife. Her laughing father. And then the remembered clang of bedpans, her mother rushing in and out of the bedroom where her father lay, sick.

Soon, she developed a certain terror of sleep, of the blank space that loomed behind her eyes, waiting to be filled. She was afraid to close them. "Mommy!" she would call out, "I have nothing to think about!"

"Think about the country," Ruth would call back, distractedly. "About the cows and the chickens and green grass."

She tried, closing her eyes again, concentrating. But the cows and chickens would flash by fleetingly, swallowed by the ominously empty darkness. "I can't sleep," she'd call out again until her mother grudgingly appeared, her arms akimbo, exasperated. But always as she drew close to the bed, her arms would drop, soft and helpless, her eyes filling with sad concern.

"What can Mommy do for you, sweetie?" she'd murmur.

"I miss Daddy," she'd say pitifully, always very sure it was a half-lie. She *did* miss him. But this whimpering admission wasn't real, she thought. How she really missed him was different; colder, harder, more difficult to form the right face for. But her goal was to get her mother to sit down at the edge of the bed and give her all her attention for once, and being pitiful often worked. Sometimes, however, it backfired, her mother's eyes becoming blank, dark discs that stared off into space, her lips trembling.

That always infuriated Sara. It wasn't fair! It wasn't part of the game!

Then one night, she developed a plan.

"Read to me," she begged. "A story."

Ruth, who wanted to be left alone already, couldn't think of a reason to say no.

> *"I was a posthumous child. My father's eyes had closed upon the light of this world six months, when mine opened on it. There is something strange to me even in the reflection that he never saw me; and something stranger yet in the shadowy remembrance that I have of my first childish associations with his white grave-stone in the churchyard, and of the indefinable compassion I used to feel for it lying out alone there in the dark night, when our little parlor was warm and bright with fire and candle, and the doors of our house were—almost cruelly, it seemed to me sometimes—bolted and locked against it."*

Sara lay back, listening. Not all the words made sense to her, yet something in her mother's soft, even tone made her eyes feel drowsy and comfortable, infusing the words with meaning. I am not alone, she thought. There were other lives outside the schoolbook readers and magazine advertisements. Children without fathers, without little houses and mothers in white aprons . . . Little David Copperfield, orphaned and cruelly treated by the world. Fatherless, yet blameless. Like David, she too had not done anything wrong. And as she digested this incredible revelation, sleep came as harmlessly as a pause between words, no more frightening or significant than turning the page.

Chapter seventeen

There was nothing left to do but wait. Ruth wondered again if the directions had been clear enough. Dave had always been the one to give the directions. What if they got lost? Or if they changed their minds? It would be unbearable after all this. After telling the children. She peered out the window anxiously, once again searching the streets below.

"What's the time? What time did they say they'd come?" Jesse paced nervously.

"Around ten. Wasn't for sure, though. So maybe ten-thirty."

"Shit. It's already ten-thirty."

"What kind of language is that?! So maybe she meant eleven. 'Around' could also mean eleven."

"And maybe they ain't comin' after all, our big, rich relatives! How'd they get so rich anyway? That big house in Wood-hurst, and all?"

Ruth chewed on her lower lip. "Not sure. The Gelts had this wine business. Your Aunt Sylvia, she's a widow. She's some kind of cousin, distant, to Mrs. Gelt . . ."

"So you'll ask her about how you start a wine business?" he pressed impatiently, bored with the crappy details of family history.

"If I can. Well, sure. Maybe, that is. OK. Anyway, when Sylvia lost her husband she went to stay with the Gelts, and she just never left. It's their house really, their money. She helps them, with the kids—"

"So she doesn't have any money at all, our rich relative! She's a babysitter for the Gelts . . . Son of a bitch!" he shouted.

"What a thing to say! What a thing . . . It's not like that at all . . . it's . . ." she began to lose track of her arguments.

"Tellin' me stories, gettin' my hopes up!" he flung the couch pillows across the room, where they thudded against the wall.

"But Jesse, Jesse," she pleaded helplessly, afraid of him and for him.

Lately, he was like a young animal that does not yet know its limits. His discipline was thin—weak bands that were stretched to the limit everyday by small disappointments. If you didn't bring him a bottle of Royal Cola, or if the Yankees beat the Dodgers, he went around slapping Sara, slamming doors and cupboards until their wasn't one damn thing in the house that wasn't chipped, cracked or dented. Something terrible was building up in him, she knew that. She found herself watching helplessly, waiting with dread for it to explode.

"But Jesse, she's bringing Mrs. Gelt with her! They're coming together!" she poured her voice like water on the glowing coals of his simmering rage.

"And maybe nobody's comin' at all!"

"You louse!" Sara suddenly yelled. "You creep!"

"So who asked you, bucky beaver?" he shot back, offended. He shoved his straight white teeth at her. "Brusha, brusha, brusha, new Ipana toothpaste, it's better for your teeeeeeeth!!!"

Tears came to the child's eyes, which narrowed into hot

slits of liquid hate. Her lips quivered as she stretched them with effort over her slightly protruding front teeth. She was terrified her brother would spoil this, like he spoiled everything. She'd been waiting for this visit for days. It wasn't that she expected a gift, something tangible, like a new doll or a dress. She didn't think of the rich relative as a person at all, but as a vast transforming presence, like a change of season; a fairy godmother who would drip sparkling silver stars over their lives.

"Oy, stop already! Stop! Jesse, leave her!" Ruth paced to the window once again. "Look!"

At the edge of the project grounds, the small squares of grass chained off with metal links, they could glimpse a long black limousine. A chauffeur in livery opened the doors.

"I'll go down for them," Jesse shouted, running towards the door, pausing only for a moment by the mirror to slick down his hair.

Up close, the car was a wonder, gleaming like patent leather, the polished chrome reflecting an inflated, concave world. Looking at it, Jesse's face stared back at him, a prosperous jowled stranger. "Aunt Sylvia," he said with sudden dignity. Both women turned to him.

Two old ladies, he saw, disappointed. A small gray one and a fat blond one. The small one was nothing special, he noted. She wore a plain cloth coat. The blond was uglier, but at least she had furs.

"This is mine nephew, Jesse," he heard the small gray one offer him up to the fat blond. He smiled uncertainly at her stare, painfully aware of each pimple on his face and the awkward stringy length of his body inside the already too-small Bar Mitzvah suit.

"My mother's expecting you. I came to show you the way."

"She's god mazal, Sylvia, your sistar-in-law! Soouch a big boy!" the blond in furs said.

Sylvia nodded. "Very lucky, Lydia. You're so right!"

In the house, Lydia Gelt took out a tissue from her pocketbook, wiped off a chair carefully, then sat down. "Comere, dahling," she said to Sara, who approached with a shy smile. "You shoed alvays be ah goot gell and do homvoik. Den ven you grow ahp you cooed voik and help your matheir."

"Teh, teh. You should get her teeth fixed," Sylvia clucked, shaking her head at Ruth.

"Whew! Vat are you talkin? Custs alot a money," Lydia interjected with authority. "Ven I got mine Eddie's teet fixed, a fahchune dey charged me, just a fahchune. You know vat?" She leaned forward intimately, as if about to reveal a secret "Tell hair to do dis." She shoved her lower teeth out like a cash drawer several times in rapid succession, giving her face a vampire-like quality.

There was absolute silence as everyone stared, amazed.

"Why?" Ruth finally whispered, wondering if the answer was obvious and the question foolish.

"Vhy? Dis vill straytin out de mout! Eef de botum teet steek oud more, so den it looks like d'top steecks oud less. And dat dunt cost nuting!"

"Lydia always has ideas for everything," Sylvia smiled appreciatively.

"Ken I look round?" Lydia Gelt asked, then, without waiting for Ruth's startled response, she walked through the house, opening and closing doors, drawers and closets. "See vat big rooms. You gotta be-you-ti-ful 'partment. How much you pay rent?" she demanded.

"Forty a month," Ruth answered uncomfortably.

She gasped. "Yuh hear dat, Sylvia? Fordy, for a nice big 'partment like dis!" The two women stared at each other, frowning in amazement. "Vat da ciddy does f' de pepul. Such a be-you-ti-ful 'partment. Such a big rooms," she almost sang. "Nice, vehra nice." She wandered back into the living room and sat down.

"You god gas?"

"What?" Ruth gasped.

"De rent, 'cludes gas, 'lectric?"

Ruth nodded unhappily.

"Yuh heard, Sylvia?"

"I heard, I heard. Wonderful. Wonderful!"

"Ven ve came t' dis conetree, ve didn't have nod even two rooms. Nod even a toylit. Nuting!! I'm happy for you, 'lieve me. Mine heartz is happy."

"This you don't know, but I tell you. When Lydia says something she means it with all of her heart," Sylvia interjected. "She is such a good person, so fine! When my husband died, she came to me and said 'Sylvia, you come to me, to stay until you feel like you want to go.' But I got so attached to the children. I love them so! And they loved me like I was their mother. I know them since they're babies. How old was Eddie when I came, maybe two? 'Auntie Vee,' he used to call me, a broocha on his sweet keppeleh. Whenever I wanted to go, the children would cry: 'Auntie Vee, don't go, don't leave us!' It broke mine heart. I could never go."

"Oh!" Lydia interrupted, overcome with some deep emotion that almost made her shake. "Mine children! Dey vere so easy to vatch! Everybody lufft dem so!" She turned to Sylvia. "And dey lufft you, it's true." She turned to Ruth. "If she vould be dere real aunt, dey couldn't loff her more."

"Sometimes I used to think I should try to find a husband, have my own children . . ."

"Dey da same to you, Sylvia. Believe me, de same like vas your own. No difference!" She placed her hand over her throbbing bosom. "Ven you see Eddie, you esk him ifs not true."

"I know, I know," Sylvia sighed, turning to Ruth: "Thank God you have beautiful children. You're very lucky. Children are a comfort to a widow, better than money!"

"So you ged Soshal Scurity? Dank God! So you haf to budgit, be a gut managair. But dank Got's nod like it vas den. Den you god nuting. You could starve. Nowdays, you see, it's a difference voild! A nice, big apahtment. A check every mont. America. Sooch a vonderful coontree! Ve so lucky, all of us! Den ven de baby geds biggair, you could voik. You know to do someting?"

"I used to be a medical secretary . . ."

"Dat's vonderful, vonderful! You'll get a gut JOB, make a nice SALARY," her voice boomed. "And you haf a big boy, he'll also voik, he'll help—"

"I want to work," Jesse interrupted eagerly, seizing his big chance.

"You could get a job aftah school. Collect old newspapuhs. Dey pay good money for dat . . ."

"I want to learn a business—"

"In high school, dey train you. Everyting nowdays dey give you. You sign vocational and den you voik in a machine shop, or printing. Ged a goot job layder."

"I thought the wine business was good!"

"Oh, vat you need vine! How hard mine poor dahling husband ust to voik. Day and night. Sooch aggravation all d'time! You don need it, 'lieve me. You a smart boy. You ged a goot job, bring home a check every veek to your mother, vit no vorries." She shifted in her chair. "So vaht time. Ve hafte get back. D'doctors."

"You're right, Lydia. Two more minutes. So." A sudden silence descended, pregnant with possibilities. "Well, the reason we came—" Sylvia began.

"Vas mine Eddie! He's . . ."

"Now don't, don't," Sylvia adjusted the trembling fur around Lydia's shoulders. Lydia wiped her nose on a lace handkerchief.

"Mine Eddie is sick." She looked around the room expectantly. They waited for her to continue, but she just sank back into her chair, making it clear she had concluded.

"I told Lydia how religious you are, Ruth. So maybe you could say a prayer for him every Saturday when you go to shul."

"Take dis," Lydia pressed an envelope into Ruth's hand. "Mine Eddie," she wept. "*Gotteinu, Gotteinu.* Dey tink even, maybe, he's got . . ."

"Don't say it, Lydia. Don't even think it!" Sylvia demanded. "And this is for you, a little something," Sylvia handed her a small box.

Lydia rose, her heavy breasts heaving like a wind-driven prow. "Ve go now. I vish you vell. You haf beyootiful chill-dren. Dey should just be helti."

Sylvia patted Sara on the head, then leaned over to peck Ruth's cheek: "Try not to worry too much about Eddie. It's in God's hands," she whispered conspiratorially.

Jesse saw them back to the car. And when he returned, the children gathered around Ruth in the kitchen, pressing against her as she tore open the envelope. Her hands trembled as she saw the familiar green with its slightly sour smell. A twenty. She turned the envelope inside out, hoping it was hiding more. It wasn't.

"That's very nice, very nice," she exhaled uncertainly, unwrapping the box. Inside was old costume jewelry. "Nice," Ruth repeated, stunned.

"Oh, dat's becauze you just such a vonderful, vooooooooonderful poison." Jesse jumped to the top of the kitchen table, his hands straining under two imaginary pendulous breasts. "Mine fat heartz is plotzing f'yous. Mine fat behind is shvitzing from dis vonderful deal ya got!"

"Look at me! I'm gonna suck yer blood. Whaaaaaaaaa!" Sara screamed, shoving her jaw in and out.

"I gots a great deal for ya, kids," Jesse shouted over her, flicking an imaginary cigar. "How wouldja like to work for me forever for nuting!!? How wouldja like t'be a niiiiiiiiiice boy!?"

Sara joined him on the tabletop, her body swaying like a man in deep prayer.

"Oh mine heartz, mine heartz! Please let mine schmuck of a son get whatever he's got, and get it good!" Jesse shouted.

"Oh, you shouldn't, Jesse" Ruth began, scandalized. Then suddenly, she felt herself convulse with laughter, tears streaming down her cheeks.

Jesse jumped down off the table, pushing his face belligerently into his mother's.

"YOU GOT GAS?" He stood there staring until she nodded, helpless with laughter.

"SO TAKE AN ALKA-SELTZER!!!"

Ruth sighed, wiping her eyes, thinking about Sylvia, Dave's older sister, in the Woodhurst mansion watching over other people's children for twenty years because she didn't have the guts to rent an apartment, get a job, remarry . . . wondering how such a human being might feel herself qualified to give advice.

Interesting, Ruth thought, how Sylvia had had only contempt for her own immigrant mother, ashamed of her accent, her clothes, her piety. So much so that she'd set her own father up with a more "modern" woman. Money, Ruth smiled to herself cynically, washed away a multitude of immigrant sins. Once you had gold, your greenness could be forgiven.

But certainly, if there was retribution in this world, Sylvia had got hers, poor dope. So that's what had been going on all those years in the elegant mansion behind the green hedges. A fat old greener—charmless, tasteless, classless, stupid—all her money couldn't change that!—and Dave's sister, the one-hundred percent American with her Friday night card parties, licking her *tuchas* and being nursemaid to her children, all the while convincing herself she was an indispensable part of the family, instead of a cheap form of domestic servant.

With odd contentment, she watched Jesse rip some tape off the plastic upholstery—neatly repaired in honor of the visit—then throw a clump of stuffing over them like confetti.

She felt a sudden flash of pride. My own home, she thought. My own children. That was something, after all.

Chapter eighteen

I was a long time coming, it seemed to Ruth. First, there was the vagueness, the confusion, the weakness. Then gradually her world began to clarify, the lens turning and turning, bringing things more sharply into focus. At last she looked at herself, her life, clearly, understanding what she was up against and the few weapons she had with which to fight her battles.

On a warm summer day in August she put on a clean white blouse slightly frayed at the collar and a carefully ironed old blue skirt. She combed her hair and pinned it back, neatly but stylelessly. The effect was clear: poor but respectable, she noted with satisfaction. She left the children with Mrs. Cohen's eldest girl, and with more purpose and determination than she had ever felt in her life, she took the bus to Far Rockaway.

The Far Rockaway Hebrew Day School was housed in four white mansions, summer homes of wealthy, turn-of-the-century German Jews who had prospered beyond their dreams. Bought up sometime during the Depression by an upstart Polish Jew who had guessed right when the snotty Germans who wouldn't invite him to dinner had guessed wrong, the houses and several acres surrounding them had eventually been donated (partially out of piety, and partially on the advice of a shrewd tax lawyer) for the "furtherance of Jewish religious education."

There were wide, fragrant lawns, a punch ball field, a basketball court. Through the tall pines and oaks and maples, the salty fresh sea air drifted languorously, bringing with it the sounds of comfortable, middle-class residents and carefree vacationers reveling on the clean white beaches.

Standing outside the buildings, Ruth imagined boys in dress shirts and slacks, girls in pleated skirts and bobby socks, children flowing through the wide halls, giggling up and down the stairs. It was an expensive school—a private, college preparatory school, with religious education thrown into the bargain.

She took a deep breath and walked into the office. "I've come to see the principal," she announced too loudly and with more insistence than was appropriate since she hadn't yet been denied anything.

The secretary looked up, surprised, even a little amused. "Do you have an appointment?"

Ruth shook her head defiantly. "But I've got to see him anyway."

"What about?"

Ruth considered that. "It's about my boy."

Hoover High—those dark old buildings near the bay; the sinister iron mesh around the entrance—filled with the rough teenage offspring of project welfare families from the inner city. And they weren't the worst. The Italian and Irish kids from Howard Beach—they were the worst. Thugs in motorcycle jackets. The future gangsters of America. She didn't care what color people were—truth be told, she felt more comfortable among Blacks than ignorant, snobbish Jews like her sisters-in-law. But Blacks, she understood, were no one's darlings. She didn't want her son to be no one's darling; to be in a place where the textbooks were worn, the teachers bored and contemptuous. She didn't want him to be forced to learn the survival tactics of outsiders. He didn't deserve to be there, after all. They weren't one of those families, not really, she often assured herself. They'd wound up in the projects by accident, like castaways, washed up on an inhospitable alien shore.

"Is your son a student here?"

She already knows the answer, Ruth thought. She can see it in the way my hair is cut, from the worn-down heels on my shoes. Her asking was a kindness Ruth appreciated. "No. Not yet. But the Rabbi's *got* to take him in. We don't have any money, but he's got to anyway!"

A warmer light came into the woman's eyes. "Please, sit down. Rabbi Lerner . . . he'll be back any time. Can I get you a cup of coffee? Tea? I always need something this time a day. Kind of a pick-me-up, know what I mean? To get through all this typing."

"Quite a load," Ruth commiserated, relaxing a little. A working woman, Ruth thought, feeling the camaraderie of secretary sisterhood. Not the Doctor's Wife, a creature with dry-clean only knits and beauty parlor hair; the kind of woman she always dreaded running into; the kind whose children, she imagined, would inhabit these halls come September.

"You must be fast if you're going to get through all that any time soon," she nodded towards the pile of papers covering the desk.

"Oh, I don't have a choice. Tomorrow there'll just be more."

"I had a job like that once. It was like one of those *I Love Lucy* episodes, you know? Where the conveyer belt keeps moving and the candy keeps piling up, then falls off the sides and Lucy keeps trying to catch up, but it just gets worse and worse."

The secretary grinned. "Oh, it's not that bad. Rabbi Lerner's a kind person. Keeps telling me to take it easy. Go home early."

"Oh, isn't that nice? Glad to hear that," Ruth smiled nervously. Very glad.

The door opened and a short, dapper little man with black, slicked-back hair, a small mustache and a dark skullcap walked in energetically. He wore a new, well-fitting suit and smelt of expensive aftershave.

"Darn pipes leaking again, Selma. Better call the plumbers before the girls' bathroom overflows into the ocean like last year. How much did they charge that time?" He suddenly noticed Ruth. "Oh. Sorry." He put on his rabbinical dignity. "I'm Rabbi Lerner. How can I help you?"

Ruth stood up abruptly. "I want my son to register here for next year."

Ruth watched Rabbi Lerner take her in. He took a deep, unhappy breath that he let out slowly, like a man who realizes that something is going to cost him money.

"Please," he bowed, gesturing uneasily towards his office door.

Ruth followed him. She closed the door behind her firmly, not wanting the kind woman in the office to witness what was about to happen next. For she had no illusions. It had taken her many long nights, many unhappy days to get to this point. But now she was finally there, she understood. There was no turning back.

"Please, sit. Tell me about your son."

"He's in . . . I mean . . . he'll be in tenth grade come September. He's a bright boy. Reads all the time," she began eagerly.

"And his grades?"

"Well, good . . . actually not so good. Could be better. Which is why I was hoping to change . . ."

"Mrs. Markowitz," Rabbi Lerner said abruptly. "You know this is a private school. We're very expensive. Do you have the means to send your son here?"

"Someone told me you take in some smart kids even if their parents can't pay. My father was very religious. I want my son to go here. I want you to give him a scholarship!"

"Mrs. Markowitz, I want to tell you something," Rabbi Lerner said, leaning forward on his elbows, smoothing down his mustache with one clean fingertip. He smiled—a little tight smile—and shrugged his well-fitting suit shoulders.

"Everybody in this town has money for everything. They've got money for new cars before the paint chips on the old ones; for finished basements in houses that are way too big to start with; for pianos nobody's ever going to know how to play; for restaurant-size refrigerators stuffed with enough lox and pastrami and corn beef to feed a congregation after Yom Kippur. But there's one thing they have no money for. Ever. Education. Jewish education," he pounded the desk for emphasis, bored and irritated by the familiar speech, "to make a *mensch* out of their kids, to give them something to live for, something to live up to, a tradition, a culture to make it all worthwhile. For that, they never have money. If only half the Jews in this town would send their children here, we'd be able to build a new gym, add classrooms . . ." his voice grew weary, "give scholarships."

How many times a day would he have to make this speech at the beginning of *this* school year, he wondered. Ten, fifty? He was sick of hearing himself talk. *Everybody* wanted a scholarship, a reduction, some way to weasel out of their obligations. Nobody got past him. If they wanted the little blue registration cards the kids handed in to the teachers the first day of school (and without which they'd be ignominiously and mercilessly sent home in front of all their little friends), they'd have to pay up.

Undaunted, Ruth met his determined eyes with her own. "Rabbi," she began quietly, just as she'd planned. "I lost my husband last year," she lowered her head, letting the words sink in, watching their effect. "I'm living on social security and even," she lowered her head still further, sinking down in her chair, just as she'd thought she would, "welfare. My son has had a very hard time, with his father dying so young. He's in Hoover High—it's a bad place! I'm afraid for him. He's so bright, you see. Reads all the time. But the teachers there, the kids. They don't let him live. They don't know how to . . ."

"Mrs. Markowitz," Rabbi Lerner interjected, shaking his head sympathetically but firmly, "our scholarship money is very limited. And your son is very old to be starting out here. We have a dual program—Hebrew in the morning, then all regular, college prep classes in the afternoon. The Hebrew is on a very high level. Most of the children here have been studying it since first grade. We'd have to put him into first grade Hebrew until he caught up . . ."

"He could catch up fast, Rabbi! I would help him. I still remember my Hebrew. My father used to teach me. He'd open the *Chumash*, the Talmud, and read to me," she looked up, beyond Rabbi Lerner's head, to a blank, clean spot on the wall.

"Well, could you pay something? I mean, for your own pride. We could make up the rest in scholarship. Let's say," he groaned and sighed, "three hundred a year?" One-tenth the going rate.

Ruth shook her head defiantly.

"Three hundred? Two hundred? One hundred? Fifty? Twenty-five?" his voice rose incredulously.

She looked up at him. He wasn't a bad fellow, she supposed. Just doing his job. But she also had a job to do. She clasped her hands in front of her and looked up into his eyes.

"I'm a poor widow with three small children," she said quietly. Her tone was perfect. Humble, downcast yet wheedling and impressive. She felt the power of the words and saw their devastating effect. "A poor widow," she repeated, knowing that thundering through his head were the words: "Thou shalt not oppress the widow and the orphan. Lest thy wife be made a widow, thy children, orphans."

With a certain perverse pride, she stepped out of herself, looking in on the scene. She almost felt herself rooting for the little man. What choice did he have against this blackmail? None, she knew. She was more powerful. And the twenty-five dollars could come out of someone else's pocket, after all, even though she could afford it. But why should I pay?—she thought defiantly. If God has cast me in this role, I'll play it to the hilt. I shall not give an inch. A penny.

"It's food money," she told him, mercilessly. "Food from my children's mouths. It's not mine to give."

She saw Rabbi Lerner lean back, take out a white handkerchief and wipe his suddenly glistening forehead. His smile was gone.

"Forgive me," he pleaded. "Who am I to judge you? We'll take your son, if he wants to come. Do you have any other children in school?"

"A girl, Sara, going into second grade." She hadn't thought of Sara. The child was happy, so far as she knew, in public school.

"Sara. We'll take her in too." He motioned with his hands, palms up, defeated. Come one, come all. Hey, you only live once, he told himself. And Yom Kippur was only two months away, at which time God, like a celestial C.P.A., would be finalizing the balance sheet—subtracting bad deeds from good ones to get the bottom line which would decide his fate for the coming year. He could almost feel the Almighty peering over his shoulder, watching this scene with profound interest; almost see the heavenly pen poised to record the results.

"God bless you. And you should have a good, healthy year. And I hope you will bring both children down soon so we can test them for grade level. Would they like hot lunches too? Of course. Good hot lunches in our cafeteria!"

He got up and walked around the desk, opening the door. "Please give Selma all the details. Address, phone number."

Ruth got up, staring at him. "Thank you, thank you so . . ." she said with abject gratitude, playing her part. But her look was knowing and full of pity. Poor Rabbi Lerner, she thought, controlling her urge to laugh out loud. Or to weep. He hadn't stood a chance.

"They'll need IQ tests," Selma said calmly, writing down all the information. "Oh, he didn't mention that, did he? Yes. And you have to pay for them. Five dollars a test. That's ten dollars."

Ruth hesitated. She considered a repeat performance, but somehow couldn't bear the idea. Not in front of this audience. "Here's five. It's for one child. All I came about was for the one child."

Chapter nineteen

"Know what? You're sick in the head, that's what!" Jesse shouted. "Hebrew school . . . with first-graders?! C'mon! Anyway, I've got other plans."

"You shouldn't speak to a mother that way! . . . Fresh! What do you mean, plans? What plans?"

"I got other plans," he repeated cryptically.

She felt like an idiot. She'd been so sure he'd be delighted, after all the complaining he'd done about Hoover . . . ! Here he had a chance to start over, to make new friends from good homes! She explained all this to him until she felt enraged, then depressed, then finally humiliated. After all that! She'd look like such a fool in front of the Rabbi and that nice secretary! And the five dollars!? A waste. A waste . . .

It was the five dollars that gave her another idea.

"Saraleh? How would you like to go to school in a beautiful white building with nice little Jewish girls?"

Sara wasn't interested either. She was happy in public school; at home in the familiar draughty red building that smelled of crayons and papers and crushed chalk. She loved the windows stenciled with snowy-looking turkeys and pumpkins. Besides, she already went to school with nice little girls. Maria of the neat tight braids and lovely, shiny black skin, the smartest girl in the class, winner of prizes for spelling and drawing. She herself had won a prize: a ticket to a Police Athletic Association Christmas party. Inside the school, she was happy.

But walking up and back from the projects frightened her. And getting safely up the elevator home. If she agreed to go to Day School, her mother had promised to walk her to the bus stop and wait for her there to take her home. Reluctantly, she agreed.

The I.Q. test was more like a game of sizes and shapes and words. She drew little boxes inside other little boxes. "What does 'afraid' mean," the man asked her.

She could feel the meaning. It sat inside her, like a meal digested. "It means,"—dark hallways smelling of pee, dark strangers in shadowy corners, groups of teenagers guarding entrances, Jesse getting mad . . . "it means . . . afraid," she repeated stupidly. But the man simply smiled and told her mother that she'd done just fine.

On the first day of school, Sara stood shyly in the classroom doorway, aware of all the eyes. She looked down at herself, noting the spots of grease that yellowed her carefully ironed blouse, the unmatched white of her socks and how they heaped around her ankles instead of hugging them with new elastic. Instinctively, she knew all this might make a difference here, just as surely as it had made no difference in P.S. 44.

She found a seat. It was not so bad. Their eyes were simply curious. Not like the eyes of her relatives during *shiva*, that probed the way a sharp fingernail probes a sore. Under those eyes, she had felt herself transformed into a creature both pitiable and grotesque, someone against whom they could measure their own happier circumstances, reveling in their achievements. They were not fatherless. They were not poor. They had watched her, she believed, hoping for her acknowledgment, for a stricken look of misery that would make it official.

She never gave it to them. She looked around the schoolroom. And never would she allow these strange children to feel with smug joy the abundance of their own charmed lives by revealing the deficiencies of her own.

No way! She would never tell, never let it show! No one had to know! Unless—could they tell, she panicked, just by looking at her? Was there something about her face, her body that revealed all those things she lacked, the things that made her different— less—than them?

At recess she escaped to the bushes, watching in safety as the girls and boys separated to their different games. The girls played punch ball and would pick teams. Marcia and Linda were the captains. They wore soft mohair sweaters and pleated skirts. As the days went by, she saw that if they wore a pink sweater they wore a pink hair band and pink tights. If they wore plaid, the headband changed magically to plaid. Marcia had short hair, layered and teased like a movie star. Linda's was long and blonde.

Sara watched as Marcia and Linda pointed their fingers at the girls, choosing up the punch ball teams. Sara was amazed and frightened at the rash courage, the blind hope, of those who stood around waiting to be chosen; fearless creatures that could not even imagine the possibility that they might be left behind, standing on the sidelines.

Each morning before leaving the house, her stomach would roll thinking of the girls and their pretty clothes, of how they stared at her when she came in late from the bus, of how they stood rashly, hopefully, waiting to be chosen, and how the lucky ones squealed with joy when the magic finger pointed in their direction.

"I feel sick, I don't wanna go," she would say, feeling her mother's cool palm against her forehead.

"You're not hot," her mother would answer, unsure.

"Oh, but my stomach. It hurts me, mommy."

Sometimes she would stay home—for two, three days—watching TV, staring out of the window, and her stomach would not hurt then. But as soon as she got off the bus and neared the school, the ache would begin again. She'd sit down to rest until it went away, oblivious of passing time. When she walked into class, the children would say "Ooooh" very loudly because she had come so late, and her Hebrew teacher—old, gray, bearded Rabbi Bender—would shake his head and sigh. He tried to teach her Hebrew.

Bais aw baw. Daled aw daw. Gimmel aw gaw.

She struggled with the strange letters that had to be written backwards. It was so hard. And her stomach hurt so much.

Bais aw baw. Gimmel aw gaw. Daled aw daw.

Rabbi Bender made her mother come to school and soon afterwards her mother bought a little notebook to write down if she ate breakfast in the morning. But she didn't want to eat breakfast. Not when her stomach hurt so much. Mama! Did it hurt!

One morning, when Sara was very late, and the class had said "Ooooh" very loudly, Rabbi Bender told a story.

"Once a man, a very good man, went to heaven. And he was a very good man so the angels made him a very good place to stay, and the man was very happy. But then one day, he looked down and he saw his little girl. And she was not listening to her mother. She was not eating her breakfast."

Sara froze, lifting her eyes to look at Rabbi Bender, terrified he was looking at her and that everyone would see.

He wasn't.

"Well," Rabbi Bender stroked his beard, continuing, "this made him so sad. Oh so sad, because he was in heaven with God and happy and he wanted his little girl to be happy too. So you know what happened?" The class leaned forward eagerly.

They're not looking at me, Sara thought. They don't know. "She started to be a good girl, to listen and eat nicely and then he stopped being sad."

Tears came to her eyes. She felt sick with hatred. He'd come so close to telling . . . so close! And the story, the awful idea of it . . . a father far away and happy to be there!! Stupid, evil man, she thought, hating Rabbi Bender. Oh Mama, did her stomach hurt now! And he was looking at her, the rabbi, but the other girls did not look so they must not know. She stared straight ahead. What if he pointed to her, she panicked. What if he told? She felt her panic rising, cutting off her breathing. What if . . .!?

If he did, he would join Mary Christina Ravirez, who lived in the projects and had told everyone her daddy had died because he was fat . . . and Jesse, who hit her everyday . . . and the worst one of all, Hesse, who had somehow come into their family and destroyed everything.

She waited for the last bell, gathering her heavy books and briefcase. Most of the children ran to waiting cars that would take them to little private homes nearby, and to expensive Tudor castles in Cedarhurst and Woodhurst. Only she, Paulette Goldberg, and a few other kids took a bus in the opposite direction, towards the modest old houses of Arverne—and only she was left when the bus rode further on to the ugly housing project in Waveside.

"I hate Rabbi Bender," Paulette said suddenly one day at the bus stop. "He always says to me 'your sister was such a good student, my favorite, and look at you.' At the beginning of the year, he said, 'The apple doesn't fall far from the tree,' and now you know what he said! 'A rotten apple!' I hate my sister and I hate Rabbi Bender," she sobbed.

She had lovely blue eyes and soft, golden hair. She looked at Sara expectantly.

"I hate my big brother. He always hits me," she offered.

"Does he go to the Hebrew Day School?"

"He goes to public school."

"Wish I could go to public school and get out at 2:30 instead of 4:30 and wouldn't have all this baa baw beh. I hate Hebrew! I hate Rabbi Bender!"

"I hate him too! I wish I could go back to public school," she realized.

"Where'd you go?"

"Forty-four."

"Yuch! That's near the projects!" Paulette said with disgust. "My Ma says it's dangerous. You don't live there, do you?"

Instinctively, she shook her head knowing it was something else to be ashamed of. Something else to hide, like stains on clothes, and not having a father. So many things to hide, she thought with anguish. "I live in a house, further down."

"My dad has a grocery store near the projects. I could go in and just take Drake's cakes and everything."

"Really?"

"I could. But he never gives me any. He says I'm eating up his profits."

"My daddy drives a big yellow taxi and we go all over in it. To the Bronx Zoo."

"Would he take me too!? Oh, please would he?"

"He can't." She looked away.

"Why not?"

"'Cause he's passed away . . ." she caught herself, "I mean gone away."

"So when he comes back then. Where'd he go?"

"I don't know . . ." she murmured, telling the absolute truth.

Paulette paused for a moment, considering. "Does he sleep with your mother?"

"He will when he comes back."

"Wanna play ball tomorrow?"

"Yes," she let out the breath she had been holding, seeing the bus in the distance.

"I'll bring mine. A Spalding."

The heavenly bus stopped, rescuing her.

They were friends. At recess, they played ball. "My name is *Agatha* and my husband's name is *Alex*, we come from *Alaska* and we sell *apples*," bouncing a rubber ball beneath their knees with graceful rhythm. The ball was firm and light, bouncing back into your hand effortlessly. It was a Spalding, not just a regular handball, like her own. Paulette had new Spaldings, and jump ropes and Duncan yo-yos, and a rubber band ball as big as a fist.

"I wish I could play punch ball," Paulette said miserably. "But they won't ask me. They all live near each other and practice together in the afternoons."

They both looked off to the playing field. It was Marcia's birthday and she was covered with corsages. From each corsage hung a number of colored ribbons—one for each year—to which something was taped: candy, a penny, or pieces of gum.

They watched her laughing as the other girls crowded around admiringly. She must have a corsage from almost every girl in the class. There wasn't even room to pin them all on! Her hair shone. Her pretty green mohair sweater and green hair band matched perfectly. Her white teeth sparkled.

Sara and Paulette sighed, linking their arms together as they watched, the way believers watch a temple goddess accepting offerings from the faithful.

"For my birthday, I'd want a red one with Bazooka bubble gum on the ends," Paulette said dreamily.

"I would love a blue one with pennies. Then I could buy anything I wanted," Sara admitted shyly.

Sara never expected Marcia or Linda to speak to her. She had not brought homage, was not in the same neighborhood, couldn't play punch ball ... Her ineligibility for the role of handmaiden was clear. Paulette, on the other hand, had hopes. Whenever Linda and Marcia were near, she would suddenly jump up; begin to tell jokes about herself very loudly, overjoyed if one of them deigned to look at her and laugh. Sara watched uneasily. Having a friend was worse in some ways than being alone, she thought, her meticulously plotted stratagems of self-defense demolished by Paulette's utter vulnerability.

"I'd love to play punch ball," Paulette mourned.

"We could make our own punch ball game," Sara suggested. Personally, she thought the game stupid. Baseball with no bat, no catcher's mitt! She was good at baseball. Jesse and her father had taught her.

"Yes! And I could be captain and I would choose you . . ." Paulette agreed eagerly. But then her face fell. "Who else?"

"Dina, Sue and Ruth!" Fat Dina, lisping Sue, and Ruth with the thick glasses and funny clothes.

"Yeah, sure," Paulette said, an odd look coming over her face.

After that, Paulette began avoiding her, hanging around the place where the teams were being chosen. At first, she stood apart, as if only watching. Each recess, she would move a little closer, making it clearer that she was a candidate, standing with the other hopefuls. And always, she was left behind when the girls ran off squealing to the playfield.

Sara watched her with quiet anguish, anxious for the ordeal to be over and for Paulette to come back to their special corner. Recess after recess she waited, bouncing an old rubber ball against the side of the white building, counting how many times she could clap before catching it, how many times she could turn around, or scoop it up beneath her leg.

She saw them coming towards her: Marcia and Linda, and all the girls who would always get chosen, their arms linked and their shining hair held back by pretty, new hair bands. Paulette was with them. Before she realized what was happening, they stood in a circle around her.

"Where do you live?" Marcia asked, charmingly.

"In . . . in," she looked at the girls, terrified, "in Arverne."

"Oh no you don't either!" Paulette said suddenly. "I live there, but you don't. You don't get off the bus with me . . . She doesn't." Paulette smiled ingratiatingly at the others.

"DO SO!" She looked into Paulette's face, pleading.

"Ask her about the other thing," Paulette said.

Then Linda stepped forward with a pleasant smile, the kind of smile she had when she would choose the girls and they would run to her, squealing, after being chosen. "Where does your father sleep?"

Sara stared at the wall of curious, serious faces; the neatly pleated skirts and perfectly matched hair bands.

"In the room . . ." she stammered.

"Which room?" Paulette demanded, looking at the others for approval.

"In the house . . ." her eyes began to swim, blinding her. "In the room . . . with my mother."

Paulette shook her head significantly at the others. "My father knows her family—her mother shops at my father's store. He told me her father passed away," she said, smug supplier of valuable information.

Sara felt their eyes turn on her, like the eyes of her small pretty cousins when her mother had come home that day smelling of chilled wool and earth.

She turned and ran.

*　　*　　*

Only when she got off the bus, did she grow frightened, considering consequences. Perhaps the school would send a policeman. She thought of the big, jolly Irish cops she'd met at the Police Athletic Association Christmas party. That would be all right. But it could also be a truant officer—they were rumored to be monstrous. They'd knock on the door and drag her away.

She would not go home, she thought. She'd run away and maybe someone would find her and adopt her and treat her kindly so she would not have to go back to the Hebrew Day School ever again. Like in a Shirley Temple movie, some kind, rich people, who would come along and rescue her, absolving all her sins and guilt.

She ran, turning towards the shanty houses and the boardwalk.

There, on the corner, was Lowitt's Drug Store, with the man who chased children out. He had a cruel red face and thick glasses, which made his eyes melt into tiny black marbles. The corners of his mouth always turned down. Lowitt's. The smell of white bandages and new cardboard boxes, iodine, and sour pink calamine lotion you put on chicken pox so they wouldn't itch. They itched anyway. She ran past. The candy store. Kramer's. The bell that jangled in welcome. Her father lifting her in his strong arms, holding her just high enough to peer into the icy rainbow of containers:

"Now which one, just tell the nice lady. You got green pistachio. You got lemon and vanilla fudge . . ."

"Chocolate!" she would scream, ecstatic. Was there any other flavor, really?

"That's my girl!" her father would roar, hugging her as he did a little dance. Chocolate with chocolate sprinkles. Sweet syrup for Coca-Cola. Good! She ran. And there was the bakery. Fresh rye bread with warm poppy seeds and cream cheese from Mr. Weiss's big tubs. Sour pickles from his old wooden barrels.

She ran.

Which way? Through the old shanty houses with their chipped and darkened wood, the swarms of small Black children with shining faces and torn sneakers hooting in laughter and chasing each other across the streets? Would they drag her into one of their dark houses, beat her?

She ran.

Lifting her head, she saw Temple Israel in the distance. Sponge cake and honey cake and salty herring. Benches of light wood, staircases to run up and down. Old women behind curtains. They turned to look at you and their faces cracked into a thousand lines. But they were only smiling. They would give you little hard candies wrapped in cellophane. And on Yom Kippur tears would roll down their soft white cheeks, falling into the grooves of their faces. *Oy vey iz mere*, they would sigh wiping their eyes. Don't look, go outside, her mother would whisper. It was *Yizkor*, the prayer for the dead. But now she would have to stay and say it. They would look at her, they would check to see if she cried . . .

She ran.

And then, right next to Temple Israel, there was the long row of bushes that hid the priest's house. If you stood on tiptoes you could see it white and immaculate behind two towering elms that arched over a wondrously red-tiled roof. It was almost like a gingerbread house in the woods. On either side of the cleanly swept steps, a garden rioted in rich glowing colors. On the wide veranda, a glider swayed, its blue silk tassels twirling gaily in the breeze. A few steps further was the church itself, which spiraled vertiginously skyward looking down with snobbish disapproval on the shanties, the projects, herself.

Sara walked up the steps and peeked through the huge doors. It was dark inside, almost black, except for the shafts of light which filtered though the many-colored windows. Eerie, ghostly. And the strange dolls on the walls—a naked man-doll— seemed to stare at her, annoyed she didn't want to play. Not with him.

She ran.

There, finally, were the old wooden steps and the powdery white sand. The sea! She ran down the stairs towards the water, her blood racing through her veins in joy, her heart lifting and falling, dancing in her chest. She threw off her socks and shoes. Awwhh! But the water was like ice, like burning ice! But so good!

"Mr. Weiss is very nice, but Mr. Lowitt gives a *schmiess*!!" she screamed, choking with laughter.

She looked out towards the horizon, watching as one after another, the waves drew themselves up with a burst of terrifying power, stretching skyward like a wall of sparkling glass. She sunk to her knees, her laughter suddenly gone. And then, always, always, the taut fury of their threat crashed down, smashing itself into gentle foam, which licked her toes like a puppy.

Who had the power, she wondered, to break that taut fury? The ultimate, hidden power to control this wild sea, turning its monster waves small and gentle? Who had the power to keep you safe?

She dug her fingers hard into the sand, still warm from the morning sun. Something was there, alive, wriggling to get free. She pulled her hand back, as if scalded. A small sand crab emerged, scurrying for shelter. She picked it up, studying the rock-like firmness of its body, but its frantic movements to escape made her heart ache with a sense of familiarity. She put it down, watching with envy as it dug its way back inside the sheltering earth.

She lay down in the sand, watching the slow movement of wind-dragged clouds across the sky. Like mountains of snow, she thought, so heavy and solid, yet they moved as lightly as smoke-rings. She, too, felt suddenly lighter. She jumped up, wanting suddenly to touch a cloud. I can catch it, she assured herself, stretching out her hands to the sky, she chased it. But always it moved just beyond her, just out of reach. She dropped to her knees, breathless, aware of her own heart pounding like some stranger begging to be let in.

He was dead. Deep in the ground. In a box. Covered with earth. He could not move. He could not smell or feel or hear or see . . . And he was never coming back.

She saw the light on the water move and change. She looked up at the seagulls as they soared into the sky, one after another, her heart slowing. A white gull, larger than the others, suddenly spread his furled wings, moving them slowly and powerfully. She craned her neck back, following his soaring progress into the clouds, until he almost disappeared.

The power!—she thought, stunned. The secret power of those strong wings that could lift the body into the sky at will, carrying it aloft to the heavens! She felt her heart stir with a strange passion. She felt dizzy, as if she were looking down from the clouds. And all at once she felt the hard shell wrapped around her heart crack open, like the clams the seagulls tossed to earth. And inside she found this pearly soft beauty. There all the time!

It came to her in an epiphany of understanding:

The earth was so lovely! Wondrous! The burning gold sun on the water, the dazzling white of the clouds, the rich blue of the sky! What riches! Perfect in every way, nothing missing, nothing needed. Perfect! And I am part of it. Here with it. I, too, am perfect.

She lay down in the sand. First, she wiggled her toes, feeling the air pass through them like the cold touch of metal. She felt a sudden strong consciousness of her ankles and the firm muscles of her calves, the long wonderful stretch of skin, so smooth and soft, that ran from her toes to the beginning of her hips. She felt aware of her stomach and the softly beating heart in her chest and her mouth and nose and eyes and ears.

Perfect! Perfectly good, with no pain, not a scratch!

A nameless joy began to rise inside her, wavelike. She felt it spread, as a wave breaks and spreads, touching the far-off shore, flooding the sand in a quick, deliberate flood. A sudden searing light, like the sun, pierced what had been dark and cold and filled with fear.

"I'm alive!" she thought, and was comforted.

Chapter twenty

The summer he turned sixteen, Jesse didn't spend more than a few hours a day at home during waking hours. His mother kept trying, with all her ridiculously transparent little hints, to find out where the hell he was. (He could tell she was worried about drinking or dirty movies or maybe she even saw him walking into stores and stuffing things into his pockets . . . !) Sometimes he thought it would actually have been a relief to her if he showed up at the door handcuffed to some cop who would reveal to her, at long last, all his criminal exploits. At least then she'd feel included in his life, even if her only role was to forgive and forget. She had no idea how way off she was.

He stretched his legs. He was already over six feet tall and still (his always too short pants reassured him) growing. His soft, childishly handsome face had grown leaner, harder. His large dark eyes, once filled with curiosity and amusement, now peered out with a wariness that he knew made people a bit uncomfortable— particularly teachers and other adults worth shit determined to favor him with their philosophy and worldview. When he declined the honor, he knew they took their revenge in his grades. Often, he studied himself in the mirror, curious at what so infuriated these little men and women. He couldn't find it. What he saw was a dead ringer for Jimmy Dean, with the olive complexion and dark eyes of an Arab.

He wasn't wrong. What would his mother say if she knew the truth? If she knew that for the last two years he had spent his summers and many of his hours after school in the same exact spot: the business and commerce section of the Queens public library?

He lingered in the cool shadows of the books, knowing that the only thing waiting for him outside was summer's harsh, scalding light; and knowing too, that between himself and success lay the useless but inevitable shouting-crying-handwringing scene with his mother. And that it was all he was likely to get in the way of immediate reward for all his brilliance, initiative, and hard work.

Geniuses always had to suffer, he comforted himself, as he had no doubt his biographer would one day put it:

In August of 1959, Jesse Marks, barely sixteen, finished a program of self-education in export-import procedures and decided to form his own company. Success came swiftly to the brilliant young businessman who made his first million before the age of seventeen. One of the first of his many generous acts was to move his family from a low-income housing project to an exclusive and spacious home in Woodhurst. From then on, there could be no doubt as to his rare genius for business dealings . . .

He saw the old geezer he had been sitting next to push up his glasses and stare and realized he must have been speaking out loud.

Embarrassed, he moved towards the exit but couldn't bring

himself to actually go outside. The library, despite the old bags and geezers with their swishing newspapers, had become a sanctuary. Cool, dark, church-like, the manuals and statistics and laws had become his prayer books.

He turned the book in his hand over to look at the loan card and the date he had first taken it out: August 15, 1956. His birthday. The year after his Bar Mitzvah. His Bar Mitzvah. He clenched his fingers, cracking the knuckles. They had all been there. Morris, his stuck-up daughters, uncles, aunts and cousins. Pushing his mother around, telling her what to do. And she had taken it, the way she always took it, damn it! All humble and thankful enough to make you puke! And they had all been at him with their unasked-for advice, their brilliant plans: Oh, they all had fuckin' plans for him all right. But not, he had noticed, the same plans they had for their own kids. How come Morris hadn't told his daughters about the wonderful opportunity of vocational training and the forty-buck-a-week job in a union factory? No. Those two were both in college. What a total shmuck he'd been! Listening to any of them! Taking them seriously . . . ! Rich relatives.

He gripped the table edge.

Old newspapers.

He remembered the women that had opened their doors to him in their small houses by the bay, their heads full of pink curlers, their small suspicious eyes like two dark lumps in a bloated sea of flesh, their "whaddaya want?" And then their laughter when they found out he wanted newspapers, old newspapers. The weeks of canvassing after school, his room dark with the stacks, acrid with the smell of dust and moist decay. The trekking with shopping carts to the junkyards to bring the papers by the ton. And each time his feet and back began to ache, being pushed forward by the image of his mother's joyful surprise as he handed her piles of money.

He had wanted to help her. "Help your mother!" Everyone

had demanded it of him at the funeral, during the *shiva*. His mother, not saying anything, just leaning on him. He'd done his best. He had put his arm around her in the hospital, at the funeral, helping her to walk and not to fall.

Why then—he thought for the millionth time with that familiar ache of bitterness—did she have to go and call Morris? His lips tightened, thinking of his uncle's somber, horsy face, the way he had taken over with his dumb questions, his stinking, dumb "arrangements." Which funeral home they'd use. Which plot. What Rabbi would officiate. Who they needed to call. How the children would have to be told. Where they would sit *shiva*. He clenched his fists, digging his nails into his palms. Should've . . . should've . . . But he had just stood there quietly, letting himself be treated like some stupid kid.

And through it all there had been the silent thread of reproach that led back to the man who could no longer defend himself. How did you do such a thing? Go into a dangerous operation without making arrangements beforehand, just in case . . . ? Morris had berated his mother. Why hadn't insurance been taken out? Why hadn't anyone thought to protect the family? Making it sound as if he, Morris, could have made it all turn out differently.

What had given him strength to pull the shopping carts loaded with old papers through the streets was simply this: that his mother wouldn't have to call Morris so often, to accept his stinking twenty bucks—charity given at regular intervals as a constant reproach, a symbol of his victory over the man that had left his family without "arrangements."

He had been prepared for everything—the fat old ladies by the bay, the heavy cart. But he hadn't been prepared for the man who had thrown the bundles carelessly on the scale, taken out a wad of bills and carefully peeled off three dollars. Thirty cents a ton. Thank you Mrs. Gelt for your wonderful business advice. And may your Eddie drop dead.

His salvation came one day on the back of a Superman

comic book, sandwiched between FABULOUS NEW FOR-
MULA CURES ACNE OVERNIGHT! and SEND IN ONE
DOLLAR FOR A HUNDRED DOLLS! It was written mostly
in lower case, and had only three exclamation points, impressing
him with its seriousness. It said: "Learn The Secrets of Wealthy
Men. You too can set up your own profitable business in your
spare time! Age unimportant. No Experience necessary." There
was a post office box number. They wanted five dollars.

He'd sent them the money—some precious cash left over
from the Bar Mitzvah that he hadn't blown on model plane kits—
and in return had received a thin pamphlet in a brown paper
envelope which he slid beneath his pillow and mattress, mortified
his money hadn't purchased something thicker. But as he began
to read, he understood that—like the ad said—this was going to
be: THE BEST INVESTMENT YOU WILL EVER MAKE!

In the intimate privacy of lamplight, he learned of "world-
wide opportunities" to sell well-made American goods to primitive
foreigners dying to enjoy them. And it was so easy! All you had
to do was look up American companies, write to them, offer them
"your talent and ability" as middleman to "broker deals between
eager foreigners and American entrepreneurs (he looked that word
up: one who organizes, operates and assumes the risk in a business
venture in expectation of gaining the profit) eager to trade in a
wide variety of American products, from refrigerators to canned
goods . . ." Apparently, "Intelligence, salesmanship and the desire
for big profits" were all you needed, the brochure said. "Anyone
can do it!"

Of course, it didn't tell him much else. But looking back,
it had been worth the five bucks. It had started him down the
road, looking up strange words like "letters of credit," leafing
through business magazines and foreign trade journals, all the
while enduring the librarian's watchful eye. The first time he'd
asked her for help, she'd lifted her badly drawn, plucked brows
and shaken her head, skeptical and amused.

Old bag.

But in the end, she'd been useful, he gave her that. Guided him to the right shelves, the right books. One day I'll come back here, he thought. Pull up in my limo, give the old girl a thrill.

He left the library, and then ran through the brilliant summer light. He sensed the blood rushing from his heart through his veins, all up and down his strong young arms and legs. He felt shot through with exquisite pain, all his senses heightened; able to leap tall buildings at a single bound, focus with x-ray vision on each small detail of beauty: the rainbow shine of gasoline on a sidewalk, the curve of a girl's ankle inside a shoe . . .

His pace slowed, his feet suddenly weighted to the pavement. His mother. Hope she doesn't screw me up! The important stuff he could do himself. The brainwork. But for the typing, the phone calls, getting a post office box and telex number, establishing letters of credit—she'd have to be his front. He relaxed, confident he could talk her into it. Into anything. She was going to do this for him. She had to.

There was something out there worth having. His uncle didn't know it existed. His mother didn't want it. But his father had seen it clearly. He had reached out and almost touched it. Entrepreneur.

He wasn't going to wait anymore. Whatever the old farts told you about getting a good education, being a nice boy, the bottom line was moolah. If you had it, you were a nic-c-c-c-e boy. Smart. A self-made man. If you didn't you were a sap, a dropout, a juvenile delinquent.

"Ma," he would say when he got home, "wish me a happy birthday. Now I'm going to tell you what I want for a present. (She won't even look up, I bet, won't even hear a word). Then he would hit her with it. "Ma! I want you to sign those papers. I'm dropping out of school!"

The details about setting up the business, he'd leave for another day.

Chapter twenty-one

On Sunday Morris took the train from Brooklyn over the bridge to the projects. It was a double-fare zone and an hour and a half ride. But a sister, a widow. What could a man do? He thought again how foolish it was to live so far out, in a double-fare zone. Of course, the rent was reasonable. But low-income projects they had in Brooklyn also. It wasn't as if the neighborhood was different. It was *schvartz* now all over, wherever you went.

He didn't look forward to talking to Jesse. A good talker, but a dreamer that boy. Now he wanted to drop out of school and start his own company! Imagine, a sixteen-year-old. He shook his head, remembering the old newspapers, and then the short-lived work selling greeting and business cards. He'd given him an order for business cards. On it he had put: *Morris Siegel, Butcher, Baker and Candlestickmaker.* For some reason, the boy had seemed offended.

He felt the candy bars in his pocket. Hershey's chocolate. Sara and Louis looked forward to it so much, those candy bars. And the dollar he'd give them to buy more sweets. Poor *kinderlech.* He sighed. What was going to be with Jesse? He could teach him the printing business. Get him into the union. He had no sons. He'd do it willingly. But would the boy listen to him? What it all came down to was laziness. Who liked to get up early, come home late? But you got a check each week, a pension at the end. You could save for your future, help your family . . . He thought of his sister and the skin pinched between his brows. Of all the people to have such *tzurus*. The boy needed a strong hand. He needed someone to teach him to grow up, to have a little responsibility. He took a deep, bracing, purposeful breath.

The cold walk from the subway made his teeth ache. But who had money for dental bills this month? This month Cynthia's college tuition came due again. He felt his shoulders slump, growing round as if under a physical weight. He patted himself in a familiar, instinctive gesture, checking for his wallet. He thought of the twenty-five dollars he had set aside for his sister Ruth. How many hours of working the machine did it take him to earn twenty-five dollars, he calculated, then stopped, guilty and ashamed. A sister. A poor widow with three children. It was a *mitzvah*. At that thought, the sorrow and the heavy yoke of responsibility lifted from his shoulders for a moment. After all, what does a man have left when he dies if not his good deeds? They would be his lawyers, defending him against the arguments of the Evil Inclination (the celestial district attorney) making a good case for his merits before God. But, he reminded himself, as the Talmud teaches, the greatest charity of all was to help make a man self-supporting. Stiff with mission, he walked quickly towards his sister's apartment.

"I can't stand it," Ruth thought. This wasn't like the other times. She felt closer to the brink now, nearer than ever to some act of desperation. It was that kid, that Jesse! He was going to kill her! Kill her! The badgering, the threats, the tantrums. There was nothing in the house that was not scarred, or chipped, or broken from him. How much more could a human being take?

She had waited patiently, with hope, these past three years. You'd think by now . . . A sixteen-year-old. That he'd be a little help. Not only was he no help, he was . . . impossible! He made her life a misery. But she was uncomfortable with that, with a full and easy condemnation. He meant well. He might even be a genius for all she knew. But how, in the name of heaven, could a sixteen-year-old have his own company?

"You're crazy," she told him a million times. But he had talked to her so long and so earnestly, and he knew so much . . . Deep down, she was so proud of this tall, intelligent young man that was her eldest son. The things he knew about! Letters of credit, how to set everything up! Maybe it could work out, she sometimes thought against her will, his arguments creating a bridge between her mature grasp of reality and his high-flying hopes that she sometimes, with great joy, allowed herself to secretly cross. (For what, after all, was so great about reality, about the clearly defined terms of her present existence and foreseeable future?)

He seemed so confident and had so many good ideas. Selling refrigerator cases to Argentina, for example. The market was wide open, he said. They were just beginning to have supermarkets over there. He'd read about that in *Newsweek*. And he now had found a supplier and all they needed were some good contacts . . .

It was so much fun to dream that she sometimes actually forgot that it was her role to hold him back, to be hard and practical and adult so that he could continue to be a child. A dreaming child. The minute she allowed herself to be seduced, she was in effect agreeing to his vision of himself as the head of the family, handing him the keys to the whole burdensome mess. And so, she fought him, fought herself, calling Morris often for an injection of anti-vision medicine, a dose of lead to keep her feet on the ground. Immunized, she would fight her son, ridiculing him, begging him, screaming back at him. But nothing stopped him. Day and night. Day and night. He pleaded, he cursed her, he threatened, and the school kept calling, kept demanding to know where he was, threatening to call a truant officer. But Jesse wouldn't go back and she had no power to make him. What he needed, she thought, as a spasm of grief and desolation passed through her, was his father. Morris was a last resort.

The *Loony Tunes Cartoon Special* had just begun, but the set was all fuzzy again. Louis began to fiddle with the antenna, but as soon as the picture got better the voice would get worse. Then the picture suddenly improved. He loved cartoons so much that he hardly noticed his Uncle Morris come in. That old bulldog was running after Heykll and Jeykll. Those two old crows. They were mean to the old dog. Dumb dog! He set down a can of dynamite under their tails then turned around and put his fingers in his ears. So of course the birds dragged it over and put it under his tail and flew away saying "My word! What a racket!" when it exploded. But there was so much noise in the kitchen, it was hard to hear the cartoon . . . Jesse, Ma, Uncle . . . Then suddenly, there was a smash, like something really exploding.

Inside the kitchen, the table was on its side. Ruth stood against the wall, covering her mouth with a fist.

"GET OUT! YOU STINKING PUTZ! YOU SHMUCK! DON'T EVER COME HERE AGAIN! WHO NEEDS YOU AND YOUR STINKING ADVICE! SHOVE IT UP YOUR . . ."

"Jesse, stop!" Ruth pleaded like a frightened child, stunned.

"WHAT DID YOU EVER DO FOR ANYBODY? YOU'RE A NOBODY AND YOU'LL DIE A NOBODY. MY FATHER KNEW THAT!"

"Your father knew everything. Left your mother in a palace with servants . . ."

Jesse rushed at him, butting him full in the stomach like a goat. Morris's tired eyes bulged. He began to gasp.

"Are you crazy!" Ruth grabbed Jesse's shoulders, but he pushed her away, a little more harshly than he meant to.

"Then you tell him to go away! Never to come here anymore. We don't need him. Go back to your rat-hole in Brooklyn! I'm the man in this house now!"

"Some man!" Morris spoke in a strangled voice. "You need a good whipping!" He backed away as he saw Jesse move towards him again.

"Morris, go! He's beside himself. He doesn't know what he's doing anymore. Stop, you *meshuganah* kid. Stop already! Morris, please go! I'll call you. I'm sorry!"

Morris looked from one to the other and the indignation drained from him. "You tell me to go?! You let him treat me like that? Me?" He was flabbergasted.

"Morris just go! I'll call you. I . . . I'm sorry."

"DON'T EVER WANT TO SEE YOUR HORSE-FACE HERE AGAIN!" Jesse screamed, but Morris was already sealed in the elevator on his way down to the street.

*   *   *

"Let's all go down to the beach," Jesse suggested the following Sunday. It was his first act of contrition. All week things had been abnormally tense. But finally, his mother had seen the light, he thought pleased. Signed his dropout consent forms. Even ordered stationary for the company. All week long, he'd been drawing the logo, trying to get it right. He was pleased with the results: a ship on a dark sea sailing towards the glowing horizon. They'd call it: the Horizon Star Company.

So now he was feeling magnanimous, and guilty. He felt that this time, with Morris, he had pushed his mother a little too far. The other times, she'd scream her head off at him, but a half-hour later, she'd come around, asking him what he wanted to eat and all. But after he'd booted Morris out on his rear end (he'd gone over the scene in his mind again and again, each time with fresh relish), she'd just sat there by the window, not saying a word. Her eyes were rimmed with black and red, as if she needed sleep or had been what . . . cryin'? Naw. For what? She even said later that she understood about Morris, how he was so different from Daddy, but that he was an older man, her brother, the only one she had to lean on . . .

He'd stopped her right there. He didn't want to hear all that crap. Ma, he had told her, you don't need Morris anymore. I'm a man. I'm taking over, he had told her, and she'd looked at him. Kind of proud, he thought. Yeah, it must have been pride, but she hadn't looked any happier.

"Come on, Ma, let's go to the beach. Like we used to."

She looked at him, her face devoid of expression. "It's so cold there," she finally whispered.

"Let's go, Ma," Sara suddenly backed him up.

"Hey, I'll even take you for a ride on my bike, Sar? How would you like that?" he said with uncharacteristic friendliness towards his sister, feeling grateful, indulgent and so much older than she; older than he had ever felt before.

Ruth looked at the two of them, her lips breaking into a reluctant smile. "Outnumbered," she said, shrugging.

Jesse balanced his sister carefully on the handlebars. He felt her long, dark hair whip across his face and enjoyed her squeals of delight at his wide, reckless turns and how she nuzzled back at him for protection. He saw his mother behind them, holding Louis's hand. The kid was skipping, laughing his head off. Jesse smiled to himself, pleased it was all going so well.

As soon as they hit the boardwalk, the cold salt air whipped up through the damp planks, tossing around their heavy winter clothes. They shivered, but no one complained. Ruth walked up to the metal railing and looked out to sea, feeling, rather than seeing, the empty expanse of greyish sky that curved towards the dull, flat horizon like a tipped cup. She looked towards the right at the stilled Ferris wheel of the boarded-up Playland, then left towards the lifeless moss-covered jetty that fell into the sea like a paralyzed arm. For as far as she could see and further imagine, there was not a single, living soul except for themselves.

She hugged herself. "Ach, such a lonely place."

"I think it's great!" Jesse shot back, an offended host.

"In Brooklyn, when I was a girl," she continued, her tone overly calm, trying not to betray her anxiety at setting her son off again, "wherever you went on a Sunday, it was so lively, so full of people walking along the streets. So many stores were open. Restaurants. Young couples with baby carriages. You could buy hot chestnuts for a penny. Imagine, a penny!"

"Yeah, I remember wonderful Brooklyn with the fire escapes and a million screaming jerks beating you up in the alleyways. Wonderful Amboy Street!"

Sara ran down the stairs to the sand, feeling the familiar peace and trance of having the enormous place to herself. Here no doors, no stingy clouded windows measured out the light and air.

Jesse took Louis down and they sat digging a sandcastle.

"You have to pack it in good," he was saying to him, impressed and touched by the child's attention.

Ruth sat at the bottom of the stairs, hugging her knees against the cold as she watched her children. A man with children never really dies, she thought. Dave's eyes, his nose, part of his wide brow—they were distributed among the children—living beings who would pass them down to other living beings, along with his capacity for hope, for living richly and carelessly, for squeezing whatever there was to squeeze out of this dry, hard planet.

She could never get used to the sheer wonder of it—their bodies combining to form new human beings, beings that were half her and half him, that united them—two separate people, two strangers—so they could never be parted again even in death. Maybe she was a fool to think about something so basic when the world was thousands of years old—millions if you believed the scientists—and this had been going on for just as long. Why, she wondered, didn't people ever give God the credit He deserved for the sheer, miraculous beauty of a system in which life was the product of love, and each multiplied the other forever?

Then her eyes met Jesse's and her heart seemed to stop. There it was, the knowledge she had been fighting against, trying to avoid. Those eyes, looking out into the distance with hope and determination.

Dave's eyes.

She felt the tidal rush of America, the richest country on earth, in all its power to entice and deny; to raise a man taller than is human and to flatten him so utterly he would never rise again, and she understood she could not compete. All her knowledge, so new and painfully won, all her experience, would not be able to help her son, as it had not been able to help her husband. He would keep on running towards the vision until he found it and saw for himself that its promises were like movie sets, beautiful fronts with nothing behind them. Only then would he turn around and go back, as she had, towards older truths, deeper rhythms. He had to, because if not, there was only the precipice and the long crushing fall. Her husband was already lying at the bottom. Not Jesse too, she prayed in utter helplessness, please God, not him too. She prayed silently, watching the rise of the beautiful sandcastle her sons were building at the edge of the shore, with turrets and towers that kept growing higher and higher even as the tide lapped away at its foundations.

Chapter twenty-two

The typewriter, which Ruth bought with a check from social security, was set up on the kitchen table. The stationery, which had cost two weeks' food allowance, lay stacked in neat boxes in the bedroom. Ruth layered the sheets carefully: stationary, carbon paper, onionskin, carbon paper, onionskin. She was in a trance, yet not unhappy. Not really. It was even exciting in a way, to have something else to think about except the dishes which needed washing, the cooking that never got done, or got done badly, the furniture and clothing that were falling apart and could not be replaced.

Her mind kept wandering to the past, as if the present were a crowded, unpleasant room she wanted to escape. There she was, nineteen (before Dave, before children, before heartache . . . had such a time ever really existed?), her face half in shadow, leaning against a white wall, her fair, fine skin glowing, framed by dark hair, her smile gleaming with shy pride. It was the picture taken of her by one of the handsome young doctors with their impressive stethoscopes and cheerful, appreciative eyes.

What would life had been like if she had fallen in love with one of them, married him? And what if he hadn't been Jewish? She tried to imagine a life without rituals, the Sabbath day, the synagogue ... And then she tried to imagine herself as a doctor's wife, in dry-clean only knits, and beauty parlor hair, who stayed home all day in her finely furnished home ... She shook her head, chasing away the visions, unable to decide which one was more ludicrous.

She'd never minded working, as long as the people were nice. She remembered the pious skinflints and shuddered. Actuyally, as bosses went, Jesse wasn't bad, she'd think, amused by the irony. But sometimes, she'd look up and the dingy, airless apartment bathed in grey light would slap her in the face, the way you slap a person who becomes hysterical. Then she'd think: What am I doing?! It's crazy, just crazy! He's just a kid!

What kept her from turning her back and walking out on him, was that it echoed unbearably of that fatal act which time and circumstance had turned into an unforgivable betrayal that would haunt her all her days. No, she wouldn't do it twice! And he looked so much like his father ... ! With this in mind, she'd lower her head, and keep on typing.

She'd forgotten a lot. Her fingers kept slipping, making mistakes that needed to be corrected with stiff rubber erasers that often tore the paper, forcing her to unroll the layers and peel them apart, staining her fingers blue from the carbon. But then, gradually, she began to make less mistakes. That in itself felt like an accomplishment.

Sometimes, she'd sit and study her hands, tracing how the rough streams of flowing time had coursed over them, aging the once smooth, pretty skin; how hot dishwater and bleach had chapped and roughened them; how mistakes with scalding pots had left tan burn scars. How could these aging stranger's hands be hers? She was not old, not yet. Her life was not over, she told herself a little desperately.

She bought cold cream. Secretly, she lavished it on her

knuckles and fingers when the children were in bed, ashamed of her vanity and extravagance. As she typed Jesse's letters, she watched with secret joy as they began looking softer, the wrinkles fading. Although the signs of age did not disappear, she came to terms with them. They were experienced hands, she decided, satisfied. Hands that had been part of life, working hard.

She had to laugh. If those people in their new suits sitting in office buildings could only see who was sending them these letters! A sixteen-year-old and . . . and . . . who? A frowzy housewife? A still young former executive secretary? The sixteen-year-old's mother? A poor widow with three children?

But she had to admit, she was proud of him, her son. Her Jesse. He seemed like a different person. Nervous, sure. He was always that. But he got up early every day and worked hard, dictating letters, researching new leads, answering his mail. He was happier than she had seen him in a very long while.

But the money! For the stationary! For stamps! For typewriter ribbons! When they could barely put food on the table and pay the rent! She'd tried to explain this to him and at first he'd spent hours talking to her in a businesslike manner, telling her he knew their capital outlay was getting larger, but that income would soon overtake it and compensate. Then he'd begged, saying they were on the verge of closing a very big deal and had to hold on just a little longer . . . ! And finally, he'd become an enraged child, throwing dishes and food around, terrorizing her.

With Morris gone from their lives, she had no one to talk to. Maybe Jesse was right. Maybe he did know best and would make their fortune. And then she would think to herself: he's still a child and he wants this very badly, needs it the way Sara needs her dolls and Louis needs cartoons . . .

So the months went by, months when some mornings there was no milk or bread or cereal . . . She wasn't afraid of Jesse, she told herself. How could she be? She was his mother. He was a child. Then she would remember what had happened with Morris and be unsure. There was something of the wild, wounded animal in him; a strange and unpredictable rage she feared and could not understand. She loved him; loved to hear him talk and make plans that turned their future all rosy and warm; loved to have someone else in charge.

She tried to tell herself off, to convince herself that it was wrong; that she had to be responsible. She must be the mother and father, the provider, the decider . . . "You are not responsible for this family," she told him often. "You are just a child. I am responsible."

She convinced no one. Not even herself.

Living in a vacuum, with only the children for companions, she sometimes found it hard to pin down reality. Was it Dave's and Jesse's world of brass rings out there for the grabbing? Or was it Morris's and Harriet's dry planet, where you survived on drops from someone else's well? And who was to say Jesse wouldn't succeed? Stranger things had happened, after all, she thought. The more she listened to Jesse, the more it all seemed possible.

Soon, letters with strange, beautiful stamps crowded their newly rented post office box. Jesse opened each one as if it were a birthday present. He would read them out loud, relishing the "Dear Mr. Marks." They were filled with color brochures of jewelry, large refrigerator cases, perfumes and novelties. Sometimes, there were even packages containing samples: an aerosol can that filled and sealed punctured tires; or blue bottles of cologne with exotic names like Breathless Mist.

But when Jesse went out of the house, Ruth would turn to Sara a bit desperately, and say: "Now he wants to rent an office! How can I rent an office? I hardly have money for food or for a pair of shoes! We can't even pay for the post office box . . . And all the postage . . . ! Letters we send, all over the world. He even made me go down to the bank to open letters of credit. What do I know from it? I thought the manager would take one look at the pair of us and laugh. They didn't laugh. They opened an account . . ."

Sara would sit by her side, at first proud to be consulted, feeling as if she were participating in a grown-up thing, until the information grew too large for her, too heavy, like the blankets her mother piled on her on cold nights to keep her warm. It became burdensome. She began to hate her brother: For making her mother so unhappy; for his constant bullying and showing off; for his screaming and tantrums; for dropping out of school (for being a *dropout*, which was only a tiny step away from *juvenile delinquent*); for being ultimately responsible for the fact that there was never enough food now, never a new thing to wear. Everything was even worse than before, she thought. Even Uncle Morris had stopped coming, drying up her supply of Hershey bars and dollar bills.

Now, no one came at all.

And it was his doing.

Often she hated her mother too, for being weak and indecisive and useless. After all, it was her mother who got the checks. Her mother who was supposed to use it to buy food and feed them. She was the one who bought the stamps and the stationary, wasn't she?

"Just tell him no, Mommy. Why don't you say you haven't got any money and you can't?" Sara would urge her mother again and again.

"Yes, yes, that's what I should do," Ruth would nod encouragingly, agreeing. But the next day, she'd be back at the typewriter again, complaining about her misery, her poverty . . . the money wasted on the stamps, the post office box, the stationary . . . until Sara ached to be someone else, to be somewhere else instead of part of this unacceptable family that did nothing right.

She would peer at herself in the mirror looking for the defects she knew must be there, binding her to these people. She never saw the striking dark eyes and gleaming, thick hair, but only the slightly protruding teeth her brother constantly mocked. Like those horrible convex mirrors in a fun house, the teeth filled the mirror.

She would never be beautiful. No one would ever look at her and say: "What a beautiful girl." Nor would anyone love her for her rich, clever father; her stylish mother, her handsome, college-educated brother, her fine home . . . All that was left then, she realized, was her mind. So she honed it with clear purpose, spending her spare time reading, losing herself in fairy tales, falling in love with Jo March and her sisters; finding the magic way to Narnia. She buried herself in her schoolwork. She'd won a writing contest at school and her English teacher now pinned her compositions up on the walls and regularly read them in front of the class.

Slowly, she began to win approval. She made a few good friends. But after school, there was no place to go and nothing to do. Often, she'd lay in bed, the pink blanket with its worn threads drawn over her head, filtering the harsh light, turning the world all rosy and warm. But soon, always too soon, someone would start screaming again: her mother at Jesse, or Jesse at her mother. It might be about money, or because the Yankees had beaten the Dodgers, or if there would be two bottles of Royal Cola instead of three . . . Any of those things would be enough to set it off, like a bomb. She'd hold her fingers in her ears and hum a song to keep the violent sounds from seeping through. Just closing the door was never enough. The sound of Jesse's feet pounding the floor, his four-letter curses, his loud, arrogant bellowing, her mother's whining, her hysterical protests.

Often, she would close her eyes and wish desperately that Jesse would die, or just go away and never come back. And then she'd feel ashamed and wish instead that she could become very, very small, a particle of dust that might simply blow out the window and float away.

*   *   *

"Where's the food, the food?!!!" Jesse was in the kitchen, emptying out the brown grocery bags. Sara suddenly heard things crashing to the floor.

"Why, I got bread and milk and chopped-meat!" her mother answered apologetically.

"Where's the soda?" Jesse screamed. "Where's the cake?"

"Well, I didn't know you wanted any," her mother answered innocently.

"You knew!! You cheapskate!! You knew all right! Now there's nothing to eat! NOTHING TO EAT!!" he bellowed.

Sara got up and walked into the kitchen. "Leave Mommy alone! Why don't you just shut up?!"

"Shut up, Bucky!" he said menacingly. "What do you know?"

"I know you waste our money on your stupid stamps and envelopes. On your stupid business! Why don't you just die!"

She felt his hand push her roughly.

He was two heads taller and five years older. But where could she run away to? The dark, menacing hallways? The evil streets? The inhospitable school? The friends and teachers from whom she needed to keep her life hidden? There was only one option open. She squared off, looking at him and not budging: "You and your stupid ideas!" she repeated belligerently.

His hand against her felt like the crack of a baseball bat.

She saw black. Then she saw red. She lowered her head and charged into him, butting his stomach and tearing at his face like a little animal. He pushed her back, hard, but she could see he was hurting. It was worth it, she thought, ignoring the stinging pain. Worth every minute. She almost felt joy at that wild flailing of fist and leg, her anger giving her strength, her fear pouring through her pores like sweat. To stand and fight for the little, tiny space left her. Inside her own home.

"*Gotteinu!!*" Ruth shoved herself between them, hysterical.

"*Gotteinu, gotteinu!!* Leave her alone, leave her! What's wrong with you! She's a child. Jesse, stop it!" Ruth cried, unaware he had been equally hurt, and that Sara was equally dangerous. Ruth looked from one to the other. Her children! Her mind went blank with dull pain.

"I am responsible," she shouted at them. "I am responsible for this family! Don't be angry with each other!" She pushed them apart. "You're going to kill me! Look what you do, the two of you!! You take a mother and abuse her! Stop already, stop! It's enough." She wept. "Sara, go to your room. Jesse, come. I'll make you something to eat. Do you want eggs? Corn? Come, come."

Sara ran into her room. She slammed the door and lay face down on her bed, covering herself with her blanket. She could hear her mother's footsteps moving slowly around the kitchen, the clang of pots, the flow of water. She knew her mother would come to her later, to dab iodine on her scratches and to cluck her tongue mournfully, helplessly. But first, she would make Jesse something to eat. She would type his letters, and listen to his ideas. Only then, only later, would she remember. Would she come.

March 10, 1959

Mr. Jesse Marks
General Manager
Horizon Star Company
POB 23554 Arverne,
Queens, New York

Dear Mr. Marks,

As per your request in your letter of January 1, I am pleased to enclose our latest catalogue and price list of commercial refrigeration equipment. *If you need further information, please do not hesitate to contact our head office.*

Sincerely,

John Delmar
Sales Manager
Pacific Freezer Corporation

Mr. Jesse Marks
General Manager
Horizon Star Company
POB 23554 Arverne,
Queens, New York

Dear Mr. Marks,

Many thanks for forwarding the information we requested on commercial refrigeration units. We are now considering the purchase of 2,000–3,000 units and are in the market to receive competing bids from a number of manufacturers and suppliers in the United States and Europe. Please let us know what quantity reductions we can expect on an order of that magnitude.

Sincerely,

Jose Fuentes
Presidente
Cooperative de Nationales de Republica de Argentina

Mr. *Jesse Marks*
General Manager
Horizon Star Company
POB 23554 Arverne,
Queens, New York

Dear Mr. Marks,

Thank you for your letter and for forwarding the positive response from Cooperative de Nationales in Argentina, which we understand is the country's largest supermarket chain. We would be pleased to consider granting Horizon Star sole distributorship for South America, and would certainly consider a serious discount in unit prices for an order of that magnitude.

In order to discuss the details of our partnership further, I would like to arrange a meeting with you in New York this month.

My secretary will call you in a few days to set up a mutually convenient time. And let me say, Jesse, that I look forward very much to meeting you and cementing what looks promisingly like a long, mutually rewarding partnership.

Sincerely,

Howard Archer,
President and CEO, Pacific Freezer Corporation

Jesse held this letter in his hand and paced around the living room, finally flinging himself into the couch where he read it aloud, his voice ringing. Then he got up and ran around the room, yelling: "Whoopee!" hugging Louis and swinging him in a circle, then calling out: "MA!" He sat her down, and read it to her once again.

"Oh, Jess. How wonderful!"

"Yeah, Ma. We're gonna make it now! You know how much one of those units costs? Fifteen thousand bucks! And he's talking thousands of them! With a five percent commission . . . ! Zippidy doo dah, zippidy day, my oh my, what a wonderful day . . ." he sang, cakewalking across the living room, while Louis followed behind him, trying to imitate. Then he crouched like Groucho, flicking off the ashes of an imaginary cigar:

"What you see here folks, is the beginning of that export company that took all the Latinos by storm, freezing the hell out of their enchiladas . . ." and then he paused, the words suddenly jogging something in his memory. He straightened up, turning serious.

"I need a suit, Ma. I know it costs money. But I need it. A business suit. And a good pair of shoes." He touched his upper lip with his fingertips and wondered if he had enough time to grow a mustache.

They went shopping in Abraham and Straus. She was intimidated by the salesmen who smiled when she told them she was looking for a conservative businessman's suit. Teenagers usually preferred something a bit more stylish and youthful, the man told her. Nevertheless, he found them one. Dark, single-breasted with small pinstripes. They would shorten the pants for nothing.

The week before the meeting, Jesse couldn't sleep. Each time his eyes would close, he would hear that sound again, that garbled, muffled threat that refused to become words. It dashed violently against the back of his forehead, making his eyes water and his throat contract in anguish. It wasn't the first time he'd heard it. At first, he'd thought it was a real noise—a radio someone had left on, or voices from the street. But when he'd get up to investigate, there was never anything there. Little green men from outer space, he'd laugh it off. A bit annoying, but nothing he couldn't handle.

But now, it was worse. Much worse. He'd get up and pace the dark hall, his heartbeat like cymbals crashing together in his chest, his stomach in some complicated Boy Scout knot. And the sound would grow louder and louder.

What? he finally begged it silently. Please! Just say it already! Just tell me, already! he'd plead. But the sound just got louder, like a subway train screeching along the rails, turning your whole body into goosebumps, giving you cold sweat in your armpits. Then, suddenly, it wasn't just noise. It was voices: grinding, jangling, harsh and rude, all yelling at him at once. He tried to hide, sitting in the dark closet where his father's clothes still hung. He draped the big red flannel shirt over his head, pressing the cuffs into his ears. That helped a little, but not much. Sometimes he'd fall asleep for an hour or two and wake up not knowing where he was or how he'd gotten there. Somehow, he'd manage to get dressed, to eat, to talk reasonably to his mother. But more and more often, the voices interrupted him in the middle of dictating letters, and simple requests. And then he'd hear bad words, curse words. Words that implied terrible, obscene, demeaning things.

And sometimes it was clear to him that he was their target, while at others, he'd realize that the words were his words and they were meant for someone else. But who?

Someone close to him. He knew that. And it made him want to go down on his knees and ask forgiveness for the terrible words. Sometimes he'd pretend he needed to pick something up and sort of get down on one knee, doing it swiftly so his mother wouldn't catch on. The voices stopped for a moment then, when he got down on his knees, he realized. So it was worth the effort.

Actually, he thought he was being quite reasonable about the whole thing, handling it well, he thought. If they responded to his being on his knees, well then, that was all right with him.

It was no big deal. A sort of compromise. A way to get on with his work.

And there was so much work! The meeting! The big chance! Only a week away, he thought. Only four days away. Only two. Only . . .

The night before he looked at the letter again, then got up and walked into the bedroom and tried on his new suit. He stood by the only full-length mirror in the house, his hands in his pockets, turning admiringly to the right and then slowly to the left. He extended his hand, smiling professionally.

All was going as planned. Never had an entrepreneur overcome so many obstacles in his path! No capital. Dubious associates and employees (he thought of his mother and sister and brother) and impossible corporate headquarters.

Daddy would have been so proud of how he was pulling this off! He was a chip off the old . . . No. That couldn't be true. He wasn't like his father. Not that he didn't want to be!

He didn't want to be.

He touched his head. The voices. They were back again. Contradicting him. And the ugly, obscene words! Louder now! But now, it wasn't just words anymore. It was sentences. And it wasn't just about him. It was about his father!

"My father would have been rich, successful!" he shouted out loud, his hands over his ears to keep out the words. But he couldn't hold them tightly enough.

"Your father was a jerk, a patsy. He was a classic mark."

He pushed harder on the sides of his head. "You don't know what you're talking about, you fuck!" Then, suddenly he felt calmer. He looked at the mirror, and his reflection showed him a serious young man, slim and intelligent. He looked at it a while, pleased, when suddenly, without warning, it began to change.

First, the face turned very young, almost into a child's. He noticed the pimples on his forehead—and the hair! He touched the mirror, furious. The serious young man had disappeared and all that was left was a gangly kid with greasy hair and acne in a glorified Bar Mitzvah suit. And that was the person that Howard Archer, CEO, Pacific Freezer Corporation, who had come all the way from California, would be meeting.

No!!

He walked to the mirror, tapping it harshly with his knuckle, trying to jog it into changing, the way you adjusted the fuzzy picture on the television set. He touched the cool glass. The voices grew louder, a thousand subway cars screeching in the darkness. He felt his fist smash into the glass and felt the cold, sharp slivers, which then grew hot and thick and very red. So red. The blood spurted out wildly, like a fountain, he thought, fascinated, watching it soak his new pants and make the floor slippery.

He heard the far-off screams and saw his mother's horrified face, his sister's and brother's terrified stares. The voices in his head grew silent. He was so relieved, that he actually smiled as he closed his eyes, welcoming the quiet darkness.

Chapter twenty-three

The house was quiet. The boxes of stationary gone. The typewriter back in its case at the bottom of the closet. And her mother didn't talk anymore about the postage money, and the stationary money. And no one bullied her or teased her, Sara thought. But her mother's face! It was awful to look at—the pinched worry lines constant now, even deeper than before. And her long silences worse than her screaming. Worst of all, was her sitting in that old chair, just staring at the walls. It brought back the old fears: again, monsters rustled in the closets, even though Sara knew she was far too old for that, eleven next birthday. But she had no control over it. She was afraid, all the time. Terrified. The disastrous tide that had borne away her father had now taken her brother too. Who was next? she wondered, filled with guilt.

She should have saved them. The fact that Jesse was still alive was of little comfort. She couldn't bear to visit him in that place where they'd taken him. She imagined deformed, dangerous people wandering the halls, or chained to filthy beds, even though her mother took Louis and visited there often. And when she came back, she talked cheerfully about the wide lawns, the nice nurses.

She was afraid, but there was anger too. Why did he have to behave that way? Why did he have to create yet another shameful secret by being in such a place! She was already hiding so much. For him to burden her with more . . . It was unforgivable!

Her whole life was painfully split in two: the abnormal child—disgraced in so many ways—that was the real her, constantly competed with the normal, young girl with the good grades that she pretended to be. And she was constantly afraid of slipping up, of letting the truth escape like some dangerous criminal, sure it would attack and destroy everything she'd tried so hard to achieve. She constantly walked the high wire, high above the crowds, without a net. One unsure step, one tilt of the balancing rod from absolute center would send her hurtling down to crushed oblivion.

Her teachers' praises were like a cleansing shower that made her feel good for the moment, even though the feeling never lasted. The next day, the next hour, she would feel her great inferiority again, needing to prove her worth all over again from scratch.

She had grown accustomed slowly to the Day School. She'd taken the hand extended by several teachers and pulled herself up to grade level and then beyond. She finally mastered Hebrew, going beyond the '*bas aw baw*' to where she could actually understand the words of the *Chumash* and *Navi*—the Five Books of Moses and the Prophets—in the original. And even though she mostly wound up translating the words into English, sometimes the Hebrew phrases caught her by surprise and she realized there were some words the two languages didn't share. The Hebrew word *tameh* for example, which was translated into English as "unclean." It didn't mean that at all, she learned. It was an impurity of spirit that had no connection to dirt of the physical kind. She understood she had to *think* in Hebrew. It opened up a whole new world, which she entered hesitantly.

While certain things in the Bible interested her—the apple of knowledge juicy with forbidden promise, the seas standing up in a wall of sparkling water to let the Hebrews pass—she had not yet grasped the point of it all. It seemed interesting but ultimately quite as useless as those fairy tales she loved in the Red Fairy book and the Russian Fairy book that lined the shelves of the local library. What was the point of studying such things, she wondered. How would it ever be useful in any way to those practical things she knew composed her real life?

When Rabbi Pinchas walked into the classroom for the first time, the girls began to giggle. He wore a baggy black suit that dropped limply from his shoulders, as if on a hanger. A wispy, small beard curled half-heartedly around his lips with an air of extreme, unrewarded effort. His teeth protruded and his large glasses slipped down his big nose. He wore a plain black skullcap so low down on his forehead it almost touched his brows.

As he faced the laughter, his face colored a silly pink.

"Ve are now gong to lun d'*Chumash.*"

Sara gasped. She suddenly felt she understood why people hated Jews. Funny and different. Ridiculous really. You could even understand why those Germans . . . She stopped, appalled at her train of thought. Yet it made sense. You couldn't admit it, but she understood all those crowds who rounded up Jews, who baited them and wanted to kill them. She stared at him, not hearing a word he said, hating him, hating herself, ashamed. She looked down at her notebook, doodling circles within circles, each one growing darker and more impenetrable.

"Ve gar lo toneh v'lo t'lhatzenu
Ki garim hoyitem b'Eretz Mitzraim
Im aneh taaneh oto,
Im tza-ok titz-ak ah ly,
shamo-ah eshmah ta-ahko

219

V'charah api v'haragti eschem bcherev
V'hyo neshchem almanos u benachem yitomim . . ." Rabbi Pinchas read from the *Chumash*.

Even the Hebrew he muddied with his mushy, old world pronunciation! There was more dignity, she thought, in the crisp vowels and consonants of her Israeli teachers, whose Hebrew began in 1948. His went back hundreds of years. It smelled of old streets and wood-burning stoves in run-down houses where little children gathered on dark winter days inbetween pogroms to learn the holy words. It had nothing to do with her, an American girl. Yet the words piqued her interest. *Yitom*—an orphan, *almanah*—a widow.

"You must not bodder a strain-jer or hoight him," Rabbi Pinchas explained in tortured English. "Thoighty-six times de Toirah tells us dis. Not any odder *mitzveh*. Not to luv God. Not to keep d'Shabbas. Not to eat koisher doz'e tell us so meny times. Vut duz it mean 'bodder and hoight?' De Talmud tells us dat *'Toneh'* is not to hoight him vit voids and *'lo telchitzeneh'* dunt cheat 'im in business. Dun't say to him: Yestarday you prayed to iduls with d'pork still stuck to your teet, and you haf de chutzpah to argue vit me, a real Jew?' " He rubbed his hands and his body seemed to rise off the ground in indignation.

He picked up his *Chumash* and read, translating as he proceeded. She began to hear the words cleanly, her mind washing away his tortured rendition, leaving behind his words as distilled ideas.

"A stranger is someone who comes alone. You might think: I can do whatever I want to him and no one will know. Don't think it! We were strangers in Egypt and they oppressed us but God heard our suffering and avenged us. *For I am the Lord who sees the oppressions that are done under the sun and behold the tears of those that were oppressed and had no comforter. And it is I who deliver every man from the hand of him that is stronger than he. In the same way, do not afflict the orphan and the widow since I shall hearken to their cry!"*

The power!

She listened, entranced by the incredible beauty of the ideas that went straight through her like a sword of light, touching her soul.

The power, beating down the waves! The power that kept you safe!

"Why the widow?" Rabbi Pinchas's voice rang out powerfully from his frail body, "Because she is alone and has no one to speak for her. The orphan," his voice became dear, noble to her now, moving her almost to tears, "because he has lost his hand in his father. He has no longer anybody to depend on, to lean on. The Torah tells us: 'Don't use their weakness. Don't make them feel it.' Isaiah the prophet told the people: 'Woe if the widow and orphan have to cry to me! I will hear them. Be just, or *I* will mete out justice. *Your* wives will be widowed, *your* children, orphans.'"

She felt her aching heart lift out of the darkness, experiencing a comfort so deep and real it seemed as if a healing hand had reached inside her to bandage raw wounds. She sensed, almost palpably, the power emanating from Rabbi Pinchas's frail, almost ridiculous body. It was the power of goodness.

Astonishment and deep shame washed over her followed by a certain horror. She had seen him with *their* eyes, the eyes of the ignorant hordes that for centuries have seen only the pale faces, the odd black clothes, blind to the spirit inside, the intelligence, the storehouse of ancient goodness. And therefore they had killed the body, destroying the repository of that unique spirit, allowing it to leave the world. How many Rabbi Pinchas's filled with words of kindness had *they* destroyed? How would they ever be replaced?

She waited for him after class, embarrassed. He too felt uncomfortable. She was a young girl, he a young Talmud scholar, inexperienced in teaching girls. It was a bit shameful to him. Yet she wanted to know more. She pursued him until he agreed to teach her and a few others after school, an hour a week. And what she discovered at these classes, was that she had a soul. It had a name: *neshamah*. There, inside her, was a living, animating presence, real, yet invisible. Not flesh, yet with definite needs of its own. You had to feed it, because if not, it hungered.

She knew that this was true. She had felt that great unanswered yearning, that heaving ache that tore her apart, the longing nothing could satisfy. The *neshamah*. It could be hurt, it could starve. But it could never die. It simply left the body and returned to God. It was a part of God, really. A piece of God inside of everyone, which connected everyone and everything. That was how God could be everywhere. How He could know your secret thoughts and deeds. She wanted God to think well of her. To love her. To protect her. Her concept of who He was began to clarify.

She thought of the Jehovah's Witnesses who had come to the projects, and the unbridgeable difference between their Bible, their Jesus, and her Torah, her God of Abraham. Their Bible was that of stern-faced farmers bending their heads before meals; it was of sin, hell fires and damnation. It was cold, dark churches with suffering, half-naked men hung on the walls.

Her Torah was funny old men in white beards drinking schnapps, dancing with the Torah scroll, hugging it like a baby. It was apples on flags, old women crying during *yizkor*, worn out synagogue benches polished from countless backs. It was pomegranates and grapes hanging from branches smelling like heaven in little *Succoth* booths, wine glowing in Passover bottles. It was her mother's soft hands covering her eyes when she lit the Sabbath candles, the silver wine goblet beaded with cold moisture cupped in her father's hand. It was Abraham and Sarah sitting in their tent at the edge of the desert, running to welcome wandering strangers inside as honored guests. It was the kind, fatherly God of Abraham, who asked only that men keep his Law and be kind to each other.

Protect the widow and the orphan.

She could almost see desert mountains erupting in flames, almost hear them thundering like falling bombs. It was as if she had been there partaking of the first Passover sacrifice, saved from the death that had touched the house of every Egyptian.

His was the power. The power to keep you safe.

She began to feel better. Not happy exactly, but calm, confident. The terrors, bluish, bulging in the night, faded into an innocent, unremarkable darkness. In the morning she would awaken surprised, refreshed, grateful.

Often, she tried to imagine God. At first, there were images: The old silver-bearded king on his throne; the giant, Neptune-like, rising from the sea. But her mind flicked out the pictures impatiently until she was able to conceive and feel a presence without form—like wind whipped through the vacuum of an immense space. It was a physical ache in her breast, the realization of God, a tugging painful joy, an unconsummated shout. She felt an invisible ear pressed to her lips, a powerful, incredibly kind intelligence hovering near waiting to hear her prayers.

Yet, too, there was always the lingering doubt that perhaps there was nothing beyond the blank calm surface of the sky, nothing beyond the warm blood that flowed through one's veins? If He was there, hiding, why didn't He speak, show Himself? How could one be sure absolutely sure?

She explored her life, looking for some sign, some clear evidence. Sometimes, she devised little tests: "Don't let me be late! Let the bus come now!" or "Let me pass this test!" And when her prayers were answered she felt a shock of recognition; and when they were not, she felt ashamed of her pettiness. She became very careful, ashamed to ask for insignificant things, feeling like the character in a fairy tale who has been granted three wishes and dreads wasting one. She felt her whole being waiting, taunt and expectant, at the edge of discovery.

She began to look forward to Saturdays, which had

now become *Shabbat*. When the day sometimes slipped back familiarly to watching old Laurel and Hardy movies and cartoon specials with Louis, she would feel bereft, almost raw with dissatisfaction. She wanted something else now. She wanted to say the Sabbath prayers, to see the Torah scroll unfurl, to hear the chanting melody of the men as they read the week's Torah portion.

Temple Israel, the synagogue across the street from the projects, had pews sparsely filled with congregants as old and creased as the yellow pages of their prayer books. But further down, in Arverne, the big white shul was filled with hundreds of young families in bright new clothes. The building itself seemed part of the present rather than a relic, an outdated reminder of an era long gone. Outside, it was whitewashed and bright as the summer sky; inside as noisy as the boardwalk in summer. For Sara, it turned the Sabbath day into a rare holiday, almost a different world, far removed from the drab isolation of the rest of the week. The chandeliers sparkled, the silver Torah chalice glittered and tinkled, the maroon velvet ark cover burned with gold embroidery. Singing in the youth congregation that was led by a young rabbi, she loved how her voice rang out with confidence as she voiced the Hebrew prayers. No one stared at her as they did at Temple Israel, where dozens of old eyes followed her every move as if she were a freak, or a small miracle.

There was one problem with the synagogue in Arverne. Getting there. Although only nine or ten short blocks stretched between Waveside and Arverne, they encompassed the heart of a Black ghetto of teeming old tenements and numerous dusty, rather sinister stores. Going through those streets was like plunging into the shadows of a dark dream. At first her mother had walked with her. But then she'd turned reluctant. "Such a long walk, with Louis to drag along. Besides, they're such snobs there," Ruth complained.

It's the clothes, Sara realized with a child's quick instinct. Her mother didn't have a small, neat, feathered hat, or a trim knit suit. She was ashamed for her. Of her.

"I'll go myself!"

"Oh, I don't know. Such a long walk . . ." she didn't say dangerous, but the word was there anyway.

"Don't care! My friends are there! I have so much fun there. What will I do home?" she suddenly turned definite where before she had only toyed with the frightening idea. Waiting to be talked out of it, she was surprised when her mother shrugged guiltily, indecisively.

"You'll come back right afterwards?"

"Yes!"

"Well, I suppose, if you really want to . . ." her mother gave in. Too easily, Sara thought, offended. Maybe she just didn't care.

By herself, outside, she immediately had misgivings. But she wanted so much for the day to become *Shabbat,* and for herself to undergo a transformation as well, from the isolation of her grey existence, to being one of the girls who sang and ate cookies and traded jokes. I just won't think about it, she told herself, striding briskly forward, brave soldier in a minefield. Block after block passed. Hardly anyone was out. Then she turned a corner and saw a group of teenagers lounging outside in abandoned chairs on an old junk lot. She looked straight ahead, full of the false courage one sometimes conjures up to fool a threatening, unfamiliar dog, knowing that a panicked run will only bring him racing closer to one's heels. There was something almost physical pressing in on her so that she could hardly breathe. Passed them! Behind her she heard laughter. "Shake, baby shake!" they called after her lazily. The words made her queasy.

But that was the last street in the ghetto. Already she saw the neat two-family homes of Arverne, the fruit stores and kosher bakery and butcher shop where her mother shopped for food, Jewish stores closed out of respect for the Sabbath day. And there, finally, was the white synagogue.

The moment she entered its safety, she felt the fright slough off like dead skin. Underneath, she glowed, newly created. She was suddenly untroubled, fearless, a bonafide member of a gentle, lovely, bright world. How the chandeliers blazed! Each light seemed crowned by its own special halo that blurred into an orb of dazzling light. She watched the men carefully lift off the Torah's rich velvet cover, almost hearing the roar of the gold lions. They handled it gently, as if holding a precious infant, unrolling the yellowing parchment. The singing and chanting of the men, the softer accompaniment of the women and girls, pierced her with its tenderness, like an exquisite piece of music. It filled her with tremulous new feelings, fulfilling her longing for peace and beauty. A soul, Rabbi Pinchas had called it. A piece of God. How wonderful that her small body, clothed in hand-me-downs, could house such a precious, valuable thing! She ached, yearning to serve that power, that goodness, for it made sense of everything. For if the body was temporary and unimportant, so was pain, so was death. The soul would outlast both and float free. The good would triumph.

The soul. It was like the wondrous sky and sea and blooming earth that had come from Him; splendid, beautiful beyond compare, perfect beyond our knowing. And it was inside her. It *was* her, the real her. She wanted to shout out this joyous knowledge. All ugliness and sorrow were like dangerous streets, but they could not taint you, touch you, harm you. Passing through them, you would soon reach the other side, where truth and goodness dwelt, and existence was brilliant, crystal clear and pure, blazing with the blinding light of diamonds.

And what were stars but holes in a thin, black curtain spread across that light? The earth and everything in it seemed to her a living metaphor, a series of instructive illusions created by a master poet and teacher. From the rain falling over the dry, brittle grass, reviving thousands of thirsty roots, she understood compassion. From the explosion of thunder, the night sky veined by lightening, she learned of power and omnipotence. From the slow unfurling of a rose, she learned patience and the slow, careful movement towards an ultimate, individual perfection inherent in every living thing. Nothing was random. Everything had meaning. Form itself was full of content.

The prayers ended. She became aware of the movement of people and felt the slight, queasy sense of loss as the harmonious voices turned into the random babble of a straggling, exiting crowd. Like air from a balloon, she felt the Sabbath, her place of safety and refuge, draining slowly away as she followed the crowd out of the synagogue doors. Fathers and mothers, older children and little babies. They walked in pairs or small groups, arms linked, smiling to each other. Inside, with the doors closed, she had felt herself part of them, connected. But now that they had separated into families, she knew she was alone.

"Sara!" It was Susan, a classmate. "Come home with me. Have lunch. And afterwards there's an *Oneg Shabbat*, with songs, stories . . ."

"I can't. I have to get home. My mother'll kill me." It wasn't really true, she thought. Her mother wouldn't care. But it was what girls said, the kind of girls who lived with their fathers and mothers in little frame houses, who had clean clothes and regular meals and rules to follow. The real reason for refusing was more the long, fearful walk home that would need to be made in the darkness if she stayed for the *Shabbat* afternoon *Oneg*. And, worse, accepting lunch when she'd never be able to reciprocate. Just the thought of her friend walking through the slums, then up the dark project stairs to her own dingy home filled her with horror and panic.

But just as she decided not to accept, something else asserted itself in perverse challenge. Yes, she wanted to go! Yes, she would go! Why shouldn't she? she thought, lashing out against the endless, self-imposed restrictions that kept her a prisoner to loneliness and pain. Why not defy those things that condemned her always to unhappiness?

It was just after four when the *Oneg* ended. It had been wonderful. So many friendly girls she knew! They'd gathered at the synagogue basement, eating sweets and drinking soda. As much as you wanted! They'd sung Hebrew songs, trying out harmonies, filling the room with their free and happy voices. They'd played games and told Bible stories. She had been one of them, no different. It was not until she'd waved her last goodbye and turned towards home that the full price of her defiance sank in.

The light was already fading. She looked down towards the dark, menacing streets. They were so dark! Darker then she'd ever seen them. And those boys! What they'd said! And they might be there, waiting. She stood unmoving, not knowing what to do. There was only one other way home. The boardwalk. Her mother had told her never to go that way in winter. Bad things could happen, she'd said cryptically, her lips prim, her eyes averted. But she'd never explained what things. Sara looked towards the beach. It seemed so much easier to go that way, towards the vast, clean, empty stretches, away from the dark rows of shanty houses, the ugly lots and dusty storefronts, the groups of menacing strange boys.

There was something heavenly about a winter beach, she thought as her feet hit the wooden boards. All the crowds with their fruit peels and sandwiches, their noisy radios and undressed bodies had been swept away, leaving behind the lovely cleanliness of sea and sand and sky. It belonged to her again. She felt so good, humming the Hebrew songs to herself, remembering Susan's family sitting around the table. Susan's nice father who had teased her kindly about her rosy cheeks, who had offered her cold, sweet wine from a silver goblet. She could almost taste it now, mingling with the salty moist air as she sang the songs of Zion in the deepening cold shadows, listening to her own voice mingle with the soft cawing of seagulls, the secret shout of waves dashing against the shore. She did not seem to feel the hard boards under her feet. She was floating. *Shabbat.* Oh *Shabbat* most beautiful!

She had never seen it in any advertisement or commercial, this *Shabbat*. Nor could you buy it. It was mysterious, hidden, like a priceless heirloom discovered in the attic.

She was alone. And then, she was not. There was someone ahead in the shadows. As he walked, a book in his back pocket crept further and further up until finally it popped free. Without a second thought, her duty clear, she ran to give it back to him.

"Mister."

He turned and she liked his face. He was white with black hair and dark eyes. His teeth were white and even as he smiled. She thought him handsome and it made her very shy.

She held out the book to him. "You dropped this."

"Thank you. You're a good little girl. Do you know what kind of book this is? Are you old enough to read?"

She nodded with uneasy pride. Reading was not an accomplishment if you were almost eleven.

"Really? That's great! Such a smart little girl." This made her prouder and uneasier than ever. He thrust the book at her pointing not to the printed words, but those he had written in himself. It was a cheap cartoon book with pictures of naked women. Certain parts of their bodies had been attacked by a pen, dark heavy circles drawn over and over.

The Seven Brothers, she thought immediately, seeing it clearly for a moment: the Formica tables encircled by red upholstered seats; the boys with glistening slicked backed hair and black leather jackets, cigarettes hanging loose from thick, cynical lips. And the girls, their bodies outlined in tight pants and sweaters, their lips pouting and red, their hair teased high. And the way it made you feel to see them sitting there together so close—all queasy and queer.

"Can you read this?" he asked again, with a little hidden smile.

Oddly, she was not afraid, not then. He was an adult and one had to be polite to adults. To do as they asked. But she didn't want to read it, not now. But his hand pushed the book at her, his eyes waited patiently, carefully. She had no way out. The words did not make sense to her. She had once had a pussy, a small brown and white little animal, fluffy as a newborn chick. Then he asked her the same question the man in the cartoon had asked the women. "Do you want me to tickle it for you?"

His face was pleasant and perfectly serious. He didn't try to touch her, but waited there as if he had asked directions, or some other simple, perfectly straightforward question that common decency demanded be answered.

"I have to go home now," she said, trying to be very polite and grown up, but carefully measuring the distance to the next exit ramp. It was not the one closest to home. It would mean a walk through the old summerhouses she dreaded. But a sure instinct pushed her urgently forward.

"I'll tell you what," he said calmly, his pace following her own, not running exactly, but a brisk measured step that did not allow her to get ahead of him. "Why don't we go home and ask Mommy if it's all right?"

The sky had gone from blue to pink-orange, to blazing red, and now it was over, fallen into twilight and creeping darkness. How cold it was suddenly! Freezing. Just the thought of being home with her mother, of laying her confusion down on her lap and letting her figure it all out made her breathe easier for a moment. But the comfort left her when she saw that he meant to go off the boardwalk with her, down the ramp. "I'm going home now," she said, and then, softly, almost confidingly, almost as if she was begging his sympathy and understanding, "I'm afraid of you."

His smile turned anxious and he fished a wallet from his pocket. It looked greasy and frayed and flat, and when he opened it and took out the only bill inside and offered it to her, all her doubts hardened into pure and utter terror, a certainty of impending pain and violation.

"Here," he said, holding it out to her, "I'll give you this."
And then she saw his eyes flick over to a row of bushes.

It was at this moment that she felt her whole life, everything she understood or believed, hang in the balance. This was the time. This was the ultimate test.

God! Her whole being cried out. My father in heaven! Help me!

And then, as if a signal had been given, the whole area was suddenly bathed in light as the street lamps went on. And then, miraculously, there were pounding footsteps. A big Black man and his small son jogged into view, the man slowing down as he saw the two of them. His glance was curious, disturbed, concerned as he slowed down, looking from her to the man. She ran back up to the boardwalk and fell in step behind him. He glanced back at her with a gruff smile. The stranger kept on moving, she saw, until finally, he disappeared. Then the three of them ran down the next ramp, through the dark streets all the way back to the projects.

Thank you, she prayed all the way home, as if addressing a flesh and blood companion, her dearest friend. It included the man and his son. It included God. This was the sign.

Chapter twenty-four

"First you clean the chicken," Ruth called out to her. "Then you cover it with water and add carrots and parsley root and an onion and celery root and bring it to a boil." She sat in the chair calling out directions to Sara who worked in the kitchen. It was Friday afternoon. The child had decided to make a Sabbath dinner like the one she'd had at her friend's house. She'd even insisted Ruth give her money so she could stop off at the fancy kosher bakery in Far Rockaway on her way home from school to buy a chocolate layer cake and sweet, raisin-filled challah bread.

Ruth, who couldn't bring herself to move from the chair, shouted directions to her in the kitchen. How to boil noodles and mix them together with eggs and grated apples and cinnamon for a *kugel*. How to pluck and singe the pin feathers on the pullet. Almost in a daze, she watched as the child ironed the frayed white tablecloth and spread it over the chipped table top; how she set up the two challah breads and covered them with the old, gold embroidered velvet cover, then folded the napkins into little fans, and polished the glasses and silverware—things Ruth never did.

She had even polished the big, heirloom silver candlesticks into something like a dull patina.

Ruth studied her daughter, wondering at the change that had come over her. It had happened that Saturday she'd come home so late and Ruth had been so worried. She'd begun to scold her, then stopped, seeing her face so pale and shaken. Instead, she'd offered her some warm soup and sat by watching as she ate. The spoon had trembled.

"Something happened?" Ruth had asked her. And the pale face had looked up wordlessly. Ruth had left it alone. But ever since, Sara seemed different. The word serene came to Ruth's mind.

Sara placed the tall candles in the silver holders. She brought the wine and set it beside the old, silver, *kiddush* goblet. She even dressed Louis in a clean shirt, washing his hands and face and covering his curly hair with a skullcap she'd brought home from school. She stood surveying her table with a shy smile, then turned expectantly to her mother: "Come on, Ma. It's time to light! It'll be dark soon!"

Ruth couldn't move.

"Come on, Mommy," Louis called, walking up to her and tugging at her hands, pulling her up and out and into another place, where it was clean and smelled of boiling soup and sweet noodles baking with apples; where the table was set with clean dishes and an ironed cloth.

Ruth walked to the table, touching it tenderly with the tips of her fingers. She covered her hair with a scarf, then lit the candles. Her hands hovered over them, then pressed against her eyes to block out the light, to make clearer the separation between the light and the darkness, the ordinary workday and the holy Sabbath day of rest. She felt something roll away from on top of her. A door opening, light pouring through. She sat down by the table.

Sara served the simple meal with pride: canned gefilte fish with scarlet horseradish, boiling soup, roast chicken with sweet *kugel*, carrots and sweet potatoes. She cut thin pieces of the precious cake, serving her mother first.

Everything was so delicious, Ruth thought, amazed. It seemed so orderly. So normal. And when the meal was over, Sara opened her book and began to sing: *Yom Shabbaton eyn lishkoach* (the Day of Rest should not be forgotten, its memory is like a fragrant odor. On it the dove found rest, there shall the exhausted ones rest). She taught Louis some simple refrains, and they sang in rounds.

Ruth returned to her chair, her eyes closed, listening to the children, breathing in the lovely warm smell of the Sabbath foods. And then a sound, like a buzz—almost like some hovering bumble bee she thought—made her open her eyes and look up.

There it was, as clear as day, up above the table: Three of them, enormous creatures with large golden wings spread before their faces, hovering above her children's heads. The first turned its face to her. It was her father, she recognized, stunned. Then the second lowered its wing just a moment and its face blazed with a shocking light. Dave, she almost shouted, paralyzed by the enormity of her vision. The third did not move, and never revealed its face.

Tears blurred her vision. She blinked them away. But when she could see again, the vision had vanished. Yet, she was sure someone was in the house. She felt it clearly. She wasn't alone with the children anymore. She felt its force, its anxiousness and concern. And then a sudden peace, a beautiful calm settled over her heart.

"I'll be all right," she whispered. "Don't worry. Don't let your hearts grieve. I'll be fine now, dear ones, my beloved. Rest now, rest. Papa, David. I love you both. Thank you. I'll be all right now." She felt the last large boulder roll away above her, leaving the opening large enough for her to push her way through.

She got out of the chair and pushed it firmly away, back into a far corner of the room. She walked slowly towards the table. The children were singing: *Mizmor le David.*

Slowly, as if making a serious decision, she sat down and joined in.

A Song of David.

The Lord is my shepherd, I shall not want.

He lays me down by lush meadows; beside tranquil waters He leads me.

He restores my soul. He leads me on paths of justice for His name's sake.

Though I walk in the valley of the shadow of death, I will fear no evil, for You are with me. Your rod and Your staff comfort me.

You prepare a table for me before the eyes of my tormentors. You anoint my head with oil. My cup overflows.

May only goodness and mercy pursue me all the days of my life, and I shall dwell in the House of God all the length of my days.

Chapter twenty-five

He got off the subway, a tall, slender young man with a small valise. He wore a nice new coat, and the polished shoes that his mother had given him on her last visit, knowing he'd outgrown the old ones after a year in the hospital. He felt, as he walked down the too familiar streets, like he'd stepped out of some time capsule: the bargain stores were still there selling the same rubber shoes and plastic flowers; the candy store window was still filled with the same dusty, bedraggled Easter bunnies and curling, faded cigarette posters of desert dromedaries. So much had happened, and so little had changed. It was comforting in a way, as well as enormously depressing.

This would be a day he'd remember, although he wouldn't think of it often. His wedding day, the day he started his own successful business, the day he bought a beautiful corner house in an expensive Queens suburb, the days his sons were born . . . all those would leave a stronger, finer stamp upon his mind and heart. But the memory of walking down those dusty gray streets would be a stone in his pocket that he would roll around on his fingertips as he went through life, a reminder of where he had come from.

His mother had offered to pick him up at the hospital, but he'd wanted to spare her. In fact, if it had been up to her, he never would have been committed in the first place. She had begged the emergency room doctors to let her take him home after stitching him up, promising to travel with him for help every day to outpatient clinics; swearing she'd take better care of him. It was he who finally made the decision not to go home; he himself who had understood, even in his rage, that he desperately needed help she couldn't give him.

Looking back, it had been an enormous risk. They could have sent him to some godawful state nut house like Creedmore, which could have easily swallowed him, chewed him and never spit him out. But some guardian angel had intervened in the form of a kind young resident at Bellevue, who had made the extra effort to find him a rare free bed at Brookdale—a five-star private clinic; a place where the disturbed and well-heeled were expected to recover. Nine times out of ten, they did.

He could see the projects looming only a few blocks away. To his surprise, they didn't look as threatening as he'd remembered, merely disgustingly harmless, like a drunk who strikes up an unwanted conversation. And there they were, those chains around the grass his sister hated. Like bars on hospital windows, or those big, ugly factories belching smoke in Newark, they had a hard, cold, almost obscenely oily shine.

He wondered: What kind of men had thought up the idea of chaining off grass? And what did they tell themselves they were accomplishing as they hammered in the stakes and soldered on the links? Protecting rare and delicate foliage from the riff raff? Maintaining the aesthetic beauty of the "grounds"? Did they ever, he wondered, at least acknowledge that they were simply the keepers of the social order, the guardians and salesmen of the great American Dream? For if the children of men without money could play on wide, fragrant lawns, safe and happy, then how could men be induced into paying almost any human price to achieve such a decent, simple thing? He leaned back against a lamppost, taking out a cigarette, lighting it, and inhaling the smoke deeply into his lungs. His hands shook.

The horror of going back into that apartment! All those things he'd done, and all those things that had been done to him. All those memories of death, mourning, insanity, and pain . . .

Give yourself credit, Dr. Golden would've said. None of it was your fault. You were a child. In your own childish way, you tried to care for your family. To take your father's place. You did your best. Your father did his best. Your mother does hers. Don't look for perfect answers, perfect solutions.

He didn't believe that, not really. Ambition was still strong in him. He had taken what he needed from the hospital, but craftily, preserving enough of his sanity to always remember who he was. He wasn't going to be Morris and Harriet's nice boy. He was a risk-taker. An *entrepreneur*. There was a spectacular shore waiting to be explored and conquered. And now he was equipped with the wisdom to navigate wisely among the treacherous rocks, the natives hooting and throwing stones on the riverbanks as he sailed upstream towards it. The most important thing his doctors had taught him was simply to respect his limitations, as one respects a resourceful and clever adversary.

He threw down his cigarette, crushing it under a determined heel. They'd be waiting, his mother, sister and brother. Slowly, reluctantly, he began to walk towards home.

Sitting in her old spot by the window, Sara watched her brother enter the building. She hurried to slam her bedroom door.

Why couldn't she be happy for him? "Be happy he was well and home, and they were all together again, just like it used to be?" as her mother had scolded her all week long.

Partly, because she'd never really believed he'd been sick.

He'd always been a bully, he'd just gotten worse. Someone had taken pity on her and locked him up. Why should she feel joy at his return? Remorse she'd never gone to visit him? Why should she pretend? The truth was that his absence had returned some precious normalcy to her existence. She'd found peace and safety within the walls of her home. Her grades had gone up. Her friendships grown. Her teachers praised her work, and gave her extra encouragement. She didn't need the challenge of her brother.

Sara was right to be worried. The years ahead would not be easy. She would have to fight every step of the way to earn her place and keep it. But she had no real reason to fear. Although many years will pass until the two of them can face each other without ghosts, closing that chasm brought about by the earthquake of their father's death, eventually the war will end. As adults, they will find each other, perhaps for the first time. They will stand together at their mother's grave reading the newly etched tombstone: "Beloved Mother, Grandmother and Great-Grandmother," and weep the way they never did at their father's, holding each other, knowing they are the only two people in the world that understand that they are now, in their fifties, truly orphans.

Sara is destined to be very lucky. In the end, the separateness forced on her by pain and loss and poverty will be transformed into a unique sense of destiny. She will leave America for good, leaving its dreams and values behind. She will never get over the loss of her father, but she will know many more answered prayers than unanswered ones. God will be with her always, warming her heart and casting over her being a mantle of unconditional love that will last until her dying day. She will try to make this love tangible to her wonderful husband, beautiful children and grandchildren, and many strangers, through her books. Sometimes, she will succeed. It will be, for the most part, a rich, beautiful and fulfilling life, more wonderful than even an imaginative child, or the father who loved her, could ever have hoped for.

Ruth heard him knock. She wiped her hands on a towel, and closed the oven door on the roasting turkey, her heart suddenly still. There was a warm apple pie on the counter with little bubbles of tart juice that rose through the golden-brown crust. She'd got the day off and had worked all morning in the kitchen. She glanced into the living room at the new couch and the new chrome lamp with its bright yellow shade, thinking: the honest work of my own hands. No one's charity, not the city's or benevolent societies, or reluctant, pitying relatives. She straightened her back. A job with the Civil Service, because she'd scored so high on all their exams. A good job, in the Board of Education, working for a professor, who told her that she was the best secretary he'd ever had. Who told her to please call him Harry, instead of doctor. Who noticed when she wore a new dress bought on sale at Abraham and Straus in downtown Brooklyn during her lunch hour.

Louis, sitting on the floor of his bedroom playing, breathed in the warm, good kitchen smells. He couldn't remember the last time there'd been so much food in the house. Usually when Sara took him home from daycare, the kitchen was cold and empty, and they'd wait a long time for their mother to come home on the subway and finally give them something to eat. He'd been allowed to stay home from daycare today, so he was happy about that too. It wasn't so bad there, but he liked being home with his mother better, playing by himself with his box of blocks, building things that other children wouldn't break.

He'd missed his brother Jesse (who'd *gone*—not *passed*— away; not like his daddy, whom he hardly remembered at all). He'd gone to visit him on long, dusty train rides, in the place full of wide lawns and doctors. He remembered the sandcastle they'd built together at the edge of the sea, and wondered why it was people had to go away.

Ruth opened the door.

"Jesse," she reached up, smoothing the fine dark hair out of his searching, still unsatisfied, eyes. Then she put her arms around him and simply rested there for a moment. "Sara! Louis! Your brother's home! Come say hello!"

Sara came out of her room, hanging back cautiously, curious to have a look at him.

Jesse took an uncertain step towards her. "You've grown." He grinned. "Not bad."

"Hi," she answered coolly.

"You know I'm just kidding," he said, surprised at her hostility. He tried to remember what had gone on between them. Some toy breaking, some yelling. What difference did it make now? He felt so far away from his childhood. Silly, childish games, all of it, that should now be put away and forgotten. "I mean, you look different. Prettier."

She stared at him. A compliment? "You too," she admitted warily, taking in the neatly combed hair, the face that had lost some of its brooding hardness along with some of its youth. She felt an inexplicable twinge of sadness that she hadn't sometimes joined her mother and brother on visiting days.

"It's your teeth."

She smiled shyly. "I had braces."

"Mom, how could you afford . . . ?"

"I have a job. A good job. I'm now a senior stenographer at the Board of Education," she said proudly.

"You'll have to find something else to torture me with now!" Sara announced.

"I'm sure I'll think of something . . ." he smiled, looking around. "Where's Louis?"

He walked though the apartment, peering into the familiar rooms, almost hearing the echoes that lingered like cobwebs in every corner. "*When the movers get here, pick out any room you want, fix it up beautiful, just like in Jersey . . .*"

It was all so familiar. All so dreadful. But in a strange way consoling too. Everything was the same as he'd left it. Or better. Nothing had been destroyed.

"Hello, Louis."

"Hello," he answered, not looking up from his blocks.

Jesse crouched down beside him. "What've you got there?"

"A bicycle. But the boy can't ride it very well." He knocked off one of the blocks, sending it flying into Jesse's leg.

Jesse rubbed the spot, then picked up the block and replaced it. "Well, why doesn't the boy get someone to help him ride then?" He picked up a few blocks and placed them in a protective circle around the first.

"Someone to hold the seat and push and run with him?" Louis said, looking up.

Jesse nodded.

"But what if he can't? What if everyone leaves and goes away and then the boy could fall off and get hurt bad, bad." His arm smashed into the middle, sending the blocks in all directions.

Jesse pulled him up, hugging the small body against his own, surprised to see how tall he'd grown. A recent haircut made his ears look tender, his neck vulnerable. "I've missed you a lot, Louis. And I'm back now. I'll teach you how to ride a bike. And we'll build more sandcastles. You'd like that Louis, wouldn't you?"

Louis wriggled free. Slowly, thoughtfully he went back to building his bicycle again, carefully balancing the block on top. "If he holds on tight, he won't fall off."

Jesse nodded gravely. "And now can I get a kiss?"

The child nodded, not looking up, passively allowing himself to be lifted again and hugged. But when Jesse tried to put him down, he felt the child's hands fly up and clench around his neck.

*   *   *

Unlike their father and uncle, the two brothers will be partners all their lives. Together they will build furniture, then kitchens, and finally houses. They will turn old buildings in the Bronx and Harlem into bright new apartments for welfare families, and the City will pay them well. Their own sons will want nothing more than to be just like them. And their families will live in beautiful homes with wide lawns.

"Come children, it's time to eat," Ruth called from the kitchen.

She stood by the table, anxiously smoothing the crisp new tablecloth, her mouth trembling. She put a kerchief on her head, struck a match and then lit the two Sabbath candles in their silver holders. The candlelight playing on her face kindly washed away some of the wrinkles and worry lines so that when Jesse looked at her, he was startled to see the mother of his youth, the one who'd stood with his father's arm around her waist behind the counter in the candy store. He loved her.

Later, much later, when she is old, he will take her in, and she will live in his house for eighteen years, helping to bring up his sons. She will love her grandsons, the room in her son's house looking out on old oak trees. And she will always say: Those were the happiest years of my life.

"Baruch ata Adonai Elohenu Melech Haolam, asher kiddish-anu bemitzvotov vetzivanu, le hadlik ner shel Shabbos."

The old words came back to him with a new, unfamiliar beauty. He looked around the table, realizing for the first time what it was that his father had done wrong. It wasn't being a sucker, giving Hesse the money—no—that wasn't an evil thing. The opposite. It was a sign of his innocent trust in his fellow man, his goodness and his loving heart that couldn't see evil. No. His father's weakness, the one and only thing for which he needed to be forgiven by his family was that he hadn't understood how much he was really worth. He'd measured his life by the wrong yardstick. He'd let it beat him to death. He hadn't understood that he'd succeeded at all the important things: at loving and being loved. At being a good man. As long as any one of them lived, his memory would be blessed, his passing mourned.

Ruth handed Jesse his father's silver wine goblet. "Please, Jesse, will you say it? We need a man."

He didn't protest, lifting the moist chilled cup and holding it in the center of his palm, as he'd remembered his father doing. He felt his obligations. But this time, they were not burdens crushing him down; but simply roots anchoring him to a nourishing earth, a place painfully cleared and reclaimed from the wilderness.

"*Veyehi erev, veyehi boker . . .*" ("It was evening and then it was morning; the sixth day. Heaven and earth and all their host were complete . . . Blessed be You, God, our God, King of the Universe, who has sanctified us with his commandments and taken pleasure in us and in love has given us His holy Sabbath as an inheritance . . .")

They sipped the wine, then washed their hands and ate the challah bread. Ruth looked around at her children. In a few months time, encouraged by Jesse and Sara, she would rent an apartment in a two-family house on a quiet tree-lined street near her daughter's school. She would hire a moving truck, call a yellow taxi, and move the family out of the projects. She would succeed in paying the rent, buying the food, the clothing, the furniture— with help from no one. And not a day would go by that she wouldn't think of her husband.

She studied her tall, handsome son, her growing daughter, and her sweet little boy and realized, amazed, that she was happy. "Your daddy would have been so proud!"

The echoes moved out of the corners, beating like wingless birds around the room.

This is not the end of the story. It is only the end of what I know. With every child born, a family's story begins anew, rolling forward into the future, further than our eyes can see, or hearts imagine; transforming the tale in ways we could not have dreamed possible, explaining it in ways we could not have hoped to comprehend ... As long as life rolls forward, no story ever ends; and no tale is ever really a tragedy.

Glossary

Alrightniks—"people who are all right", the formation derived from the way people who live on a Kibbutz are called "Kibbutzniks"

Bar Mitzvah—the rite of passage moving a child into the responsibility of adulthood regarding the Jewish Mitzvot (religious obligations), established for a boy at the age of thirteen. The ceremony for boys, as we know it, probably dates back to the Middle Ages; it is also an entry into formal Jewish education, since historically parents provided education for children in their early years.

Bubbies—Yiddish for 'grannies', old women

Challah—Hebrew for "dough offering". Egg bread is used for ritual purposes for Shabbat and festivals, in the form of a braid to represent the mystical Sabbath bride's hair, braided and round for Rosh Hashanah to represent the cycle of the year. There are always two challot for Shabbat, to remind Jews of the double portion of *Mannah* they received on Fridays in the desert so they would not have to gather food on the Sabbath.

Chumash—The Five Books of Moses

The Four Questions (also known as *Mah Nishtana* in Hebrew)— a high point of the Pesach (Passover) Seder night service in the home, when the youngest child present recites this.

Gefilte fish—fish that has been filleted, the bones removed, and usually cooked with breadcrumbs and carrots to give it a sweetish taste. A delicacy often made with carp, left to set and gel; it is eaten cold, often with horseradish.

"Gotteinu!"—Yiddish exclamation, "God help us!"

Haftorah—Weekly reading on Shabbat and holidays from the Prophets, following the main Torah reading. Its theme reflects and amplifies the weekly Torah reading.

"Im Yertza Hashem"—Hebrew, "God Willing"

Koshered chicken—chicken soaked and salted to remove any excess blood in accordance with Jewish dietary laws that regulate the lives of observant Jews. Kosher literally means "fit", and it can be used to refer to religious items that are fit for use (such as a kosher mezuzah on the threshold of a Jewish home) as well as for food that is kosher or non-kosher (such as pork or various kinds of seafood) or food preparation itself, where dairy and meat dishes, ingredients and utensils are kept strictly separate.

Kiddush—benediction over the wine for the Sabbath and specific Jewish holidays. For example, the Sabbath kiddush tells of how God completed creation on the sixth day and rested on the seventh.

Kinderlech—Yiddish for "children", after the German, Kinder (CK)

Kneidlech—dumplings made of *matzah* meal and egg that is cooked and eaten with chicken soup

Knishes—festival dish of pastry or noodle dough with a sweet or savory filling, very popular are cheese knishes or knishes made with a filling of savory mashed potato

Kugel—baked vegetable dish, see 'Potato kugel'

Matzah—unleavened bread, used as the symbol and staple for Pesach (Passover) often referred to as the "bread of affliction"—indicating the time of the Israelite slavery in Egypt. It is said that the Israelites did not have time to allow their bread to rise on escaping Egypt, so instead they baked the large flat, dry crackers that, in the plural, are known as *matzot.*

Mazal—Hebrew: "good luck", "good fortune"

Meshuganah—Yiddish, from the Hebrew *"meshugah"* meaning someone who is crazy, wildly unstable

Minyan—a Jewish prayer quorum requiring a minimum of ten males, Bar Mitzvah age and older

Mitzvah—loosely, a "good deed" but it refers to a specifically designated set of 613 commandments (positive and negative) traditionally acknowledged to have been given by God or decreed by the Rabbis. Generally used to refer to a good deed.

Mensch—Yiddish: literally meaning "man," referring to someone who is a good human being

Nebbech—Yiddish: someone inept, unfortunate, to be pitied

Oneg Shabbat—Literally "Sabbath joy or delight," refers to the enjoyment of the Sabbath on Friday evening or Saturday, and includes a reception-like affair, with some refreshments, singing, or a lecture program.

Potato kugel—baked dish, of potatoes and onions

Putz—Yiddish: stupid, fool

Rogelach—little yeast-based cakes, with cocoa-chocolate filling

Schmuck, or shmuck—Yiddish: idiot, inept clown

Shul—Yiddish for "synagogue," and often referred to as temple in more liberal circles, the house of worship for a local Jewish community. Following the destruction of the Temple, the Jews had no choice but to erect shuls wherever their wanderings took them; there is evidence, however, that the Temple co-existed/overlapped with some ancients shuls for a period of time.

Schmiess—Yiddish: from the German, to throw, or hurl—meaning a hard slap

Shlepped—Yiddish: to carry something heavy or burdensome; to take a great deal of trouble over something

Shandah—Yiddish: something shameful, a scandal

Shikker—Yiddish: from the Hebrew: *shikor:* drunk

Shiva—Hebrew: the traditional seven-day mourning period after a death, during which the family stay at home and receive condolence visits from family and friends

Shvartzes—Yiddish: from German *schwarz,* a Black person.

Shegetz—a gentile; can also be used sarcastically for an irreligious, or anti-religious Jew

Talmud—Hebrew for "teaching," the name applied to the Babylonian Talmud and Palestinian Talmud, in which are collected the records of academic discussion and judicial administration of Jewish Law by generations of scholars during several centuries after 200 C.E. The Talmud consists of the Mishnah, together with the Gemara, a commentary on the Mishnah.

Tateleh—Yiddish: affectionate term meaning "little father"

Tefillin—Phylacteries, or prayer boxes, strapped to the head and arm, worn during the daily morning prayer, but not on holidays or Shabbat. They are the sign of the covenant between God and his people.

Tuchas—Yiddish, from the Hebrew, *tachat*, bottom

Tzimmes, also spelled tzimmes—a Jewish hotpot, its flavor depends on long, slow cooking in which the sweet elements in it—be they carrots, dried fruits, sweet potatoes, squash, honey—slowly caramelize, giving rise to a glorious aroma. Some *tzimmes* dishes are purely vegetarian, others include brisket meat, either in cubes or as a joint, giving added richness

Tzurus—Yiddish: troubles, woes, from the Hebrew: *tsarot*

Yontiff—derived from the Hebrew—Yom Tov: religious festival

Yosom—Yiddish: from the Hebrew, *yetom*, meaning "orphan'

Zetz—slap, flick

About the Author

Naomi Ragen

Naomi Ragen is the author of four international best-sellers: *Jephte's Daughter, Sotah, The Sacrifice of Tamar,* and *The Ghost of Hannah Mendes*. Born in New York, she earned a BA from Brooklyn College and an MA in English from the Hebrew University of Jerusalem. For the last thirty years, she has made her home in Jerusalem. The translation of her books into Hebrew in 1995 has made her one of Israel's best-loved authors. An outspoken advocate for gender equality and human rights, she is a columnist for *The Jerusalem Post*. Ragen's first play, *Women's Quorum*, was commissioned by Habima, Israel's National Theater.

The author welcomes reader comments and can be contacted at P.O. Box 23004, Jerusalem 91230, Israel or through e-mail: Naomi@NaomiRagen.com

The fonts used in the book are from the Garamond and Helvetica families

Other works by Naomi Ragen are published by The Toby Press

Jephte's Daughter

Sotah

The Sacrifice of Tamar

Available at fine bookstores everywhere. For more information, please contact The Toby Press at www.tobypress.com